OBSERVATIONS ON A POTENTIAL PEST

by Noah Hellstrom,
owner of Wanderlust Tours

...another day in the bush. Our plans are coming together well, and I stand to make quite a fortune from the poaching operation. This alliance with the Texan will prove very profitable indeed. I worry—needlessly, I'm sure—about the American park ranger, Wynne Sperling. She is as intriguing as she is infuriating, arresting my men as if she were some kind of savior. I cannot afford to let her disrupt my most exciting venture yet. But I can't say that her fighting spirit doesn't compel me, even though her prim rebuttals of my advances annoy me. And the albino leopard that follows her every move like a kitten is equally disturbing. But that's part of Wynne's charm—she is as rare as that damn beast, and twice as beautiful. What a wonderful trophy my pretty little ranger would make....

Dear Reader,

What's in *your* beach bag this season? August is heating up, and here at Bombshell we've got four must-read stories to make your summer special.

Rising-star Rachel Caine brings you the first book in her RED LETTER DAYS miniseries, *Devil's Bargain*. An ex-cop makes a deal with an anonymous benefactor to start her own detective agency, but there's a catch—any case that arrives via red envelope must take priority. If it doesn't, bad things happen....

Summer heats up in Africa when a park ranger intent on stopping poachers runs into a suspicious Texan with an attitude to match her own, in *Rare Breed* by Connie Hall. Wynne Sperling wants to protect the animals under her watch—will teaming up with this secretive stranger help her, or play into the hands of her enemies?

A hunt for missing oil assets puts crime-fighting CPA Whitney "Pink" Pearl in the line of fire when the money trail leads to a top secret CIA case, in *She's on the Money* by Stephanie Feagan. With an assassin on her tail and two men vying for her attention, Pink had better get her accounts in order....

It takes true grit to make it in the elite world of FBI criminal profilers, and Angie David has what it takes. But with her mentor looking over her shoulder and a serial killer intent on luring her to the dark side, she'll need a little something extra to make her case. Don't miss *The Profiler* by Lori A. May!

Please send your comments to me c/o Silhouette Books, 233 Broadway, Suite 1001, New York, NY 10279.

Best wishes,

Natashya Wilson
Associate Senior Editor, Silhouette Bombshell

Please address questions and book requests to:
Silhouette Reader Service
U.S.: 3010 Walden Ave., P.O. Box 1325, Buffalo, NY 14269
Canadian: P.O. Box 609, Fort Erie, Ont. L2A 5X3

Connie Hall

RARE BREED

Published by Silhouette Books

America's Publisher of Contemporary Romance

SILHOUETTE BOOKS

ISBN 0-373-51368-2

RARE BREED

Copyright © 2005 by Connie Koslow

This edition published by arrangement with Harlequin Books S.A.

www.SilhouetteBombshell.com

Printed in U.S.A.

CONNIE HALL

is an award-winning author whose writing credits include seven historical novels, written under the pen name Constance Hall, and four screenplays. Her novels are sold worldwide. An avid hiker, conservationist, bird-watcher, and painter of watercolors and oil portraits, she dreams of one day trying her hand at skydiving. She lives in Richmond, Virginia, with her husband, two sons, and Keeper, a lovable Lab-mix who rules the house with her big brown eyes. For more information, visit Connie's Web site at www.erols.com/koslow.

To Julie Barrett at Silhouette for her vision and for giving one hundred and ten percent of herself to her writers. To Anne McLaughlin, Camelot McAren and John Remmers, my worst critics and best friends. I love you guys.

Chapter 1

Lower Zambezi National Park, Africa

Wynne Sperling held the steering wheel of the Land Rover with one hand and pointed at the vultures with the other. "Look, you can see them for miles. There must be hundreds of them."

"A sure sign we're close," Eieb said, speaking very proper English, but slowly, lacing it with a Tonga accent. In his ranger rags, he resembled a black Dudley Do Right, save for the shoulder-length dreadlocks and the Garfield baseball cap, a thirtieth birthday gift from Wynne. He looked like a guy who would go out of his way to avoid stepping on a beetle, but Wynne had seen him wrestle a grown lion to the ground. Perhaps his deceiving appearance made him such a good ranger. Wynne usually worked alone, but when she needed backup, she chose Eieb.

He checked the compass on his watch, then glanced back at the vultures. "It's close to where Aja said the meeting would go up."

"That's down. Go down."

"Right, down." Eieb frowned at his attempt at American slang and seemed to file the word away for later use.

"It looks like we're about ten miles from the site." Wynne swallowed hard and asked, "How many elephants do you think they've killed?"

Eieb glanced through the windshield and narrowed his eyes. "I don't know, but I'd say a lot by the amount of vultures."

"I hate this part of the job. We work so hard to keep them alive, and in a few seconds they're destroyed."

"You feel responsible for all the animals we protect. Not good."

"I can't help it. It only takes one person—"

"To make a difference," Eieb finished for her. "I know. I know. But even an army can know defeat."

He had a point. Not that the underfunded Zambian Wildlife Authority could pay an army of rangers. Comprised of one hundred and twelve rangers—including Wynne, and Commander Kaweki, the unit warden— ZAWA was expected to police twelve thousand square miles. Still, she couldn't help feeling responsible. She gripped the steering wheel until her knuckles shone white and said, "This happened on my watch. I should have been more vigilant, patrolled longer—"

"You're the only person I know who makes Nelson Mandela look lazy."

"I feel like I've done nothing. Poachers are hitting us more often, right under our noses. Why didn't we know these guys were operating right in the park? We should have known. They've been here at least three days." Wynne remained pensively quiet and stared at the road ahead.

"It is as if they know our every move." Eieb studied Wynne a moment. "You think we have a spy in camp," he said with certainty.

"How else could they be killing animals right in the park?" Wynne asked, aware Eieb knew what she was thinking. He probably knew her better than she knew herself sometimes. "Someone must be directing them, and that someone has to know where the rangers are at all times. And if we don't catch them, they'll expand. I'll bet that if we hadn't kept this sting to ourselves, we wouldn't have been able to set it up."

"We were lucky Aja received that tip from the villagers about the poaching."

"If Aja hadn't come to us with the information and arranged the buy, we wouldn't have known a thing." Wynne thought of Aja. He had been her first friend in Zambia, and her teacher. Without his help, she would never have learned to survive the harsh extremes of Africa. He was the most revered tracker in Zambia and a poacher's worst nightmare.

"We have to find out who it is." Eieb rubbed his jaw and seemed to be ticking off names in his head.

"I know."

"It will be a good mystery. Something to look forward to when we get back." A hard, unrelenting glint twinkled in Eieb's eye, an unusual contrast to his typical restrained facade.

Snow, one hundred and ten pounds of white fur, perked up in the cargo area of the Rover. The leopard's unusual pink eyes gleamed in the mirror as she lifted her nose and scented the buzzards. Or the kill. Wynne didn't know which.

"Some powerful and dangerous predator you are,"

Wynne said to Snow, the irritation still in her voice, though it was directed at herself for allowing this poaching ring to thwart them at every turn. Wynne finished with a guttural moan, cat language Snow understood.

The leopard responded by rubbing her whiskers against Wynne's arm, nudging her into the side of the door.

The Rover veered toward the ditch. Wynne jerked the wheel back. Her collection of *Simpsons* bobble-head dolls on the dash nodded in unison.

Eieb frowned at Snow and said, "You know, you're going to have to take her to another reserve one day and set her free."

"I can't until she's hunting on her own."

"Uh-huh. I saw her drop a kill at your door yesterday."

Wynne didn't answer him. Snow had been hunting on her own for three weeks now. Wynne thought she'd done a pretty crafty job of hiding it, until now.

"You've tamed her so much she may never assimilate back into the wild." Eieb reached back and scratched Snow behind the ears.

"We've bonded, that's all."

"Uh-huh. What about the Big Five Habitat? You bonded with those creatures, too. You keep *bonding* as you say, the habitat will be overflowing." Eieb gave her his most critical glance.

"Hey, we just turned a bush baby and an eland loose last week."

Wynne thought of the Big Five Habitat, one of the few accomplishments in her life of which she felt completely proud. She had convinced the park's veterinarian to train older school children in helping to care for wounded or motherless animals. It aided in recruiting volunteers for the reserve and educated the children on the delicate ecological balance maintained by all living creatures. They not only learned the importance of conserving the big five wild animals of Africa—the elephant, rhino, buffalo, lion, leopard—but all wild animals and their habitats. Some of the happiest moments in Wynne's life were watching the smiles on the children's faces as they released the animals back into the wild.

"But you do nothing to set Snow free." Eieb motioned toward the cat.

"I raised her from a cub," Wynne said, hearing the desperation in her own voice. "I won't throw her to the poachers and hunters. You know her white fur is prized."

"Survival is not guaranteed in the wild, as you know. But if you do not let her go, she'll never have a normal life or live free. Want to know why I think you keep her?"

"No, but you'll tell me anyway."

"I think you're using Snow as an excuse to remain alone."

"That's not true. I don't keep her on a leash."

"No, just in your hut at night."

Wynne thought she'd hidden that as well, but obviously nothing escaped Warden Freud here. "She'll leave when she's ready," she said, her voice adamant. "I won't drop her somewhere and abandon her, and that's that."

She knew firsthand what it felt like to be disowned, severed from those dearest to her, and she wouldn't discard Snow in a strange place to fend for herself. One day she would let Snow go, when they were both ready.

Eieb lapsed into silence, and Wynne was glad when they neared the site. For now, the third degree was over, but Eieb would bring it up again. He was just as stubborn as she was.

She couldn't stop thinking of the Judas in their operations base as she left the main road, keeping her eyes on the vultures. The Rover bumped through the tall grass, past a herd of blue wildebeest. The lead bull raised his head and shot them a casual glance, then went back to grazing.

She breathed in the scent of dung, fresh pasture and last night's dew, the raw scent of vastness, primitive earth and pulsing life. The self-reliant, adventurous part of her craved that solitary open scent. She felt needed and wanted here.

"Let me out up ahead." Eieb picked up the rifle resting near his right leg and hung it over his shoulder by the strap. He checked his walkie-talkie to make sure it was turned on. "Frequency four?"

"I'm already there." Wynne patted the unit inside her vest pocket, and the handcuffs in an adjacent pocket rattled slightly.

"I'll circle around through the forest and come in on the east side."

"I'll go in from the west side."

She parked the Rover near the forest's edge and cut the engine. She checked to make sure the leather slingshot wrapped around her waist was secure. It wasn't a modern slingshot with an elastic band attached to a forked base. No, she was schooled in the art of the sling; a ballistic weapon David had made famous in the Bible when he slew Goliath. It had been one of the most important weapons in an ancient army's arsenal. It was still used in some African cultures today. Two long cords were attached to the ends of a leather strap. The strap held the projectiles—she preferred smooth stones—and the cords allowed her to whirl the stone overhead or at her side. The cords were long enough to go around her waist, and she had disguised the slingshot to look like a belt from a Ralph Lauren Congo collection. But in her trained hands it was a lethal weapon.

Eieb's expression turned grave. "If I was hard on you earlier—"

"I needed to hear it." Wynne grinned at him.

He tried for a smile, but only managed to pull his lips into a thin sober line. He tugged on her long braid twice, the closest thing to a hug she had ever gotten from him, then he said, "Godspeed."

"You, too." Wynne did the same with his dreadlocks, then he slipped off into the woods. For a six foot guy, he moved through the forest like a ghost, disappearing into the foliage.

She lifted the left cuff of her pants and checked the small dagger and sheath there. For the undercover operation, she had worn her most loose-fitting civilian clothes, a white oversized safari shirt, a hunting vest, and tan cargo pants. The pants were wide enough at the bottom to allow her easy access to the dagger.

She dropped the cuff and reached across the stick shift. Strands of blond hair escaped her braid and fell in her face. She blew them back and found the packets of money she had wrapped in waxed canvas and tied with twine. Carefully, she shoved the neat little package into a vest pocket.

A .22 rifle, a Winchester, and a dart gun were in the trunk, mandatory equipment for a ranger. She used the dart pistol when she needed to sedate an animal, but the other guns she rarely utilized. She had seen firsthand the damage guns could inflict. They were made for taking life, not preserving it, and there had never been a time in the two years she'd been a ranger that cunning and wits hadn't won out over bullets.

She slipped into the forest, Snow shadowing her. Wynne found a well-worn elephant path and the going was easy. She kept her eyes trained for movement. Poachers were infamous for setting traps and had murdered a ranger six months ago.

A blue striped skink skittered across the path in front of her. Out of habit, Wynne paused and found what the lizard was running from. A slender mamba slithered after its prey.

Snow paused behind Wynne, curious, but inherently cautious.

The snake wasn't quite four feet long and still olive-green, a juvenile. Mambas turned black when full grown and Wynne had seen them fourteen feet in length.

The snake sensed her, but mambas were as poisonous as cobras and they had an attitude to back it up, so it didn't challenge her and pursued its skink-a-la-mode dinner.

Lack of fear was the snake's first mistake. Wynne whipped off the slingshot, loaded a rock in the leather strap and followed the mamba.

It reared its head at her.

One snap of her wrist and the slingshot's cords wrapped around the snake's slender neck and mouth. Wynne grabbed the back of its head and loosened the cords. She forced open its mouth and drained the venom on a log.

"Don't worry, little guy, you'll be free soon," she said, thrusting the snake in a cloth pouch she kept for capturing poisonous snakes.

The skink looked at her as it scurried off into the under-brush, as if to say, "Thanks."

The snake thrashed and writhed in the sack as she secured it to her belt and continued her approach.

Another twenty yards, and she paused at the sound of male voices. She imitated the call of a sparrow weaver.

Eieb's whistle answered.

Everything was in place. She gave Snow a hand signal to stay, then peeked past the underbrush. Five elephant carcasses littered the ground. They had been butchered, only meaty bones and tendon left, the choicest morsels for the vultures and blowflies. By the smell and look of the carrion, the animals had been killed a good three days ago. It surprised her that the meat had been butchered so quickly. Five bull elephants amounted to tons of meat. It took a tribe of hunters a day to butcher one good-size elephant. These guys had killing down to a science.

It made her sick to see the senseless carnage, and she glanced down at her hands, feeling a tightening in the region over her heart. It was part of her job to monitor the elephant herds in the park. There were only one hundred and fifty elephants in the reserve—now only one hundred and forty-five. She had named some of them by their personalities. Which ones had she lost? God! She didn't want to know.

Thirty feet from the kill, standing near the tusks, Wynne spotted Aja and three poachers. Aja was about fifty, elderly for an African, with graying temples and the expression of a sage. Strands of beads covered his legs, arms and neck. He wore a loincloth. A leather slingshot, identical to Wynne's, hung down the side of his hip. Despite the development and exploitation of Zambia, some Africans hadn't lost their sense of heritage. Aja valued the old ways of his ancestors. He truly was one of the people of the earth, and he wore his pride in his bearing. They made eye contact, but he had been expecting her and didn't give her away. He continued to converse with the poachers.

She assessed the other three Africans. Young, not locals, probably from another province. They donned camouflage fatigues, urbanite garb from a military store. They held Remington M70s, enough firepower to take down the side of a house. More than likely they had herded the animals here and mowed them down like a firing squad. Wynne tried to take a long calming breath, but she kept picturing the slaughter, and the air sat in her lungs like she had just breathed fire.

The tallest of the three men wore a tan beret. An ivory earring dangled from his nose and ear. A belt crafted from giraffe hair and elephant tail hair was threaded through the belt loops of his pants—nothing like flaunting the contraband. He glanced around as if expecting trouble; the leader, she presumed.

She stepped into the clearing, a Teflon smile pasted across her face, while inside she seethed.

The men grew wide-eyed with confusion and concern.

Did they know she was a ranger? Had her cover been blown? Fear pulled at her. She reached for her slingshot, but the men's uncertainty quickly segued into obvious disdain and she slowly relaxed her hand at her side.

The leader took her measure and spat. He looked at Aja. "We wish to do business, but not with a woman," he growled in Nyanja, one of over seventy dialects spoken in Zambia.

"Her money is good."

"We don't deal with women."

Wynne had come up against men like these many times before, killers who didn't respect women or any living creature. To them, she was nothing but a lowly woman, beneath them and not to be trusted. She pulled out the money from her vest and spoke in their language. "Here's the seventy pounds as agreed upon."

This softened the leader's expression.

Wynne tossed the packet to him.

He snatched it out of midair and grinned, white teeth flashing. "Maybe we can do business."

The other men drew close as the leader tore into the packet.

Wynne stepped back and smiled, focusing on the miniscule cloud of brown dust flittering down as he dropped the covering.

For a moment Aja met her eyes and they shared a knowing glance.

"It's all there." Wynne watched the leader fan the bills, more dust scattering in the air.

The others stared, rapt by the sight of so many greenbacks.

"I'll have my men pick up the ivory." Wynne walked toward the tusks, each weighing about seventy to eighty pounds, flesh still attached to the ends. She had to look down at her hands.

"Wait." The leader shoved the money in his pocket and nudged his companions.

They walked toward Wynne. Her gaze shifted between their eyes and their guns.

"Ivory is prized," the leader said. "One hundred fifty pounds, or no deal."

"We agreed on seventy," Wynne said. "That's all I've got on me."

"You can pay us the rest tomorrow."

"What about the meat? Is it for sale?"

"No meat." The leader shook his head emphatically. "All bought."

Wynne had a horrible suspicion brewing in her. She hedged, then said, "Where shall I meet you?" How many other poachers were in the area and involved in this ring? She looked forward to interrogating them.

"Here."

"No, not here. I passed rangers on the road about twenty miles north. What about your camp?"

A moment of indecision, then he said, "We'll meet you at this location."

"Very well, but I may not be able to come up with all the money right away."

The leader eyed her up and down. "You're not a bad-looking woman, you can think of something."

Wynne gave him her most winning smile, while she visualized what she'd like to do to him later. It involved the mamba and a knife.

The leader nodded at the tusks. "Get them."

"Wait! They're mine!" Wynne stepped between the tusks and the two men. She held up her hands and tried to look as if she were at their mercy.

Aja stepped next to her and crossed his arms. "They are the woman's."

The men glanced at them: a woman and an old man. They found it amusing as they aimed their cannons at Wynne and Aja. The leader's teeth glistened in a Cheshire grin. "I keep the tusks until full payment."

"I don't think so." Wynne looked at Aja. "Do you?"

Aja nodded. "No, I do not think so."

Snow chose that moment to step out of the woods and pad toward them.

The leader saw Snow. Fear registered in his expression. He whipped his gun around to shoot....

Wynne already had the sack in her hands. She tore it open and hurled the snake at the leader. It landed on his head.

"Get it off! Get it off!" He screamed, dropped his gun, and flung the mamba into the forest.

It was the diversion Wynne needed. She kicked him, then knocked him down on the ground in a tantui move, a martial arts form of kickboxing. In seconds she'd wrestled his hands behind his back and cuffed him.

Abruptly the other two men groaned and grabbed their stomachs. They staggered several feet and dropped their weapons.

Wynne was on them in a flash, throwing them to the ground, cuffing them, while Aja grabbed their rifles.

"It took a long time," Aja said. "Did you use enough lobelia on the money?"

Lobelia—a tobacco derivative—contained poisonous caustic latex, more potent than digitalis. It was one of the tricks Aja had taught her. "I did, but I didn't want to kill them. Next time, I'll make the powder more potent. But I did bring the mamba as a diversion."

"Huh, a mamba." Aja shook his head, then the wrinkles stretched around his eyes in disapproval. "I would have found a cobra."

Wynne was used to Aja's criticisms. He was the master in the African bush; she was only his student. She knew how fortunate she had been to have his friendship and tutelage, and she always showed him the deference he deserved, though it never stopped her from hoping to hear him compliment her one day.

Her gaze shifted to the three downed men as Snow sniffed them. The thought of losing five elephants to these creeps ate at her. However, it gave her pleasure to watch them trembling not only from sickness but from having a full-grown leopard breathing down their necks. An idea came to her.

One hand signal from her and Snow paused, bent down and sniffed the leader's neck.

He stiffened, his body trembling all over.

"You probably don't know this, but albino leopards stay hungry all the time. Has something to do with their genetic anomaly." Not true, but sounded good. "And Snow here hasn't made a kill in days."

"P-please…" His voice was a raspy whisper.

"I know you were trying to make a little extra cash with this deal. Was it your idea, or your boss's?"

"Ours alone."

"Whose?" Wynne motioned to Snow and the big cat plopped one paw on his back.

"Mine." He struggled not to move.

"Where is the meat?"

"Packaged for b-bush meat.…"

Wynne grimaced. Bush meat. The most devastating kind of poaching. It was the illegal use of wildlife for meat and had caused the near-extinction of animals in Africa. Also it exposed consumers to diseases such as Ebola, and twenty-six kinds of SIV—Simian immunodeficiency virus—two of which had been identified as the origin of AIDS. Bush meat poaching meant a highly organized, commercial illegal operation. They could wipe out the park's wildlife in a few weeks.

"How are you transporting the meat?"

"Supposed to drop it at a contact point."

"When?"

"Tonight…midnight." His eyes squeezed shut as Snow sniffed his ear, and his trembling turned to full-blown shudders.

"Where?"

"Near Sausage Tree Camp.…"

"How is it moved?"

"Z-Zambezi River."

"Through Zimbabwe?"

"Yes."

"Where does it go from there?"

"I don't know. I-I swear."

"Who is behind this ring?"

"I don't know."

"Okay." Wynne shrugged. "Snow, it's poacher dinner for you, girl." She signaled the leopard with one finger.

Snow let out a roar that Wynne felt deep in her chest and she was certain rocked the poacher's eardrum a little. Then the big cat flopped down across his back.

"Haah! Please... Please! I-I don't know! Money and in-structions come through e-mail." Perspiration streamed down his brow, and he blinked it back.

Wynne believed him, not because he was scared out of his wits and wouldn't dare lie to her, but because the ring leader had been clever enough to set up a bush meat ring right under their noses, even had a spy, or two, in their camp. He'd definitely be clever enough to keep his iden-tity hidden. She motioned for Snow to back off.

Shots rent the air. Wynne's head snapped up. Buzzards scattered into a black haze.

Aja glanced into the forest and asked, "Where is Eieb?"

"Oh, my God! Eieb!" Wynne should have known this ar-rest had gone down too easily. There must have been a look-out. She snapped a hand signal at Snow. "Guard." She pointed to the poachers and heard another staccato blast of shots.

"Please, watch them," Wynne yelled over her shoulder at Aja as she ran into the forest, whipping off her slingshot. Wynne prayed Eieb was still alive and that the poachers hadn't won this round, too.

Wynne slowed as she neared the gun battle. It was sev-enty yards ahead of her. She crept forward, using the dense undergrowth as cover. She couldn't see Eieb or the poach-ers. Only heard them. A semiautomatic rapid fire, *rat-tat-tat-tat,* layered by Eieb's shotgun, *ka-plow.* At least she knew Eieb was still alive. It sounded like the middle of a war zone.

Abruptly the shots stopped, the quiet deafening.

Her pulse drummed in her ears. She smelled the bitter scent of gunpowder, thickened by the humidity. The air pressed in around her as she searched for movement, a quick rapid scan. Left. Right. Only lush green jungle. She tuned into the faint sound of moaning, jagged breathing. Was that Eieb?

She didn't dare call out. Poachers could still be in the vicinity, ready to play the Kill the Warden game. She prowled toward the sound, then heard…

Whisper of leaves. Footfalls behind her. She loaded her slingshot and whirled it, arm poised, ready to fire.

"It's me," Eieb whispered, his voice wired from the gun battle.

She relaxed, relieved to see him, and let the slingshot drop. "Any more around?"

"Only one. The shots came from this way. Pretty certain, he's down."

Eieb headed toward the sound, Wynne on his heels. They spotted the fallen African at the same time. He was barefoot and wore ragged civilian clothes. His body was curled into a fetal position and he held his stomach. Blood oozed between his fingers and ran down his arm. An AK-47 lay next to him.

Wynne kicked the rifle away. Then she and Eieb must have seen the young man's face at the same time, for they gaped at him.

"Mehan?" Wynne said, aware she shouldn't feel empathy for a poacher who had tried to kill Eieb and probably other rangers. But she had seen Mehan's smile every morning in camp for the past two years, knew his wife and four children, and the promise within him; he was an artist and had carved a leopard out of wood for her. It resembled

Snow. How could she distance herself from someone she had called friend?

"Why, Mehan?" Eieb looked as tortured and in pain as Mehan.

Mehan squeezed his eyes shut, as if he couldn't bear to look at them or face what he'd done. "Need…" he spoke in Nyanja. "Feed…family."

It was always about need. Mehan needed to poach to feed his family. Wynne needed to stop bush meat poachers. She grabbed a nearby Balsam plant, stripped the leaves with one glide of her hand, then crushed them between her palms. She pulled her dagger from its ankle sheath, tugged her shirt from her waist, and cut the bottom off; Mehan probably had two shirts to his name—if he was lucky.

Wynne squatted on the other side of Mehan and looked at Eieb. "Help me roll him on his back."

Mehan grimaced but didn't cry out, the African male warrior in him refusing to give way to pain.

"Hold his hands." She waited for Eieb to grasp Mehan's hands, then thrust the leaves against the bullet hole.

Mehan tensed, agony scorching his dark eyes. Perspiration trailed down his forehead. He clenched Eieb's hands as if he were dangling from a cliff.

"Just one more thing." She wrapped the shirttail around his middle, packing the leaves against the wound. He was so thin, she knotted the strip of material twice. Mehan bit his lower lip, and his eyes glazed as if he might pass out. "That should help the bleeding. We'll get you some real help."

"Who is behind this?" Eieb bent over Mehan, his voice soft, but his expression hard with resolve.

"LZCG.…" Mehan's lips quivered, the name dissolving in his throat. Then he shuddered and passed out.

"LZCG?" Eieb and Wynne both spoke at the same time, openmouthed in disbelief.

"I don't believe it." Eieb shook his head. "The LZCG behind a poaching ring?"

"Not just a poaching ring," Wynne said. "A bush meat ring."

"Are you certain it's a bush meat operation?"

"The carcasses have been butchered and one of the men we caught confirmed it."

"I still do not believe it. Mehan could be lying to cover for someone else."

"I don't think so. It's like he was clearing his conscience."

"But without the LZCG we wouldn't have the air and ground support. They just paid for the new animal tracking system," Eieb said as if trying to convince himself it wasn't true. "They gave us the funding. No, I cannot believe it."

"Now that's the kicker, and what the orchestrator of this ring would like us to believe," said Wynne. "If you think about it, it's the perfect setup. No one would suspect someone in the LZCG of poaching." The Zambian Wildlife Authority had been fortunate to have the LZCG base their operations in Zambia. Wynne knew the Lower Zambian Conservation Group, or LZCG as most people referred to it, had done more for saving wildlife than the Zambian government. It was a nonprofit organization started by safari tour owners and tradesmen who catered to wealthy tourists, photographers, and licensed hunters. In the 1970s and '80s, safari owners had witnessed the near extinction of wildlife in Zambia, and they realized their livelihood was dying. Thus they created and funded the LZCG. Without its financial support and added manpower, Zambia wouldn't have begun to make an impact on poaching. The lack of funding from the government made it impossible for the understaffed rangers to cover all of Zambia's vast lands. LZCG's employees took up the slack, covering borders and patrolling areas, working alongside the rangers. Some of them had been deputized and could make arrests. They were constantly assisting every ranger on the force, including Wynne when she asked for help. No one would suspect the LZCG insider of poaching. It was the perfect smoke screen.

The furrow on Eieb's brow loosened and he seemed a little more amenable to the idea. "Okay, just suppose you're correct. Who could it be?"

"I don't know. Hey, it could be anyone." The LZCG board members flashed in Wynne's mind and for some reason the enigmatic handsome features of Noah Hellstrom stuck. She had seen the way he walked into a room and owned it, his charisma and presence electrifying the air. With just one smile, he had the ability to charm anyone out of anything. Four months ago, LZCG's board members had unanimously voted him in as their new chairman of the board and head of operations.

She didn't know how Hellstrom had the time to volunteer at the LZCG and operate Wanderlust Tours, one of the largest safari companies in Zambia. Unlike some safari owners, Hellstrom always followed the laws. On her patrols in the bush, she had never arrested any of his scouts or hunters for not having the proper licenses in the game-managed areas where hunting was allowed. Still, she couldn't ignore the fact they hadn't had a poaching problem until Hellstrom took over.

"What about Hellstrom?" Wynne threw out.

"I don't know. He's so well liked."

"I know, but he did shoot down my idea of getting a

DNA wildlife crime lab. He said it was too expensive and wouldn't even take the idea to the board to vote on it."

"I remember. Strange was it not, since it's more effective in ferreting out poachers than the tracking system."

It had been a dream of Wynne's to see a lab established in the park, but she needed the LZCG behind her and the influence they had with the Zambian government. It certainly wasn't going to happen while Hellstrom was chairman of the board.

"His safari business would be a great way to transport the meat," Eieb said, his voice uncertain.

"True, and he knows our every move, but so does all of the LZCG staff." She glanced down at Mehan. "We need to keep him safe. If the leader of this poaching ring knows he's alive and talked, they'll try to eliminate him."

"I'll protect him." A heavy frown stretched across Eieb's brow.

"After Doc Mukuka treats him, we should move him somewhere safe. Aja can help us." Dr. Mukuka ran an AIDS clinic about two miles from base camp. It was the closest thing they had to a hospital.

"I know of a place." Eieb nodded.

"Take the Rover. I'll deal with the prisoners."

Eieb hefted Mehan in his arms like he was a child, the tendons in Eieb's long forearms straining. But the weight didn't seem to slow him as he hurried through the forest.

"Don't tell anyone about our arrest just yet," Wynne called to Eieb's back.

He didn't answer her, and she wondered if he was too far away to hear her. If word of the capture got out, the meeting at Sausage Tree Camp would be cancelled. The poacher had said he was to turn over the contraband to-night. The camp was twenty kilometers away, near the southern edge of the park, next to the Zambezi River. She could easily slip down there and see who turned up. Maybe follow them and find out the smuggling route the poachers were taking.

Wynne picked up Eieb's and Mehan's rifles, then hurried back to Aja and the poachers. She thought of the LZCG again.

She didn't want to believe one of the board members could be corrupt, but it was obvious someone was, maybe even more than one person. She didn't know who to trust any longer. And she couldn't risk offending all the board members by accusing one of them of poaching without definitive proof. It was the golden handcuff principle at work. And whoever was head of this ring had probably anticipated that advantage.

She knew finding the identity of this person would be like playing chess with the devil. One wrong move and she'd not only lose the job she loved with all her heart, she could lose her life. Tonight, just maybe, she could get one move ahead of the devil—if that was possible.

Chapter 2

The sun had just set and the soft evening moonlight cast a long sparkling shadow down the center of the Zambezi River as Wynne crept along its bank. The water current and bellows of hippos drowned out her footsteps. An occasional splash warned of a croc looking for a snack. A rich brew of animal musk, vegetation and the dank scent of fresh water clung to the air.

There was enough moonlight to see across the river to Zimbabwe's shore. The Zambezi River acted as a natural boundary between the two countries. It also gave poachers a quick escape route into Zimbabwe. It was September; the end of the dry season, and the river had shrunk to a fourth its size, making it easier for poachers to cross. Poaching was rampant in Zimbabwe. Endangered species were all but wiped out. The country was too impoverished to control it and animals had fled into Zambia for protection.

It made sense the bush meat poachers would transport the meat along the river into Zimbabwe. And she wasn't surprised she hadn't come across these men in her nightly patrols of the river. The rangers never made a move unless they cleared it with base camp and LZCG headquarters. Since they worked so closely together, they both needed to be updated. Whoever was on duty would know she regularly watched the Zambezi at night. It was common knowledge among the rangers. She never failed to catch small-time local poachers, but never these new bush meat poachers.

Wynne paused as she spotted five female elephants with a three-year-old calf and an infant. She scanned the underbrush for a bull following the herd. Usually bull elephants traveled separately from the females and either foraged for food alone or in small herds with other male juveniles. But if a cow was in season, bulls trailed the females. They were also larger than the cows and easily spotted. She didn't see one with this herd.

In groups like this one, a matriarch usually led the herd. She could be fifty or older and her experience in finding food and water, and in sensing danger maintained the social order of the herd. But this lone group of cows seemed frightened and unsure of approaching the river, raising their tusks and scenting the air, keeping their young at their sides. Obviously this herd had recently lost their matriarch—most likely one of the five elephants poached today.

The mother of the calf turned and Wynne saw that she had one broken tusk. Wynne had named her simply Broken Tusk. She was part of Bright Betsy's herd, but Bright Betsy must have been one of the elephants slaughtered by the poachers. Wynne called her B.B. for short. B.B. had grown accustomed to Wynne and had let her get within thirty yards of the herd while they fed.

Years of poaching and the slaughter of thousands of elephants had made them fear man and they would rarely take the chances of drinking in the open along rivers and streambeds during the day, nor would Wynne have ever been able to get as close as she had to B.B.'s herd. But since the park had cracked down on poaching, the elephants had been overcoming their fear. At seeing this herd disoriented, afraid and mourning the death of their matriarch, Wynne felt a stab of guilt and anger in the pit of her gut. She'd failed them today, broken their trust.

She waited as they eased forward and drank, then plodded back into the forest, following Broken Tusk and her infant. Wynne vowed to see them unafraid and drinking out in the open again.

She spotted the place where the poacher had said he was supposed to hand over the goods. Sausage Tree Camp was nothing but a bush lodge, named for the huge sausage tree that marked its location. The tree grew along the river's edge, centuries old, its boughs as thick as the tires on her Rover. She could see the phallic-shaped fruits hanging from its branches. Some of the gray-green fruit was well over two feet long and had to weigh at least twenty pounds. Several blue monkeys lounged on the branches, munching on the fruit, a much-prized treat of monkeys and elephants. Some native healers pulverized the fruit and applied the paste to treat skin problems, venereal disease, rheumatism, and cancer. She had used the paste a time or two herself on heat rashes and bee stings. Sausage tree fruit was also employed in a secret ritual that supposedly predicted the size of an infant's penis when he reached adulthood.

Wynne cracked a smile at the thought, then shifted her gaze to the lodge. It could sleep nine, but it was hardly more than a massive tent with a cement floor, though its lavish description on a safari tourist pamphlet made it sound much more inviting.

Tonight it looked empty. No trucks, or tethered horses— they were often used on bird-watching safaris. Bolts of mosquito netting stretched across the open tent windows. Zambia was a malaria zone; a fact reserved for the pamphlet's fine print. She had slathered her own skin with mud, a natural and readily accessible mosquito repellent.

Wynne was attuned to the sounds in the bush: the shrill chatter of monkeys; the trumpeting of an elephant; the cough of a hunting leopard. The sounds were always present, a gauging of normalcy, comforting in a way. She heard none of them now, only her own breathing and a dead eerie silence. Had the poachers gotten here before her?

She scanned the area behind the lodge. The trees. Along the road. She was about to take off her slingshot and follow the herd when someone touched her shoulder.

Wynne screamed in surprise and wheeled around. She kicked her attacker in the side, but the large man grabbed her leg and tossed her to the ground. As he came at her again she countered with a knee cut that knocked him off balance.

He staggered back and hit a tree trunk.

Wynne leaped to her feet, ready for the next strike.

He used an aikido side arm thrust this time. She deflected the blow and got in a lucky kick to his ribs.

He flinched a little, but stood his ground, solid as a mountain.

They circled each other, hands up, on the defensive. His face was in shadow and she couldn't see his eyes. It was important to see an opponent's eyes; they gave away every intended movement. She felt blind fighting him.

For a broad-shouldered man his movements were decisive and quick and hard to anticipate. He was a head taller than her five foot eleven inch frame. She looked most men in the eye, not this guy.

"We could do this two-step all night," his voice was deep, honey-coated by a Texas drawl.

"You're American?" It took her aback for a moment, but she didn't drop her guard or stop circling him.

"Last I checked." Amusement laced his voice. He paused and looked too at ease, hardly out of breath.

He'd been sparring with her, not using his full strength. What would have happened had he really felt threatened? "Who the hell are you?" Wynne paused because he'd paused. They stood three feet from each other. She kept her gaze on his hands.

"I was going to introduce myself when I tapped you on the shoulder—that is, before you attacked me like a cat with its tail caught under a rocker."

"I didn't hear you behind me. It was a knee-jerk reaction."

"Guess I should have cleared my throat." He sounded genuinely contrite. "My mistake. Bygones?" He shoved a hand at her.

Wynne leaped back as if avoiding a mamba attack.

"Whoa, there. Touchy thing, ain't you?"

"Keep your hands where I can see them." She narrowed her eyes at his dark form. It seemed massive against the back drop of the moon. She wished she could see his eyes.

"Anything you say." He slowly raised his hands.

"You didn't answer my question," she said, certain he was enjoying toying with her and had this pleasant harmless act honed to perfection. She felt her patience slipping. "Tell me your name."

"I could ask you the same, darlin'."

"I'm a ranger, and *so* not your darlin'. Your turn."

"Jack MacKay—nice moves you got. You study under a *sifu?*"

"Fifteen years." She wasn't about to tell him his form was as good as hers—a different discipline than the karate kick boxing she had studied, but impressive. His eyes were hidden in the dark, but she could feel him eyeing her up and down. "And you?" she asked.

"Ex-SEAL."

A good old boy and a SEAL, a lethal combination. That explained why she didn't hear him sneak up on her. "Okay, Lone Star, what are you doing in this area? The park closes at night."

"Most people call me Jack. And I was just walking. Any law against that?"

"The park's dangerous at night. Big cats and crocs hunt at night along this river, and so do hyenas and wild dogs. Stick to walking in daylight when the park is open. And don't ever sneak up on someone again. Now, I'm going to have to frisk you."

"Help yourself, darlin'." He turned and assumed the position with his hands outstretched and feet apart all too willingly. "I'll warn you, I'm packing," he said.

She stood behind him to be on the safe side and patted his ribs none too gently and enjoyed it when he winced. "Guns are not allowed in the park."

"It's a man's God-given right to protect himself."

"This isn't Texas, or the Alamo." She felt the shoulder holster, then found the gun. A massive thing, a .44 Magnum. Dirty Harry had nothing on this guy.

"Careful now. It's loaded. Wouldn't want a lady hurting herself."

He had just pushed the wrong buttons. She hurled the gun as far as she could. It plunked into the river with a loud splash.

"Hey, that was the first gun I ever bought. I'm attached to that gun." The sugar coating left his voice, a steely edge in its place.

Was that the true MacKay surfacing, a hint of dark center behind the Texas buttercream icing? "No guns in the park." She finished patting him down.

"Y'all really know how to show a guy a good time around here."

"Jeez, I'm sorry our social director is off. You got stuck with me." Wynne finished patting down his legs and decided not to search his crotch. He might like it too much. "You're clean."

"Do I get to search you now?"

"You can, if you want to be staked over a termite mound." Wynne listened to him laugh loudly, an exaggerated roar from deep within his chest. She rested her fists on her hips and said, "Now, I suggest you go back to where you came from."

"Can't. My jeep broke down." He gestured to the dirt road that led into camp.

"You said you were out walking?"

"I was. I knew the camp was here, so I walked here to find out if there was a phone."

"A phone?" Out in a bush camp. Malarkey. And he'd snuck up on her in a perpendicular direction to the road. What was he up to? Was he the contact the poacher had spoken about?

"What were you doing driving here to begin with?"

"You're mighty nosey."

"Technically you're trespassing on a Zambian national park and a game-managed area. I could bust you for having a gun. So answer my question."

"All right, no need to get your hackles up. But I kinda think you like gettin' 'em up."

She heard the smile in his voice and said, "Just answer the question."

"I heard of the bush camp and wanted to check it out and see if I might want to spend a week or two along the river."

"Why?"

"Let's just say I'm the outdoorsy type. Isn't that what lures most people to Africa?"

She suspected there was a lot more to his motives than he was admitting. "Where are you staying?"

"Why, you wanna join me for a drink?"

She wanted to toss him in the river, too, and said, "Just answer the question."

"At Hellstrom's Tours. Signed up for a safari."

Wynne's gut clenched. Hellstrom. There was his name again. Was Cowboy Jack just a tourist? Or sent here to throw her off, or perhaps alert the poachers? The way to the truth stood before her, one hundred and ninety pounds of Texas machismo packed nice and tight in a pair of jeans and a denim shirt. For some reason the sausage tree fruit ritual popped into her head.

She quickly squelched that line of insane thinking. He was the enemy. She said curtly, "I'll take you back to Hellstrom's."

"I'm fishing Jefferson Davis out the river first."

"Jefferson Davis?"

"My gun."

"Help yourself. I'll keep watch for the baboons."

"Baboons?"

"They like to tease the crocs, so it's like a natural alarm. But there's no warning for hippos."

"I don't care how many crocs or hippos I got to fight to get my gun. I'm gettin' it." His voice held an Alamo, Davy Crockett, do-or-die tone.

Something told her this was just the beginning of her night.

* * *

MacKay had refused to leave until he'd found the gun. The man was determined, she'd give him that. It also had helped that the gun had landed close to the shore and sunk in the mud. They had walked back the two miles to where she had hidden the Rover, and now they bumped along the road. The faint clicking of *The Simpsons* dolls and the road noise filled the interior of the truck. Hellstrom's compound bordered the Great East Road, a forty minute drive from Sausage Tree Camp. With MacKay in the truck, the miles seemed to drag, the trip taking forever. He seemed unusually quiet, distracted.

She chanced a few quick glances at him while driving. She hadn't really looked at him before. Damp jeans stuck to long muscular thighs. His soaked forest-green shirt was glued to washboard abs. His gun holster crossed over his broad chest and hung beneath his right shoulder. Dash lights glowed along his chiseled features and short cropped blond hair. He had a Brad Pitt face on a Schwarzenegger body. Not a bad combination, she had to admit. But it was obvious he was an expert at using his facile charm and good looks to his advantage.

As if he felt her gaze on him, he said, "Thanks for letting me find ol' J.D. here." He used that affable tone of his and patted the gun in the holster.

She didn't deserve his gratitude. The whole time he was searching for the gun she had visions of a croc running him out of the water. No such luck. She could have confiscated the gun, but if he were going to use it he would have long ago. And he seemed genuinely attached to it, like it was some kind of Texas security blanket, and she had to be at least civil to him. He was the key to getting inside Hellstrom's compound. Since he was feeling indebted to her at the moment, Wynne figured now might be a good time to find out if he was connected to the bush meat operation, so she said, "No problem. So how did you hear about Hellstrom's safari tours?"

"Internet—you never did tell me your name." He pulled off a soggy river reed stuck to his shirtsleeve, then flicked it out the window.

She didn't want to be on a first-name basis with him, and said, "Sperling."

"Your first name?"

She hesitated and said, "Wynne."

"Wynne Sperling?" He tried the name out. It sounded like *Spuhlin'* when he said it. "Sperling. I knew some Sperlings. You got family in Amarillo?"

"No."

"Where's your family from?"

"Washington, D.C."

"Visited the District once. Climbed the Washington Monument in the summer. It was one scorcher of a day—"

She interrupted his tourist anecdote and said, "Washington can be murder in the summer, but probably not any hotter than Texas. What part of Texas are you from?"

"All over, but mostly Austin. My life is pretty boring. Now yours is different. How'd you get all the way from D.C. to Africa?"

She didn't like the adroit way he kept turning the conversation back to her. "I majored in wildlife ecology with a minor in criminal justice. I thought I could do the most good here on the front lines. So what do you do for a living?" she asked, getting back to his life.

"I'm a businessman."

"What kind of business are you in?"

"Just about everything. Whatever strikes my fancy and turns a profit."

Was bush meat poaching one of his fancies? "How do you go from ex-SEAL to businessman?"

"I kinda teach aikido to kids, too. Keeps me in shape."

"I see."

He reached over and touched Bart's head, watching it bob. "What's with *The Simpsons* fetish?"

"Birthday gifts. From my little sister, Cody. It was one of our rituals to watch *The Simpsons* every week. She likes to tease me because I don't own a television here."

She recalled snuggling on the couch with Cody, a bowl of Doritos between them, watching *The Simpsons.* Wynne missed hearing Cody's nasally laugh, the peachy-bubble-gum teenage scent of her hair, the way she always used to get in Wynne's makeup and wear her clothes and swear she hadn't. The dolls connected Wynne to home, to her sister, to a life that was no longer her own. Wynne cherished the six dolls. She couldn't bear to see him abusing Bart's head and said, "Please, they're fragile."

"Sorry." He drew back his long arm and let it rest on his thigh. "You miss your family?"

His insightful question surprised Wynne and she said, "Very much."

"What about your folks? They alive?"

"Yeah, but divorced." Wynne thought of her father and smiled. "My father is a veterinarian for the National Zoo in Washington, and my mother…" Her smile melted. What was her mother? A bulldozer in stockings, heels and a Chanel suit. "She's in corporate law," Wynne finally said, realizing she'd said too much. "What about your parents?"

"My parents?" He gave a little taut laugh. "They consisted of the nuns at St. Anthony's Orphanage, and Clarence, the grounds man." A wistful tone entered his voice.

"Clarence?"

"Yep, old Clarence kinda took me under his wing, taught me how to box, work on cars and how to hunt—the sisters didn't like that though. He took all us boys hunting on weekends, told the sisters it was a camping trip to commune with God. Ha! I think they were wise to him, but they didn't say a word. Beside the priest, he was the only male influence in our lives—not knocking Father Reilly, he could go a round in the ring with the best of them, but he liked gardening. We boys just weren't into perennials...." His words trailed off, and he seemed lost in memories.

The kind of silence that accompanies too much personal disclosure dragged between them. She wished she hadn't asked about his parents. Was he lying to gain her sympathy? No, there had been an unmistakable honesty in his voice. All she really wanted to know about him was if he was involved in the poaching.

"This is a mighty fine ride you got," MacKay said, glancing around the interior of her truck. "It's not standard issue."

"It's mine."

"How does a warden in Zambia afford something like this? Isn't the government strapped? Your salary couldn't be but so much. You probably can't afford to put gas in it."

"I didn't exactly take this job for the Wall Street salary." He didn't need to know she lived off a trust fund her grandmother had left her. Any momentary sympathy she might have felt for him flew out the window. He was becoming annoying again.

He lifted his beefy hand and began methodically cracking each knuckle. "So are you one of those bleeding-heart, bunny-hugging activists? That it?"

Make that extremely annoying. She jabbed back, "Are you one of those guys who prays to Charlton Heston every time you pay your NRA dues?"

"Touché." He wrote an imaginary one in the air, then went back to work on his knuckles. "Score one for the liberal. But don't you use a gun in your job?"

"Hardly ever." The popping sound of his joints grated on her eardrums like sandpaper.

"Now that is different." He spoke as if he didn't believe her. He stopped torturing his knuckles, then said with a smirk, "But you gotta admit being a warden is not a fit job for a woman, even if she were packing."

She fought the urge to stop the truck and leave him for roadkill, but she wasn't going to give him the pleasure of letting him know he was getting to her. She smiled at him as if she'd just been impaled by a rhino. "And what kind of jobs *are* fit for a woman in your opinion?"

"I don't know...." He shrugged and rubbed his chin. "Air traffic controller, astronaut, lobbyist, lawyer, veterinarian, detective. See, I'm not as chauvinistic as you thought, darlin'."

"It's a good thing you can't read my mind."

"Maybe I can."

"You don't seem psychic to me."

"No, but I know you're probably the only female warden in all of Africa. Hell, there's probably not that many in the States."

"I don't defend how I live my life to anyone."

She'd had to do enough of that with her mother, who would never understand why Wynne stayed in such a dangerous job. It wasn't just about preserving the last great wilderness on earth, but also about the challenge. She thrived on overcoming the danger and the obstacles, and experiencing the amazing rewards which kept her here, like watching a lioness teaching her cubs to hunt, or the beauty of a herd of impala or zebra grazing. Africa had a wild but beautiful rhythm to it, and that rhythm was in her heart. It was well worth the fight to save it. Something this arrogant Texan would never understand. Or her mother.

"Are you a thrill-seeker, or you just got a death wish?" he asked.

"Do you?" Wynne added enough bite to the words that they came out as a threat.

It actually worked and for once he was speechless. He crossed his arms over his chest and stared at her in a probing, contemplative way.

She didn't realize she'd driven past Hellstrom's compound and she skidded to a stop. *The Simpsons* dolls whiplashed on the dash and MacKay braced himself, uttering something about female drivers. She shifted into reverse and pulled into the drive then slammed on the brakes.

A man stood in the headlights, a rifle pointed at her.

Chapter 3

Wynne stared into the face of the guard. The headlights glowed along his dark skin and sunken cheeks and eyes. He wore a tan uniform with Hellstrom's Tours embroidered on the shirt pocket. One hand held the rifle, while he grabbed a walkie-talkie on his belt with the other. He looked at her license plate, then spoke into the radio.

"Hellstrom's got good security here." MacKay grinned over at her.

Maybe too good. It hadn't seemed extreme to her before now because all wildlife ranches and safari owners had secure compounds. But as she gazed at the ten-foot-high barbed wire fence that encompassed the compound and the guard's AK-47, a rifle more suited to stopping armies than people, she had to wonder what he was hiding. "I guess he has his reasons for it."

"You ever been here before?" MacKay asked while he rolled down his window, his attention on the guard.

"I ride by on my rounds sometimes." Hellstrom's compound was about twenty-five miles south of base camp, in a valley surrounded on one side by rolling hills, a prime area for grazing wildlife. When elephant herds went in search of fresh pasture, she sometimes drove past his compound to monitor them. She remembered the area before Hellstrom built the compound, when nothing was here but open spaces and herds of buffalo, eland, zebras, wildebeest and giraffe. She felt a tinge of loss.

"Can't blame a man for putting up a fence." MacKay didn't wait for her comeback and stuck his head out the window. "It's okay, Cephu. She's giving me a ride."

Cephu dropped the gun, smiled and said in English, "Oh, Mr. MacKay, it's you." The guard's joy at seeing the Texan beamed in his face and a broad smile showed his white teeth. He dropped the walkie-talkie and stepped aside, waving Wynne through. "Have a nice night, *Bwana* MacKay."

Bwana was a Bemba term for "Mr." or "Master." Wynne didn't know if MacKay deserved such deference.

She narrowed her eyes at him. "Do you know all the staff?"

"What can I say? I kinda grow on people." He shrugged, then gave her a sympathetic glance, as if the only way she could grow on someone was if she were toenail fungus.

"I can grow on people, too." The moment the words were out, she regretted them.

"I bet you do darlin', I just bet you do." Good-humored irony laced his voice.

Wynne couldn't believe what she'd just blurted out. Why did she care what he thought? She didn't need his approval. She let it drop and looked out at Hellstrom's compound. It consisted of two hundred acres. Most of the ground had been plowed. Rows of tobacco, yams and maize grew along the drive.

MacKay saw she was looking at the fields and said, "I hear Hellstrom donates food to the Zambian government for the indigent."

"I know. He also started an LZCG trust for local orphanages and AIDS clinics."

"I believe someone told me he worked at a mission feeding the poor, too. Gotta respect a man who's generous with his wealth."

"Everyone respects him, no doubt about that." Wynne frowned. "He knows how to win friends and influence people."

"I wonder when he finds time to kick back and raise a little hell," MacKay said, forcing a smile. "Everybody's gotta have a little fun sometime. I sure have to."

"Around here living is about survival, not about fun."

"It's gotta be godawful taking life so seriously. You gotta kick back." MacKay chuckled. "You're about as uptight as a beer can without a pop-top. You're gonna explode one day and it ain't gonna be pretty...although come to think on it, it might." His lips turned up into a sensual grin.

Wynne realized for the first time he had deep dimples, and she said, "Thank you for your candid six-pack psychological evaluation." Wynne glowered back at him. Was he one of those American guys who hadn't outlived his adolescence? Or was this part of his happy-go-lucky facade that was meant to fool her. "And you may think life's an amusement park, but it's not."

"Nobody knows that better than me, but it doesn't hurt to jump on a ride sometime." He winked at her, his long-lashed eyes gleaming purplish blue in the green dash lights.

She could have fun. Couldn't she? She loved her job, but she couldn't remember the last time she'd really had fun. There had been the picnic she'd arranged for the kids at the Big Five Habitat, yet she hadn't been able to go. A lion had been caught in a poacher's snare and had gotten his head loose, but the snare had remained embedded in his neck. Wynne had been forced to dart him, while Dr. Leonard, the on-staff veterinarian, worked on him. Had she been in the bush so long she'd forgotten what fun was? She didn't need the answer to that and certainly not from some stranger involved in poaching.

At her silence MacKay spoke. "In case you haven't noticed, darlin'," he motioned toward the fields they drove past, "Hellstrom doesn't look like he's having any trouble surviving."

The Texan was more right than he realized. Hellstrom was too good to be true. Wealthy. A philanthropist. Conservationist. A living breathing paragon. He had to have a dark side. Didn't he?

MacKay pointed ahead of them. "Just drive right on up to the front door—looks like Hellstrom's got himself some company. Maybe another fund-raiser dinner. I hear he has lots of them. He'll probably hit me up for a donation before I leave."

"When will that be?"

"You sound like you're in a hurry to get rid of me," MacKay said, pretending to sound hurt. Or maybe he really was.

"Do I?" Wynne said it in such an innocent Scarlet O'Hara way that MacKay chuckled.

She glanced toward Hellstrom's house, an expansive two-story Spanish Colonial Revival with iron-railed balconies, arched windows, cornices and parapets. A row of bungalows flanked the right side of the house, the servant and guest quarters. In the back were two large garages, a barn and a landing strip. It was bigger than some villages in Zambia.

She remembered taking a tour of Hellstrom's house when he had finished building it several months ago. He had given a housewarming party and invited all the wardens and the LZCG members and supporters. Wynne hadn't wanted to go, but the commander had made it mandatory.

Hellstrom had been his normal charismatic self, delighting everyone with anecdotes and playing the perfect host. At one point he had singled Wynne out, and she had sensed his attraction to her. Thankfully Kaweki, the commander, had interrupted them and introduced Hellstrom to his wife. Wynne had slipped away, relieved, feeling as if she had just escaped before Hellstrom had asked her out. After the incident at the party, she felt self-conscious around him and tried not to be alone with him ever again. No matter how handsome and appealing Hellstrom might be, she didn't approve of how he made his living.

Safari owners, like Hellstrom, reaped most of their income from wealthy hunters—mostly English and American. Hunters paid safari operators large fees for supplying guides to take them into game-managed areas to hunt. The problem arose when corrupt hunters paid safari owners under the table and killed more animals than their government-issued licenses allowed. Coupled with native poaching, bush meat poaching and loss of habitat, animal populations just couldn't recover. But Hellstrom did have an altruistic side that made him more likeable. And other than his dismissal of her DNA lab idea and the interest he appeared to have in her, he really wasn't a bad leader for the LZCG. They had a good working relationship so far, and she meant to keep it all business—unless he proved to be the duplicitous head of this bush meat ring.

She pulled in behind a line of Toyota Land Cruisers,

Rovers and Hummers. Some of the trucks had zebra-striped tops with logos from local tour businesses. She parked at the end of the line. Then she spotted the Zambian Wildlife Authority jeep. Rangers weren't allowed to take the only ZWA jeep out for personal use, which meant the commander must be in attendance. It didn't surprise her. Commander Kaweki worked closely with Hellstrom, and he was invited to all of Hellstrom's social functions to represent the ZWA.

"Thanks muchly for the ride, darlin'. It's been real interesting." MacKay saluted her and opened the door.

"Wait, aren't you going to ask me in?"

MacKay's sandy blond brows rose a fraction and a lazy victorious grin spread across his mouth. "You change your mind about that drink?"

To make her plan work, she had to play along and seem interested. He probably knew she wasn't. But the pretense would give her a reason to get inside Hellstrom's office and do a little reconnaissance, and it would keep MacKay guessing. "Let's just start with the drink, shall we." Wynne jumped out of the Rover and breezed past him.

"The night is young yet, darlin'." He sugarcoated the epithet, then fell in step beside her.

Wynne rolled her eyes. She could stand one libido-horned Texan for a few minutes. She stepped into the path of the lights that shot out through the front windows and glanced inside. It was a large solarium type room. A yellowish haze of cigarette smoke bathed a sea of white and black faces. She recognized the LZCG treasurer, Mr. Masamba, and the vice president, Mr. Njobo. They were talking, their wives at their sides, nodding. Thankfully, the commander was nowhere to be seen. She really didn't want to explain why she had lied earlier and radioed that

her 10-20 was the Rufunsa game-managed area and not
Sausage Tree Camp. She couldn't risk tipping off the
poachers. She didn't know who at the LZCG might be
monitoring the transmissions.

Abruptly the door opened, and Hellstrom himself stood
in the doorway as if he were expecting her.

"Wynne, so nice to see you. Jack." Hellstrom's sophisticated English voice held a warm welcome. His yellowish gold eyes brightened. "Come in, come in. A pleasure."

"I got a bone to pick with you, Noah," MacKay said,
stepping past Wynne.

For once Wynne didn't mind the Texan. He had gained
Hellstrom's full attention. She followed MacKay up the
steps, adrenaline flowing, her body wired. Stay cool.
Breathe. Search his house for evidence, then leave. How
hard could that be? Yeah, right—about as easy as falling
off a cliff with no parachute.

Once inside the foyer, Wynne paused next to MacKay,
still feeling that roller coaster ride sensation that left her
stomach in her throat. A set of closed double doors stood
to the right and left of her. Muffled voices and Beethoven's
Moonlight Sonata drifted from behind them.

MacKay was rambling on about the jeep breaking
down. The guy knew how to beat a topic to death. "You
need a new mechanic. That radiator had a leak. You
couldn't miss it."

Hellstrom was listening, nodding, with a gracious smile,
but his deep-set gold eyes were on her. His straight black
hair tapered to a razor-sharp widow's peak on his tanned
brow. Several strands fell on either side of his temples and
made him look younger than his thirty-something years.
His features were sharply chiseled, beautiful in a Michelan-

gelo's "David" sort of way. He was a walking Ralph Lauren ad. Charisma oozed from him and she found herself unable to look away.

Was he wondering why she was here? She felt the roller coaster take another dive. Just breathe. Smile. Be friendly.

MacKay seemed to realize he'd lost his audience and he said, "Better have your vehicles checked out by someone competent." Then he remembered Wynne and said, "Look what I dug up." He gestured toward her.

"Wynne, how have you ended up with my guest?" Hellstrom's voice held a hint of an apology.

"I found him lost down by the river. Next time a guest ventures out alone at night, I'd make them take a guide along—for their own safety. And make them aware of the park's hours."

"Of course, how remiss of me."

"And you might want to instruct them about firearms."

"Of course." Hellstrom pulled at a ruby cufflink.

"Don't read the riot act to the man. It's my own fault." Oddly MacKay's grin had been replaced by a sober expression. "I thought it would be all right to look at the park. He didn't know I took off and went sightseeing."

Wynne thought MacKay had jumped at that too easily. And there was a note of falseness in his voice. He was covering something. He and Hellstrom were probably better acquainted than MacKay had let on.

"You'll know better next time, won't you, Jack?" Hellstrom said smoothly.

"Sure." MacKay nodded, not at all contrite, just unusually curt with his one-word reply.

"I'm sorry he took you away from your duties, Wynne."

She waited for the invitation. It didn't come. Hellstrom seemed to be giving her an entry for an exit.

"I should go." Wynne turned to leave.

MacKay said, "Wait. You've come this far. You can't leave now."

Hellstrom shot MacKay a glance, but the four hundred-watt smile never left Hellstrom's face. "Quite right." He took in her appearance. "But you might want to freshen up a bit."

Wynne glanced at her torn shirt. The slingshot was wrapped around her waist, bits of leaves stuck in it. Her hiking boots were slathered in river mud. The mosquito remedy still caked to her neck and her face was beginning to itch. She hadn't realized just how grubby she was. In her line of work, she was used to getting dirty. She had never been more aware that her femininity had taken a back seat since coming to Africa.

She maintained a smile and felt her cheeks straining in an attempt to be civil. "You'll have to forgive my appearance. I've been working."

"I wonder how she cleans up?" MacKay said, while his blue eyes roved over her body. "Versace might look real nice on her."

Wynne smiled sweetly at MacKay, though it was slowly killing her. "I'm afraid I'm all out of designer dresses. There isn't much use for them in my line of work."

A door opened and a beautiful woman in a strapless black evening gown glided through. The woman's complexion was so smooth and white it looked transparent. Her dark curly hair fell in waves to her shoulders. She was model thin, maybe in her late twenties.

A cacophony of voices followed her into the foyer, along with the cloying scent of her perfume. She gently closed the door behind her and muted the sound. She stepped over to Hellstrom and touched his arm possessively. "Noah, dearest, we've run out of champagne," she spoke in a British accent.

Slight annoyance flashed across Hellstrom's expression, then it disappeared into his usual polite demeanor. "Jacqueline, you've met Mr. MacKay, but I don't think you've met Wynne Sperling."

"Charmed, I'm sure." Jacqueline gave Wynne an uninterested passing glance, then her gaze settled on MacKay. "Jack, it's always a pleasure." Her smile turned sensual.

MacKay's blue eyes glittered as he winked at her. "The pleasure's all mine, darlin'."

Did MacKay flirt with every woman within eyeshot? Or was Wynne picking up on a kinky factor between the threesome? Did they pass Jacqueline around like a pool cue? Maybe she'd found Hellstrom's dark side. If she had any doubts that MacKay and Hellstrom were more than business associates, they were gone now.

The pool cue turned her attention back to Wynne. "And are you one of Noah's customers?"

"I'm a ranger. We kinda work together."

"Oh." Jacqueline leaned so close to Hellstrom her breasts touched his arm.

Gracious as ever, Hellstrom said, "And she'll be staying for the party. Wynne, I'll have a servant show you where to freshen up—"

"Thank you."

"I should change, too." MacKay winked at Wynne and said, "I'll definitely see you later, darlin'."

Wynne wanted to say "Fat chance," but she had to play the game. She watched him walk out the front door, grinning like a hyena. He must be staying in one of the guest quarters.

"My servant will show you where to go," Hellstrom said to Wynne, then clicked his fingers.

A short slender African came running down the hall. His head reached the top of Wynne's rib cage. He was enrobed in a white gauze tunic and scandals. The Pygmy looked more child than man. How he heard Hellstrom's summons over the music and conversation puzzled Wynne. He kept his head bowed as he listened to Hellstrom's orders.

Hellstrom spoke a dialect that Wynne recognized as one of several languages Pygmies used, then said to Wynne, "Tungana will take care of you."

"Thank you."

Tungana motioned for Wynne to follow him, but didn't lift his eyes up to her face.

Wynne trailed Tungana down the hall, feeling Hellstrom and Jacqueline's gaze on her. She wondered about the extent of the relationship between Hellstrom and MacKay, and when they were out of Hellstrom's hearing range, she casually asked Tungana, "Is MacKay an old friend of Mr. Hellstrom's?"

"Don't know." Tungana spoke in broken English and shook his small head.

"You've never seen him in Mr. Hellstrom's company before?"

"Don't know."

Okay, she was getting the parrot message. He was loyal to Hellstrom and he wasn't going to talk. A lot of people were loyal to Hellstrom, including MacKay, it seemed.

They passed the dining room, decorated in ornate antique French furniture. Guests huddled around a massive table laden with enough food to feed ten Zambian families for a week.

The memory of the tour flashed back to her, and she knew the next room they passed would be the music room. It had been in this room where Hellstrom had approached her, and she had felt his attraction for her. Had she been imagining it? He hadn't pursued her in any way since. Maybe she had read more into it than really had been there. She was good at reading animals. But men? They were a whole different species.

A grand piano graced the music room's center. A musician in a tux sat playing Bach now. Commander Kaweki's balding head caught her eye, the chandelier light bouncing off his dark, shiny scalp. He stood behind the piano, speaking to Colette, his wife and another couple Wynne didn't recognize.

Colette had short curly ebony hair and wide, impish green eyes. Her smile lit up her face. A simple, yet elegant black gown covered her hourglass figure. Colette was originally from France, but had worked as a missionary in Lusaka, the capitol of Zambia, before Kaweki married her. The only time Wynne ever saw the commander smile was when he was with his wife. He appeared enthralled by what she was telling the other couple now and didn't notice Wynne and Tungana move past the doorway.

After they cleared the music room's entrance, Wynne relaxed a little. She really didn't want to explain to Kaweki what she was doing here until she'd had a chance to nose around.

"You really don't have to show me the way," she said. "Just point me in the right direction. I can find it myself."

"Oh, no, no. *BaK para* would not like that."

BaK para meant "master" in the Pygmy language, a term of fear and obedience. Wynne frowned as she said, "You know, Tungana, you're employed by Mr. Hellstrom. He's not your master."

Tungana nodded, but still wouldn't look at her.

"How long have you been with Mr. Hellstrom?" She asked as they slipped past an African couple, strangers to Wynne.

Tungana avoided all small talk by merely shrugging.

At seeing Tungana reduced to servitude and away from his home, Wynne couldn't help but think about the life he'd left behind. Pygmies had a wonderful nomadic lifestyle, centered on their love for the forest world and their family. She had visited the Belgian Congo once when she first arrived in Africa. She spent several days with the BaMbuti Pygmies and fell in love with their warmth and gentleness and the simplicity in which they lived. The sad thing was they had existed for millennia, even ancient Egyptians wrote of seeing Pygmies in the heart of Africa, but now their hunting and gathering way of life was quickly eroding. The destruction of rain forests and the overhunting of food sources were taking their toll. Nothing saddened her more than the slow extinction of a once proud, self-sustaining culture. Part of the beauty of Africa was its diversity and even that was disappearing.

"Do you miss your family?" Wynne asked.

Tungana nodded, an unmistakable sadness in his eyes. Then he seemed to realize that he'd actually answered her and slipped back into self-protective mode.

The din of the party drifted away as he led her up a flight of stairs and into a deserted wing of the house. She recalled the area from the tour.

He paused before a door. "Tungana draw you a bath. You like?" he asked, his words clipped.

"I can manage alone. All I need is a hairbrush and a washcloth and towel."

"Brush in closet." He opened the door to the room and waited for her to step inside.

"Thank you. I can find my way back."

The bedroom was done in a Spanish motif. Red wallpaper complemented the rich mahogany furniture and four-poster bed. A woman's photograph hung above the bed. Her hair was coal-black and worn in a French twist. Golden eyes, similar to Hellstrom's, stared out from the photo. Her dark hair accentuated her pale skin. The photographer had captured an isolated, detached gleam in the woman's eyes. They reminded Wynne of a doll's eyes, inanimate and blank. Wynne didn't remember the painting on the tour and said, "Who is that?"

"*BaK para*'s mama."

"Oh."

Tungana walked to the closet and opened the door. A row of women's dresses hung neatly in the closet.

"Wow, does Hellstrom keep those for his female guests?" It looked like thousands of dollars worth of designer labels.

"He best host." Tungana nodded and seemed to be looking for one particular evening dress. He pulled out a slinky red gown and a pair of red heels.

The gown might fit her, but it was a little more revealing than she would like. It was ankle length and low-cut with rhinestone spaghetti straps. The same red rhinestones formed starburst patterns randomly all over the dress.

Tungana laid the evening dress on the bed. "For you?"

"But I don't—"

"*BaK para* want you to wear."

Leave it to Hellstrom to anticipate every female guest's need by supplying them with dresses. If it would bide her some time to search the house, she'd comply. "All right." She nodded.

Tungana left the room and closed the door behind him.

She pressed her ear to the door and listened as the soft tread of his footsteps faded.

She hurried into the bathroom. When she looked into the

mirror, she didn't recognize herself. A mud wrestler, after a fight, probably looked better than she did. She recalled MacKay's comments about her cleaning up okay. Her female vanity wanted to show him just how well she cleaned up. But then she reminded herself, it didn't matter what a woman looked like, he'd flirt with anything breathing and wearing a bra.

She scrubbed the remnants of mud off her face, neck, arms and her boots. Then she untied her hair. She brushed the bits of mud out of it around her face. There wasn't much she could do about the limpness. Her hair always had the texture of thick straw. It hung down her back, stick-straight.

She quickly changed into the dress, wrapping her slingshot around her thigh and sliding her knife into it. The shoes actually fit her size nine feet, but the heels felt strange. It took a few strides to get used to them.

She surveyed herself in the full-length mirror behind the bathroom door. Wide hazel eyes stared back at her from an oval tanned face. She didn't like the pronounced dimple in her chin and her mouth seemed too wide, genetic gifts from her father that couldn't be helped. But her tanned skin was clear and glowed from the scrubbing—so she wasn't drop-dead beautiful and her cheeks weren't sunken and she didn't have sticks for arms and legs like Jacqueline. She was built of sturdier stuff. She'd like to see Jacqueline freeing a baby rhino from a mud bog.

The thought brought a smile to her face as she decided she didn't look half-bad in the dress. She had to go braless and a hint of her nipples showed through the lined silk. The dress actually clung to her curves in a flattering way, and the starbursts on the dress only made her body shimmer. Not bad. It was the first time since coming to Africa she had felt feminine. It felt pretty good. She cracked the door, checked that it was clear, then slipped back out into the hallway.

The moments ticked off in Wynne's mind, keeping time with her heartbeat. She remembered one room that had been off-limits during the tour. Hellstrom had said it was his office, and they wouldn't find anything of interest in it.

She reached the door.

Locked.

She heard guards laughing in the hall ahead of her. Before they rounded the corner, she darted into the opposite door. She was standing inside a linen closet. She moved so the shelves wouldn't cut the back of her knees and she realized her dress was caught in the door. She couldn't open the door. The guards were too close, their voices right in front of the closet. What kind of excuse could she use for being in there: "Can you point me to the ladies' bathroom, I seem to be turned around." That was lame. Oh, God!

She held her breath.

The voices faded.

She dared let herself breathe and opened the door.

A clear coast.

She stepped out, lifted her dress and pulled out her dagger. She shoved it in between the doorjamb and the lock. The lock clicked open.

Wynne stepped inside. A desk lamp bathed the room in dim light. It was a massive room. Shelves of books lined the walls. Above the shelves was a gun case that covered the whole perimeter of the room. Guns of every make and description were arranged in a collage of shapes, numbered brass placards beneath them. He must be anal about his guns.

African tribal masks formed a patchwork of color on the wall behind a massive mahogany desk. She recognized the local Bemba tribal masks, and the monkey shaped expressions of the Boa. They weren't the mass-marketed copies bought off the Internet. These were aged, the wood cracked from wear. The real thing. Probably worth a fortune and sacred to the people who had made them.

Across from the masks, a computer and copier sat on a credenza. She didn't have time to bring up the computer. Hellstrom probably had a code to open it anyway.

She stepped over to the desk. Books on Africa were stacked in piles. An Underwood manual typewriter—a dinosaur—sat in the middle of them. A spot had been cleared for a small mountain of typed pages. A manuscript? She picked up the first page and read: *Musings of an African Safari Owner* by Noah Hellstrom. Add author to Hellstrom's accomplishments.

On the edge of the desk, she spotted a picture of Hellstrom standing over a felled elephant. She grimaced. Next to it was a photo of a couple. She recognized his mother, the same deadpan face from the portrait in the bedroom. The man wore the uniform of the British army, medals emblazoned across his chest and shoulders. He had a sour expression like his face would crack if he ever smiled. Hellstrom's father?

Guards approached the door, talking.

She tensed, ready to jump beneath the desk.

They strode past.

She let out her breath and walked to a filing cabinet. She had no idea what she was looking for, but when she found it she would know.

LZCG ledgers were in the top drawer. Another drawer, more ledgers for his tour businesses and a row of books.

She read the titles: *Mein Kampf* by Hitler, biographies of Churchill, Patton, Mussolini, Genghis Kahn and Alexander the Great. Did Hellstrom have a secret god complex?

Another drawer revealed old tax forms, business licenses and rubber-banded envelopes of past due notices on loans from the World Bank. There were a lot of them. Hellstrom must be in financial trouble. Three of them were from Springhill Mental Health Sanitorium. Why did he have past due notices from a mental hospital?

She spotted the drawer on his desk. She should have checked there first. Isn't that where all the crucial stuff was always hidden?

She tried it. Locked. She grabbed the letter opener and worked the lock. James Bond made it look so easy. "Come on…" She jiggled the opener in frustration.

The lock clicked open.

"Thank you." She peered inside and found a bundle of letters rubber banded together. The return address label read, Edna Hellstrom, Springhill Mental Health Sanitorium, Yorkshire, England. Were there some unglued genes in Hellstrom's family? If only she had the time to read each one.

She found the rest of the drawer empty. So where would he hide illegal documents? She felt for a secret compartment on the desk. Nothing.

She closed the drawer and stood in the middle of the room and really looked at it as Hellstrom would. Something drew her gaze to the tribal masks, and a large mask near the bottom caught her attention. It was painted white, the facial features outlined in black. It was a striking, almost frightening, *ngil* mask. The male societies of the Fang tribe wore the gorilla mask during initiation of new members and for persecuting wrongdoers. It was a mask of dominance and retribution. If Hellstrom had a hidden narcissistic side, he would be attracted to it.

She lifted the mask, expecting to find a safe hidden behind it. What she found was a wooden sleeve secured to the back of the mask by screws. The open top-end of the sleeve revealed a blue folder, stuffed with papers.

She reached for the folder, but instinct stopped her. This was way too easy. She sniffed the leather pouch and recognized the woody scent of nuts: Physic nuts, to be exact. Africans ground the nut with palm oil to make rat poison.

Wynne grabbed several sheets of paper from the typewriter and used them as makeshift gloves to pull open the folder. It was stuffed with bills of lading for a company named LiBolo International Trucking. It had a South African address. Crates containing dry ice, some flown in from Zimbabwe, had been trucked to Botswana, Zimbabwe, Mozambique, South Africa, Malawi, Namibia and almost every city in Africa. Some even went to the U.S., England, and China. The bush meat would have been packed on dry ice, then shipped.

She'd found what she was looking for.

She had never seen such a well-organized, sophisticated ring. Usually the operations were kept locally. Dealers contracted and paid hunters up front for the number and kinds of meat. The hunters hired a crew of bearers to cut out the tusks, butcher the meat, and dry it. In villages near game-managed areas, there could be fifteen commercial poachers operating at any given time. After the kills, the hunters met the dealers and trucked the meat to marketplaces in Zambian cities where it was sold illegally. Wynne had been in on many of these stings, arresting the commercial poachers with the meat. But this dealer operation was outside of Zambia, so it hadn't been discovered.

The bills of lading only proved LiBolo International trucked something on dry ice. Even if she could convince the Zambian government to investigate this company, proving Hellstrom was tied to it would be another hurdle. It would take prosecutors and accountants months, maybe even years, to go through international courts and subpoena the company records from South Africa. And she couldn't take the paperwork to the LZCG board. It would be too risky without definitive proof he owned the company.

She heard voices in the hall. How long had she been gone? Fifteen? Thirty minutes? She had to hurry.

The voices were getting louder. They sounded angry. Doors were slamming.

Her hands shook and the ersatz paper gloves were getting in her way. *Hurry, Sperling, or you're toast.* She managed to stuff the folder back in the wooden sleeve, crumple her makeshift gloves, clean side out. She tossed them in the trash, then plopped the mask back on the wall.

The door's lock was turning. She ran to the door just as it opened.

Chapter 4

Wynne gazed into Hellstrom's face. For a nanosecond they stared at each other with a wrong-restroom look.

Hellstrom recovered first and waited for an explanation.

"Sorry, I—um, was looking for the party and somehow got lost." Lame city. He'd never buy that.

"A lost ranger? Don't you have a keen sense of direction?"

"Only outside. Give me the outdoors and I'm fine. You can always find your way by the sun or the lay of the land. But in closed quarters, forget it. All the walls and hallways look the same to me." Could he tell she was lying? It didn't show in his face.

"I thought this door was locked." His golden eyes probed her face.

"It wasn't. I just walked right in." Wynne wanted to step past Hellstrom, but he was holding the doorknob and blocking her way. "Now that you're here, can you show me the way back to the party?"

His gaze fell to the red dress. For a moment her body held his attention, then his expression softened. "You look so different in that gown. Quite stunning." He stepped inside and closed the door. "I thought the red would look good on you."

"Thank you for letting me borrow it." Wynne felt trapped as she watched him close the door. "We really should get back."

"You've caught me." He stepped closer, his eyes taking on a strange dynamic glow.

"Caught you?" Wynne tried to sound surprised, while her insides churned. Was this it? A showdown? If he knew she was on to him, he might move the operation. Or worse, eliminate her before she could find proof against him. Every muscle in her body tensed as she waited for his answer.

"Yes, my wretched attempt at novel writing." He motioned toward his desk, his gaze glued to the dress. Or her body in it. She wasn't certain.

"Novel writing?" Relief flooded Wynne as she glanced toward the desk. That's when she noticed the mask…hanging crooked. Just a tiny bit off kilter. But definitely not how he'd left it. Oh, God! Had he seen it? From his angle, the stack of books on his desk blocked the bottom of the mask. Hopefully he wouldn't notice.

"I really just stumbled upon your office," she said. "So I really didn't see much."

"It's fortunate the door wasn't locked." He cocked a brow at her and grinned, but it was a tight smile that didn't reach his eyes. "I believe in fate. There are no coincidences. I was meant to find you at this moment."

And I was meant to find those bills of lading. "I have to disagree. I think man controls his own destiny."

"You speak your mind, don't you?"

"I am pretty direct."

"You're one of a kind."

"Not really."

"I must disagree. Most women of my acquaintance flatter and dissemble. But you, you know your mind and are incredibly honest. I admire that. I think I can trust you with my secret."

"Your secret?" She wanted to look toward the mask, but held his gaze.

"My writing secret." There was an intimate depth to his voice that she'd never heard before.

"Sure, I won't tell anyone."

"Thank you." He smiled, his even white teeth gleaming. "At least not until I get it published." He paused, his eyes dipping to her breasts. "Now that you know my secret, it's only fitting I know one of yours." He stepped closer, their bodies almost touching.

She could smell the starch in his white shirt, mixed with a musky aftershave and smoke from the party. A strand of straight black hair had fallen over his left brow, giving him a handsome, rakish look. If she didn't know what a hypocrite and fraud he was, she might have been attracted to him. He was only a few inches taller than her and she was forced to look him straight in the eyes.

"I'm a pretty open book." She shrugged and then pointed to his gun collection. When she did, she stepped to the side so that in order for him to face her, his back would be toward the mask. "I did notice your gun collection when I came in. It must be worth thousands."

"It is, but you're avoiding my question. You must have a secret."

Wynne almost glanced at the mask, but forced her eyes back to his face. She had to give him something and make it sound convincing so she said, "Um, my mother and I are estranged."

His expression turned inward. "My own dear mother is ill, I don't see her as much as I would like."

So the letters she had found from the mental institution must have been from his mother. She recalled his mother's photo and the peculiar look in her eyes. Now Wynne knew the reason for it.

She really wanted to change the subject and get out of this office, but as long as it kept him occupied and not looking at the mask, she'd have to go with it. She sensed he didn't want to talk yet and waited patiently.

After a moment, he came out of his musings, but dark shadows lingered in his eyes. "My father was a bloody bastard. He gambled away all of my mother's inheritance. He died leaving her penniless. Don't get me wrong, I love my mother and I don't mind aiding her now, but it all could have been avoided."

She recalled the past due notices in his desk. How much aid could he afford to give his mother? He hadn't paid his own bills or her mental hospital bills in months. "I'm sorry," she said, trying to sound sympathetic.

"Don't be. It wasn't the worst of my father's contemptible qualities."

"There's more?" She really didn't want to hear anymore, but she had to keep him talking.

"He had a wicked temper." Hellstrom paused and appeared lost in bleak memories. After a moment, he said, "My mother stood up to him. Sometimes I wish she hadn't."

Wynne suddenly could see Hellstrom, a frightened little boy, cowering in the corner, while his mother protected him from a beating. This was getting way too deep for her, so she said, "I'm not that brave. I ran to the other side of the globe from my mother." Wynne frowned at that self-realization.

"I'm sorry," he said, then cleared his throat. "I digressed about my mother. Please, tell me about yours. Why are you estranged?"

"I committed a cardinal sin."

"What was that?"

"I refused to go to law school and become a partner in her law firm. You don't say no to my mother. She couldn't understand I wasn't cut out to work behind a desk. And she never understood why I came to Zambia."

"Solicitors can make a difference. You could have worked in environmental law. What made you come to Africa to become a warden?"

"Partly my father. He's a vet for the National Zoo in Washington, D.C. and used to let me go to work with him. He instilled in me a love for animals. But that isn't exactly what brought me. I guess it was…" She paused.

"What?" He stood there transfixed on her face, his golden eyes glowing with a rapt yellow light.

He seemed totally absorbed by the conversation, so she continued. "I guess I was about twelve. And I was watching this *National Geographic* special on the plight of African elephants. I can't even remember where it was in Africa, all I remember seeing was this herd of females with their calves. The local government declared they had to be killed because they were destroying crops. Hunters had cornered the herd and circled them. As you must know, when you kill a herd of female elephants, the oldest alpha female turns to protect the calves and younger elephants with her body. Then the other females join her. They make a circle around the calves. The shooting started, and I'll never forget watching them go down. One by one. Then the calves. The look in their eyes. The fear…the pathetic resolve, as if man had failed them. I somehow felt the bullets enter my own heart. I knew in that moment that I had to fight to protect them, to protect all the wildlife here." Wynne had overemphasized her last words, still feeling the painful impact of the memory.

She glanced at Hellstrom. She'd told the story partially to make him feel guilty and to see how he'd react. But his eyes gave away nothing.

"Would you have them destroy the crops?" Hellstrom asked, his voice terse.

"No, but they could have been moved. They could have been taken to zoos, or other wildlife parks. They could have done something, anything, other than the easy way out. Wildlife is a gift to man. He should be a steward of that gift. The answer is rarely a bullet."

"I agree." His voice softened slightly. "Conservation is always the better choice."

"I know you feel that way or you wouldn't be chairman of the LZCG." Wynne searched his eyes for the deception behind his words, but his expression remained inscrutable, hidden by a mask of what looked like sincere concern.

"Quite right. We can help the animals together." His gaze moved over her lips as he stepped close again and touched her jaw, tracing it with his fingers. "You'd like that, wouldn't you, Wynne? I like seeing the fire alight in you. Your eyes a moment ago were like torches when you spoke about the elephants, brilliant defiant hazel torches…."

Oh, God! His fingers felt like a spider crawling along her skin, and yet a part of her felt an undeniable magnetism in his touch. Every nerve in her body grew aware of him. She wanted to pull away, but she couldn't risk him seeing the mask.

He gently wrapped his hand around the back of her neck and pulled her face toward his. He leaned in to kiss her.

Abruptly, the door opened.

Hellstrom stepped back, but not before Jacqueline walked inside. Relief washed over Wynne.

Jacqueline stood there, her gaze shooting fire at Wynne. "I've been looking everywhere for you. I came to see if I could offer some makeup or anything, but—" she cut her eyes at Hellstrom, tears gleaming in them "—I see you don't need any help." She turned and swept out the door.

"Jackie, love, wait!" Hellstrom paused long enough to say, "I fear she'll pout all night. I'd better go after her. We'll continue this later."

"I look forward to it." She would play along if it meant finding concrete evidence against him.

He waited for Wynne to step outside the office, then turned to close the door.

That's when he saw the mask.

His gaze held for just a split second, but long enough. His expression changed right before her eyes. The charismatic public pretense melted, and the emotion in his face turned raw and ugly. His gaze dissected her, piece by piece. She felt like a specimen under his microscope.

In that instant she realized he fed off the weakness of others, like animals of prey. It hadn't been the fire in her eyes as she'd spoken of the elephants that had turned him on, but the pain he'd seen in her face. As she did with any animal of prey she met his gaze squarely and showed no signs of vulnerability.

Briefly they mentally circled each other in a he-knew-that-she-knew moment. An old African legend said that true enemies shared their souls, their strengths and their blood. Wynne felt that connection with Hellstrom like a blow to her gut, and she sensed that when it came down to the final battle, only one of them would survive.

He broke the momentary trance and slammed the door and locked it. Now that there was no need for pretense between them, he wasn't smiling, nor did he glance at her. He hurried past, yelling, "Jackie, wait!"

Wynne followed in his wake, wondering if she had the strength to take Hellstrom on.

Wynne found the bedroom Tungana had taken her to and slipped inside. She went to the bathroom, put her hair back in a ponytail, then changed into her working clothes. Hellstrom had given orders to Tungana for her to wear the red dress. It was just another avenue of his manipulation, and she had to let Hellstrom know she wouldn't be controlled by him.

If she was going to face Hellstrom, she'd do it in her own clothes, battle clothes. She retied the slingshot around her waist, then secured the dagger at her ankle. Next came her combat boots. As she stared at the ranger in the mirror, she felt ready to face Hellstrom again. This time on her terms.

The thought of leaving occurred to her, but she needed to question MacKay and probe him for information about his involvement with Hellstrom.

A few moments later, she left the room and strode down the steps, toward the dining room, avoiding several servants whose arms were laden with crates. A girl trailed behind them, a basket loaded with food and canned goods balanced on her head. Wynne knew this hallway led directly to the house's kitchen and back exit, close to the garages. Hellstrom's party preparations certainly had to have been done by now. So where were these provisions going? And for what?

"Someone moving?" Wynne casually asked the girl, blocking her way.

The girl looked maybe fifteen, with beautiful bronze skin and eyes that appeared shy and frightened of everything. "Don't know, miss. Please, I'm behind." She nodded to the men in front of her.

Wynne knew this girl wouldn't talk, so she let her pass. She started to follow them, but someone tapped her on the back. She wheeled around and saw Tungana looking up at her.

His lips pursed with suppressed fury, and she realized she was seeing another side of Tungana that he kept well hidden. The voices she'd heard outside of Hellstrom's office must have been Tungana and Hellstrom looking for her.

"Where you go?" he demanded.

"I got lost." She quickly changed the subject. "Where is everyone?"

"The gallery. I take you," he said in a petulant tone one would use on a naughty child. It was obvious she wasn't getting out of his sight again. "Where is dress?"

"I put it back and left it on the bed."

"You found bedroom okay?" His lips hardened into thin lines.

"Yes." She didn't offer an explanation. There was no need to lie now.

They passed the music room. Commander Kaweki and his wife were no longer there, she noticed. Only servants moved about the room, picking up empty glasses and plates. The piano player had moved on to Streisand tunes.

Wynne followed Tungana. Now that she had seen evidence Hellstrom was shipping the meat, she hoped to find out what part MacKay played in all of this. And she had to do it quickly. Hellstrom knew she was on to him. He'd either make plans to get rid of her or move his operation somewhere else. Obviously MacKay had been at Sausage Tree Camp to intercept the meat shipment. And what were the servants doing with all those provisions? It was nonperishable food. The kind eaten on a long safari. What was Hellstrom planning?

Tungana paused before the gallery door and opened it. Hellstrom's mesmerizing voice drifted toward her. He must have soothed Jacqueline's jealousy. He was probably an expert at manipulating women and prided himself on it.

Tungana thrust his hand toward the doorway. "You go in."

Wynne obediently stepped inside, uncertain if she liked this new Tungana.

He closed the door behind her.

The gallery had not yet been decorated when Wynne had last toured the house, and she recalled how eerily her footsteps had echoed through the massive empty room, and how she felt consumed by it. Now it just sickened her.

She felt taxidermied eyes staring at her from all directions. As she crossed the room, her gaze was drawn to cases of stuffed animals lining the walls. Exotic birds in one. Reptiles and small mammals in others. Along the walls were the mounted heads of buffalo, antelope, zebra, impala, kudu. Stuffed monkeys were posed on top of the cases, their blank faces shaped into bizarre smiles. Any other person might have walked into the room and been impressed by the collection. She saw it for what it was, a monument to death, to extinction. What she was fighting against in Africa was embodied in this room.

The party crowd had gathered at one end of the gallery. Hellstrom stood before a captive audience, pointing to a stuffed baboon. "We were three weeks into the bush, and we'd run out of food. This male wanker charged us, and we had baboon ballocks fricassee."

Everyone chuckled.

"It sounds horrid." Jacqueline sipped her drink, the only evidence of her tears was the smudged mascara near the corners of her eyes.

"Baboon is quite good, a delicacy," this from Mr. Masamba. He nodded and smiled at Hellstrom, his white teeth stark against his dark skin. Masamba's face beamed with confidence as he looked at the new chairman of the LZCG.

Could Hellstrom sway the LZCG treasurer into agreeing with just about anything he wanted? She glanced at Mr. Njobo. The LZCG's vice president looked as equally vulnerable to Hellstrom's charisma. Were they involved in the poaching ring, too?

Wynne hoped they were only beguiled by Hellstrom's charisma like everyone else was. She paused at the back of the crowd, struggling with the impulse to turn and walk out of this hall of horrors. She could feel the animals' dead eyes still watching her. A waiter walked past her, and she grabbed a cocktail from his tray. The scotch tasted bitter as she drank it.

Hellstrom noticed her. He continued to speak, while he took in her appearance. A flicker of a memory passed over his face. He studied her, the plastic smile in place. What was he thinking? Would he derive pleasure and power from her disgust of the room? It took all of her concentration, but she kept her expression blank. Blank and impenetrable as the golden leonine gleam in his eyes.

"Let's ask Ms. Sperling what she thinks." Hellstrom pointed to Wynne.

All eyes turned her way. Commander Kaweki frowned

when he spotted her. Colette followed her husband's gaze and waved at Wynne.

Wynne smiled and nodded a greeting. At least someone was happy to see her. Kaweki sure wasn't. The furrows in his brow were deepening by the minute. He reminded Wynne of a bloodhound when he wore that expression. It meant he'd just sniffed out insubordination and his authority was being challenged. She was in big trouble. Wynne gulped the scotch.

"What do you think of baboon meat, Wynne?" Hellstrom asked, putting her on the spot. He stared at her, his dark eyes probing.

Wynne's attention shifted from Kaweki. "Shouldn't the question be, what would a baboon think if he tasted a human?"

Laughter bounced through the crowd.

Hellstrom laughed, but it was exaggerated. It was obvious he didn't like being upstaged. "You make light of it, Ms. Sperling, but I have seen baboons maim natives," he said, his voice less hospitable. "It's not pretty. They can be a real danger."

"If they are provoked."

"Are you saying they are selective in their killing habits?"

"Left alone in nature, animals only kill to survive."

"The same could be said of man. We must steal other forms of life to feed our own. It is the law of nature."

"That's true, everything kills to eat in the food chain. But man doesn't need to kill to survive. There are other forms of protein."

Hellstrom looked her directly in the eye, his expression so intense it was aggressive. "Are you saying we should all be vegetarians?"

"That's my preference, but I don't fault others for eating farm-raised animals. I just don't think they should kill endangered animals and eat bush meat."

Jacqueline joined the conversation. "But who would give up venison? I, for one, will not. I like the taste of wild meat." She made a dramatic show of rubbing up against Hellstrom's right arm, smiling, and batting her eyes.

The crowd caught her meaning and laughed.

Hellstrom looked slightly embarrassed by Jacqueline's overt display, then he seemed to realize he could capitalize on it. He stroked her cheek as he would an object, not really seeing Jacqueline, looking at her as if she were an inanimate possession to be fondled when it pleased him. He said loudly, "You, my dear, have had too much to drink."

"I have not," she said, in a slightly pouting, sexy voice. She captured Hellstrom's hand against her cheek and held it there for a moment, before he drew it back. Disappointment registered on her face as she said, "I was merely making a point about wild meat."

A large woman, standing next to a thin man with a potato-shaped head, spoke up. "And a good one it was. I see nothing wrong with hunting and eating what you kill."

Mr. Njobo raised his hand as he spoke. "I have to agree. The wild game raised for hunters on our game-managed area lands and ranches bring in handsome revenues for this country."

Wynne said, "The theory of the game-managed areas is all well and good, if wild animals reproduce faster than they are being killed. But that's not the case."

"How is that?" Mr. Njobo cocked his head at her and looked like a confused ostrich for a moment.

"It's not only licensed hunters who are killing the animals, but impoverished locals who have to poach to eat.

And then there are the commercial bush meat poachers."
Wynne's eyes met Hellstrom's and their gazes locked for
a second. "Not to mention drought, population growth.
Every species has had a fifty percent reduction in the last
ten years, and the rhinos have been hunted to the point of
extinction."

"What is your answer to the problem?" Mr. Njobo asked.

Wynne sipped her drink, then spoke. "We should explore other ways of getting revenues into Zambia and work
on preserving and regenerating game resources. We also
need to educate local people that the long-term effects of
preserving the game will be to their benefit. Right now,
they see little of these revenues from issued hunting licenses. It stays in the hands of the affluent and the government, while the people go hungry. And if they are hungry
they kill the wild game or poach it. But the locals are not
the real problem. It's the organized bush meat poachers that
have driven wild game to extinction. And the locals have
become a part of these operations because they are forced
to provide for their families." She thought of Mehan and
said, "So it a vicious cycle."

Mr. Masamba chimed in. "And do you have an answer?
Because you should mail it to the newly elected president.
Mwiinga needs all the help he can get."

A titter of laughter. Wynne's gaze shifted over to
Kaweki. He wasn't smiling. In fact, his eyes had narrowed,
the whites all but gone.

She downed the rest of her drink and a tight smile
stretched across her lips. "I would put more money into the
tourist trade. Draw tourists and photographers and re-
searchers to the parks—"

Mr. Masamba interrupted her. "But won't that disturb
the animals' natural habitats?"

"Not if we control the number of safaris during breeding season and allow a fixed number of people in the parks at any given time. Right now we don't have the resources or the staff to do this. But with a new direction, our game-managed areas could be kill-free and self-sustaining. Locals could be hired to work in these parks. If we employ the people living near the reserves and they see how preserving the animals will feed their families, then they will naturally make an effort to protect the game. Explore other avenues of revenue besides killing."

Jacqueline lifted her chin at a challenging angle. "What's wrong with killing wild beasts? I couldn't care less if all wild animals in Africa disappear. It's a matter of selection. The strong survive."

"What gives us the right to live at the expense of other creatures? When we do that we are jeopardizing our own future."

"That's ridiculous." Jacqueline waved a bony hand through the air. "Who cares if rhinos go extinct. They are odious creatures with no real value to humans except at a zoo, maybe."

"You should care because rhinos are part of an ecosystem and all ecosystems are connected in a way that sustains life on this planet. No species can survive in isolation. Think about it," Wynne said, her voice growing more impassioned as she realized people were really listening to her. "Take the declining hives of honeybees for example. No honeybees, no pollination. No pollination, no grain or corn to feed the livestock that come to your table."

Jacqueline crossed her arms over her chest and said, "We'll find another way to pollinate crops."

Hellstrom broke in. "Man will always overcome every obstacle before him."

"Will he," Wynne questioned, "or will his arrogance be his downfall?"

He kept smiling, but his eyes turned a coppery blaze of yellow.

Commander Kaweki grabbed Wynne's arm and said, "As usual, Officer Sperling, you have given us a lively topic for discussion." He was from South Africa and his English was laced with an Afrikaans dialect, a seventeenth-century distinctive Dutch language that caused a commanding rise in tone at the end of his words.

"Wynne must be considered an asset to any party." Hellstrom nodded at her, a salute to an opponent. "You must allow me to extend an open invitation to you. Please feel free to enter my home at anytime. You will always be welcome."

She smiled back at him for the double entendre. She knew he was referring to her searching his office. A waiter took her empty glass from her hand as she said, "I'd like nothing better."

Kaweki pulled Wynne's arm. "Now if you'll excuse us, I need a word with Officer Sperling."

Hellstrom nodded graciously as Kaweki dragged Wynne over to a corner. Wynne looked around for Colette, the only person who could sooth Kaweki's anger. But the large woman had trapped her in a corner, her hands animating her every word.

He paused and whispered, "What are you doing here?"

"I brought one of Mr. Hellstrom's guests here and he invited me to stay. I couldn't say no."

"I thought you were out in the field. Why haven't you checked in? I almost sent out a search party."

"The truth is, I caught commercial bush meat poachers today." Wynne tried to gauge his anger by the number of wrinkles on his brow. Three. Not good.

"Where are they? You brought no prisoners in today."

"I have them tucked away."

"Why?"

"There was supposed to be a meeting at Sausage Tree Camp, but it didn't go down. I didn't bring them in because we have spies in the camp."

His bushy brows narrowed and more worry lines appeared over them. "On my force? Are you certain? This is a grave accusation."

"Yes, I'm certain. Mehan was shot during the bust. We took him to the clinic." Wynne saw the skeptical look on his face and waited for him to absorb this, before she continued. "And I'm certain there are more. The only reason we were able to arrest the poachers was that we didn't tell anyone or radio it into camp."

"You could have told me." He clenched his fists at his sides.

"I really didn't have time to include you, sir. And I didn't want word of it getting out. If we involve others on the force, the security level would have been compromised and the poachers tipped off. I couldn't risk that."

"Do you have any idea who the spies are?"

Wynne lowered her voice. "No, but I think I know who the ring leader is."

"Who?"

"Hellstrom."

"What?" Kaweki's face went from openmouthed to incredulous. "You must be wrong."

"I've seen evidence in his office."

"Mweo mutakatifu!" Bemba for Holy Ghost. Kaweki's jowls shook as he spoke. "What did you find?" He cut his eyes at Hellstrom, who was smiling and entertaining his guests with a hunting story about a stuffed massive lion

with a huge beautiful mane. The lion's unanimated glass eyes reminded Wynne of Hellstrom's when he unleashed his Mr. Hyde side.

Wynne told Kaweki about Mehan's naming the LZCG, about finding MacKay at Sausage Tree Camp, the shipping manifestos going to ports all over the world, about Hellstrom catching her in his office, about his duplicity, and she finished with, "He's covered his tracks well. We cannot accuse him without hard evidence, or we risk losing LZCG's help."

"How well I know this."

"We'll have to catch him with the meat."

"That won't be easy. He has men everywhere in camp, and monitors our radios. I speak to him every day. He knows exactly what we are doing. So where are these prisoners? I wish to speak to them myself."

"Secure in the bush."

"See that they get to camp ASAP."

"I will."

"And how did you find these poachers?"

"A tip."

"From whom?"

"Sources in the village." She didn't tell him about Aja. Aja had an ill-disguised dislike for the commander. She had always believed it had to do with the commander's abrupt manner with the local people. He was harsh on local poachers.

He hesitated a moment, his dark brown eyes searching hers. "And have you learned how they transport the meat?"

"I believe they move it along the river into Zimbabwe."

His expression didn't change and he said, "And I guess Eieb was with you, since he hasn't checked in either." The grooves in Kaweki's brow deepened.

"I asked him to help me, sir."

"Where is he now?"

"With Mehan."

"Before you leave, take care you do not offend the supporters of the LZCG with your idealistic zeal. If we lose their support and financing, our work will be in jeopardy. I may even have to let rangers go. And don't think because you are the hardest worker I have that you won't be affected."

Was that a compliment? "Yes, sir."

He shook a beefy finger at Wynne. "And make sure you check in with me. I'll be worried about you from now on."

"Yes, sir."

"I will watch Hellstrom's every move myself." Kaweki gave Hellstrom a long assessing glance. "Now that we know him for who he is, we'll get him. Together."

Hellstrom's voice rang in her mind, "We can help the animals together." A chill crawled down her spine.

"Perhaps you can find out what this MacKay person is doing here. Your assumption about him must be correct."

"I'll try." Wynne searched the room for MacKay, but didn't see him.

Colette stepped up to her husband's side. She mouthed *I'm sorry* to Wynne, then took his arm. "Wynne, so nice to see you. Are you having a good time?" she asked, the words laced with her native French accent.

"Uh, yes." Wynne gave her a silent plea for help. Colette knew how domineering her husband could be.

Colette touched Kaweki's cheek, and his shoulders relaxed as he stared down at her. "Come, *mon chere,* let Wynne enjoy the party. I'd like you to meet Mrs. Ramoodu."

Kaweki gave Wynne a long pointed stare, then allowed his wife to escort him over to the overweight lady. Wynne had noticed that Kaweki seemed on edge. He had a right to be. She had just dumped a huge, deadly snake in his lap. It felt as if a boulder was lifted off her chest though. She knew she could trust him. He had been the commander for ten years. No one was more dedicated to saving Zambian wildlife. He fought hard to curb poaching, had even taken her idea of a DNA crime lab to Hellstrom.

And he held a special place in her heart. He'd hired her despite protests from the other men on the force. It was true, she had gone through the American embassy and petitioned the Zambian government for a visa to stay in the country. And the American embassy might have put the pressure on Kaweki to review her résumé. But he didn't have to hire her. He'd gone out on a limb. She felt he'd done it because he assumed she was a wealthy American and would bring financial resources to the camp that he couldn't otherwise get from his own government. In many ways she had done just that. She had also made a promise to him he'd never regret hiring her. She worked hard to overcome the prejudice of having a woman on the force, and a white American, at that. And she had proven to the other rangers she could do the job as well as they could, or better. Tonight, she hoped she had proven her worth to Kaweki.

She noticed that the crowd had broken up and people stood before display cases pointing and talking. Hellstrom was speaking to Masamba and Njobo. They seemed to be hanging on his every word.

MacKay entered the room, hard to miss. Tall and broad-shouldered, he towered over the crowd. Wynne had to admit he looked pretty *GQ* in a black tailored suit, a white shirt and bolo tie, and yes, cowboy boots. Amazing what clothes could do. Now if he could only put a tux on his tongue. His gaze swept the room.

Too late. She made eye contact.

He winked at her and stepped toward her, but three women chatting near the door saw him and blocked his path. They seemed to have been waiting for his entrance and swarmed around him like a fan club. He lapped up the attention, wearing a playful invitation in his long-lashed blue eyes and an infectious grin. But his gaze found her again.

Wynne pretended to examine a display case next to her. When she saw the contents, she became genuinely interested. Carnivore fangs were carefully labeled. The smallest started with *Herpestinae:* meerkat, and the true mongoose family. *Hyaenidae:* hyena and aardwolves. *Ursidae:* all bears, and worked its way up to *Felinae:* lion and tiger. Below them, in neat rows were *Machairodontinae* fangs, those of the saber-toothed tigers. One tooth, an upper canine, was unlabeled. It was smaller than the saber-toothed variety. Wynne had her head bent low over the case, deep in concentration, so when she felt someone step up beside her she jumped and looked in Hellstrom's ever-suave smile.

Chapter 5

"Do you think it's safe to be near me?" Wynne asked, glancing at Jacqueline whose gaze was shooting poisonous darts at her.

"Jackie is fine." He shrugged, his body language saying, *she's easily manipulated.* "And what sort of host would I be if I were remiss in showing you my collection? I see you've found something that interests you?" Hellstrom stepped closer, his arm touching hers.

Wynne felt a quickening—not the butterflies in the stomach variety, more like there's a scorpion nearby. She had to force herself not to pull away. This was his way of intimidating her, making her squirm. She wasn't going to give him the pleasure of seeing her discomfort.

"Quite a collection." She looked down at the unlabeled tooth.

"Yes, a hobby of mine. I thought you might be interested in it."

"Why is that tooth not labeled?"

He seemed pleased that she had noticed. "That tooth is in question."

"Why?"

"It was found in Zambia."

"Zambia? What kind of tooth is it?"

"Some kind of lesser scimitar as far as I can deduce."

Wynne recalled her college paleontology. Lesser scimitar cats were related to the better known sabre-tooth tigers. They were lion-sized and contained razor-sharp, flattened, stabbing teeth. "But weren't scimitars more prevalent in North America, Europe, and Asia before the Ice Age?" she asked, her brows knitting as she tried to remember what she had learned.

"The specimen *Homotherium ethiopicum* and *Homotherium hadarensis* have been discovered in Africa," he said, his voice amused as if he were enjoying impressing her with his knowledge. "But this tooth does not belong to those two species, through it is in the *Homotherium* genus. Therein lies the rub. A definitive classification cannot be made. Radio carbon dating has been done on the tooth, and it dates to 1998. So you see, I'm quite in a quandary. I can't label it until I know what the damned thing is." There was that smile again, as if he had labeled her in some way and was adding her to his collection.

1998? "The carbon dating must have been wrong."

"It was done twice, once at Oxford, and once at the University of Rochester with Dr. Gove, the coinventor of Accelerator Mass Spectrometry. The chap knows what he's about." He leaned closer, his hot breath on her ear. His voice was a raspy whisper. "The data is irrefutable. The scimitars have found a niche somewhere in Zambia, and still exist."

"That's a pretty wild theory."

"You know yourself new species are found every day. One example, the coelacanth."

It was true a dinosaur fish thought to have been extinct for millions of years had been found in the 1950s. And it was true species existed in nature that man hadn't recorded. But scimitars alive in Africa? "It's still a little farfetched in my opinion."

"It's not solely my theory. There is a Bantu legend that the cats still exist here."

A memory sparked. Just last week, Wynne had investigated a report of a man mauled by a huge cat near a northern Bisa village. A ranger's duty included relocating or even exterminating large cats that began preying on humans—she always tried to relocate them. After she had looked for the lion and found nothing, she had examined the man's puncture wounds more closely and decided they didn't look like any wounds she had ever seen from a lion attack. The gashes were too deep. They could have been self-inflicted or he had gotten into a brawl, been cut by a knife, and made up the story about the lion. But now she remembered how strangely Snow had acted that day near the site, crouching and pacing. Wynne had never seen Snow act that way when she scented a lion. Snow hadn't relaxed until they left for home. Had the man been telling the truth? It couldn't have been a scimitar. Could it?

She smiled and said, "When did you start believing in superstition?"

"Superstition is based loosely in fact. But I grant you, I didn't actually believe the legend until I had this tooth carbon dated. I'm intent upon tracking the cat." He'd thrown that out like a challenge.

"Tracking it?"

"There is no endangered species list protecting it. It's free game."

"If this thing exists, which I doubt seriously that it does, you'd kill it?" Wynne couldn't keep the contempt from her voice.

"If I don't, some other chap will. And can you imagine the ads that I could run on the Internet, the prices I could command for hunting them. Every hunter worth his salt will be there bidding." His golden eyes bored into hers.

"You're not making enough money now?" She recalled seeing the overdue notices in his office drawer.

He motioned around the room. "This doesn't come cheaply."

"No, it doesn't." No one knew better than she what price had been paid.

Hellstrom's nice guy facade had dropped away. She could have been looking into the eyes of a cobra, for all the humanity she saw there. Well—that wasn't really true. Cobras killed for reasons of basic survival. Hellstrom was much more dangerous, he killed for greed and for the feeling of power it gave him. She understood why he had shown her the tooth. He wanted to see the concern in her face when he'd spoken of killing the animals. It was all about control with him. And after speaking to him about his childhood, she deduced his need to dominate and control others stemmed from the helplessness he'd felt during his father's brutality.

She wanted to pull back and look away, but she held his gaze and said sarcastically, "Happy hunting."

"Thank you. You know, Wynne, we're alike, you and I."

She wanted to say, *You're all wrong, jerk. I'm nothing like you.* But she had to be honest with herself. If it came down to stopping him from poaching, she could easily turn as ruthless as he was. The realization that he could manipulate her into becoming a predator like him sent a prickling sensation over every nerve ending in her body. She whispered back, "How's that?"

"We both like the excitement, the challenge. I sensed that the moment I met you." His voice conveyed an upsetting calmness.

She felt trapped by his closeness, caught in his powerful undertow. She knew this was part of his manipulation game. Unnerve her. Create fear and dismay. The intimidation of an aggressor.

He eyed her clothes. "Why did you take off the dress, Wynne?"

She hated the sound of her name coming from his lips. "Because I have to leave," she said.

"Take it with you as a gift from me. You looked so lovely in it."

"Thanks, but no thanks. I can't wear it in the bush." She managed a nonchalant shrug.

Just then MacKay slapped Hellstrom on the back. "Well, well, you two are mighty cozy over here. You can't keep her all to yourself."

Hellstrom's public mask slipped back in place. He leveled a winning smile at MacKay. "How careless of me. She's all yours." Hellstrom pulled at his right cufflink, then strode back over to Jacqueline, who seemed to be measuring Wynne for her coffin size.

MacKay grinned at Wynne and thrust a martini in her hand. "Here. You look like you could use a drink."

Something can be said for extroverted Texans. She downed the contents in one long gulp, even though she hated the taste of gin and vermouth. It burned all the way down. An intense rush crept from her stomach up to her head.

"You and Hellstrom are right chummy." MacKay chugged down three fingers of what looked like whiskey on the rocks.

"We understand each other." Wynne looked at him over the top of her empty glass.

MacKay grinned like a naughty little boy, his dimples beaming. "You could understand me, too."

"I already do."

"I don't know if I like your tone, darlin'. I'm nothing but a big lovable teddy bear. You got to know that."

"A teddy bear stuffed with thorns, you just don't find out until you prick your finger."

"Not me, no thorns. I'm all sugar."

"An ex-SEAL that's all sugar? Now that's a new one. How many men have you killed exactly?" The thought crossed her mind that he could be a hit man as well as a poacher. Who would suspect such a likable guy? Perfect cover.

"You don't expect me to own it." His blue eyes glistened like sapphires, brimming with secrets. "Anyway that was a long time ago. I make love now, not war."

"That's comforting." Wynne looked at him like he could be her next headache.

"So what do you say? Let's get to know each other better. We can talk in my bungalow."

Wynne hedged. Talk? That was the farthest thing from his mind. Still, she might be able to find out Hellstrom's next move through this dimpled lover-boy. It's not a date, she reminded herself. It's about life or death. It's about carrying out Kaweki's orders and finding what MacKay is doing here and what he's planning with Hellstrom. But she had to retrieve the prisoners and check on Mehan tonight. Yet she couldn't close the door entirely.

"Aw, come on. You won't be sorry." His grin promised pleasures beyond any woman's imagination.

How long did he practice those looks of his in front of a mirror? She plopped down her cocktail glass on the edge of the cabinet. "I'll call you. It's time for me to go back to work."

"No work and all play, that's my motto."

"I can see that, Lone Star." She saw that Jacqueline had grabbed Hellstrom's arm and was hanging on for dear life. "Please give my regrets to our host."

Wynne left, feeling MacKay's, Hellstrom's and Kaweki's gaze follow her out the door. She thought of MacKay. She wasn't good at using her feminine wiles to get the truth out of men. She used threats to get it out of them, or used a little muscle if she needed to. It was more straightforward and a lot less messy. Instinct told her that her normal operating procedure wasn't going to work with MacKay. She remembered sparring with him, and she knew he could have easily won that fight. He was as dangerous as Hellstrom—doubly so because of the Brad Pitt factor he had going on. She had to keep him at arm's length and somehow interrogate him for information. Easier said than done.

She put him out of her mind and recalled the servants carrying boxes and food in the hallway. Hellstrom had said he was going on safari to kill the scimitar. She had to make sure that wild-goose chase was all he was up to.

Once outside, Wynne took a detour to the Rover. She ran around the side of Hellstrom's house, then huddled near the bushes. A steady stream of servants walked to the garage, Tungana directing them. Several men carried crates. Wynne moved in closer to hear what was being said.

"Hurry, we have three sunrises to get ready. Don't put those tents there," Tungana said. "*BaK para* says they'll mold."

"We can put them on a shelf," one servant said.

"No, no. In the corner. We'll crate them and have more room for his guns."

"I don't know why he needs so many guns," another man grumbled.

"Big game."

"You can only shoot one gun at a time."

"But he likes to think he can shoot many."

They chuckled. Tungana didn't. He followed them into the garage and disappeared inside.

Wynne had heard enough. Guns. A tent. Food. Hellstrom was going on a safari in three days. Was his disclosure of the scimitar hunt a ruse so he could poach more animals? Or was he really after the scimitar? She still had a hard time believing they were nothing more than legend. She had to question Aja about the existence of the cats; he would know something. But first she had to take the poachers off his hands. And then check on Mehan. He was her only witness. She couldn't call Eieb on the walkie-talkie for fear the frequencies were being monitored by Hellstrom's men at base camp.

She jumped in the Rover and maneuvered past another jeep. Something drew her gaze to the rearview mirror, and she saw Hellstrom standing on the front steps, watching her. She felt that strange primal connection to him, saw herself in his eyes. A shudder coursed through her, and she jammed her foot on the accelerator.

Wynne had parked the Rover and was climbing up the escarpment to Aja's camp. The moon shone like a giant ball above her head. The night sky in the African bush was like no other in all the world, clear, brilliant, unadulterated by everglowing city lights. The stars looked so vivid she could reach up and pluck one out of the sky and hide it in her pocket.

She moved up the rocky path only a foot wide, carved by the wildebeest that used to migrate to the valley by the millions, before their numbers were depleted.

Sometimes Wynne felt as if she had been born in the wrong century. There was a place in her heart that longed for the other Zambia, long before country boundaries, copper mines, power plants and English settlements, when the bush was wild and beautiful and free, where sky and night met in an endless undisturbed cycle of life. Where the native people lived in peace with the land, and there was no need for game reserves because there was no such thing as poaching, or greed for ivory, or fear of slave traders.

Thoughts of her work brought back Wynne's last memory of home. She had been climbing into a taxi on the way to Dulles Airport, full of dreams and great expectations for her new life in Zambia. That was before she had bid her mother farewell.

Her mother had followed Wynne out the front door and stood in the driveway, words spewing out of her mouth. "You'll fail at this like you failed at being my daughter. I tried to give you everything and this is how you repay me. You could have been somebody, been a partner in my firm, but no. No! You toss away law school for animal ecology. Foolishness, that's what that is, a government grant course for the gullible. Then you run off to a third world country to live in squalor for some idealistic conservationist bull. And if you drive away in that taxi, I won't waste my time worrying about you. You won't be my daughter any longer. You understand me. I won't be hurt any more by you—"

"I never wanted to hurt you, but I have to live my life," she'd said, turning to look her mother in the eye.

"Go and live it then. But I mean what—"

Wynne had slammed the taxi door, nodded to the driver

to leave and left Maria Van Warren-Sperling standing in the driveway, in front of her million dollar home, her petite face red with rage. And as the taxi had threaded its way into the traffic on Connecticut Avenue in the heart of D.C., and every word her mother had uttered left an indelible scar in her memory, Wynne felt a forty-ton steel resolve welding its way into her fiber. She was determined to make a difference in Zambia, to prove to herself that her mother had been wrong, that she was doing something that mattered.

But she had given up hope that one day her mother would ever realize that.

Wynne still held fast to her resolve, but days like today, losing those five elephants and learning of Hellstrom's poaching ring in camp, brought back her mother's parting tirade like a broken record in her mind. Yet up here, looking out at the beautiful wilderness, her mother's voice was a shallow empty whisper, and she knew no matter how dangerous it became here, or how many failures stood before her, she would keep trying. Because all of this was worth it.

As if a lion heard her thoughts, it roared, its voice echoing through the Zambezi valley like thunder. Another lion answered it.

Wynne smiled inwardly and realized she was getting close to the top. She whistled, her distinct impression of the fish eagle's song: *keeh-kaw, keeh-kaw*. She listened for Aja's answer.

Nothing but the wind blowing along the escarpment, a solitary sound, lonely and desolate.

Why hadn't Aja answered her? He should have heard her. Why didn't he answer her? She hurried up the path now, leaping over rocks. She slowed as she neared his camp, her footsteps soft enough to melt into the wind. It was in a small culvert, surrounded by thick bush, away from the wind. Wynne slipped through to the clearing.

No fire. No Aja or Snow. No prisoners.

Had Hellstrom's men been here? God, she prayed not. How could they have known? She and Aja had made sure they weren't followed.

Wynne surveyed the site for signs of a struggle. No broken leaves. No spent cartridges. She sniffed the ground. Snow's feral scent reached her, and she located the spot where the leopard had slept. It wasn't warm. They'd been gone some time. She found no evidence of blood, a good thing. The poachers must have taken Aja and Snow with them. They would take Snow to a location close to their camp so they could kill her and strip her hide without having to carry her any great distance. And Aja, he was stubborn and proud. They'd kill him, unless of course Hellstrom was keeping him hostage. She couldn't track them along the rocks. That it was night made it almost impossible to pick up their trail.

Let them be all right! If something had happened to them...

In her mind she saw Hellstrom in the rearview mirror again, watching her drive away from the party. Had he already known his men had managed to escape?

She felt as if Hellstrom had opened up her chest and was hacking away pieces of her heart. She let out a cry that reverberated across the valley and melted into the night. Only the echo came back to haunt her.

By the time Wynne reached the Rover, visions of Aja and Snow hurt, bleeding and maybe dying had played over and over in her mind. So she didn't see Aja and Snow sitting on the hood of the Rover, until she was almost upon them.

"Oh, my God!" Wynne had never been so glad to see

Aja's beautiful dark leathery face. She ran to him and threw her arms around his thin neck.

He braced his feet against the side of the Rover to keep from falling back on the hood. Wynne was taller than he was and outweighed him by twenty pounds and she could have easily knocked him over.

When he stiffened and didn't return the hug, Wynne realized she was making him uncomfortable. He was her teacher and friend, but utmost a Bantu guide and warrior. Such displays of emotion were awkward at best. She stepped back and said, "You don't know how glad I am to see you."

"And I you." He frowned at her, still ill at ease from the embrace.

That's when Snow leaped on Wynne. Woman and panther hit the ground. Snow commenced licking Wynne's face.

"I missed you, too." Wynne nudged her face against Snow's muzzle and ran her hands over Snow's furry ears and neck, the familiar warmth against her fingers flooding her heart. How could she ever let Snow go? Just those few moments of believing the cat was lost to her tore her up inside. She spoke to Aja. "When I couldn't find you, I was worried." She wouldn't admit she'd had fears they were both dead.

"I couldn't stand their complaints. Nag like women. I moved them so I couldn't hear them."

"Where are they?"

"In the *bucinga*." Aja jumped down off the Rover.

The *bucinga* was a game pit carved in the rocks by ancient tribal hunters. They used it to lure game to their death, before guns, when hunting with spears and arrows depended on starving or surviving. It was considered haunted by the spirits of the animals and a deserted place by most locals. Aja liked to go there to commune with nature and pray.

"How did you know I had arrived to pick up the prisoners?" she asked. "The *bucinga* is over a mile away."

"I heard your heart speak. It have loud echo," he said, his voice edged with annoyance.

Wynne felt a moment of embarrassment at having lost control and giving voice to her fear.

"Did you think so little of my abilities that I would be taken by poachers?" The wrinkles around his mouth stretched with chagrin as he finally addressed the real reason he was provoked by her.

"I didn't know if they had many cohorts who might overpower you and try to release them." She wouldn't ever offend him by pointing out he was elderly and she worried about him.

Aja snorted in disgust. "Legions of cowards. Cowards are arrogant, easily defeated."

"Their chief isn't a coward. He's cunning."

"Who is this chief?"

"Hellstrom."

Aja nodded, his wise expression never changing. "Hellstrom, huh? The one with the lion eyes. He stalk during day and wait for his prey to fall asleep, then makes his kill."

"No one will be falling asleep around him. I'll see to that. I need your help though. Can you alert other villages in the area about Hellstrom's poachers? The more eyes we have the better."

Aja nodded. "I will start tonight."

As they walked back toward the base of the escarpment, she told Aja about finding the shipping documents, Hellstrom discovering her in his office and their conversation about the scimitar. Wynne ended with, "Hellstrom says there is an old Bantu legend that revolves around the giant cats?"

"Most of the African population in Zambia are Bantu in origin. Many Bantu clans," was all Aja said.

"I know. So how can I find which clan believes in these animals? Obviously Hellstrom has found them. He says he's tracking the animals. He cannot track them without a guide."

Aja stared off into the night. After a moment, he said, "All is not lost."

"You know of these people?"

Aja nodded. "Bemba. I know of them. They claim to be the keeper of the *mweo mfumu*."

"Spirit chief?"

"The vessel of *kakoba*."

"So the *kakoba* lives inside the *mweo mfumu?*"

"Correct."

"Isn't *kakoba* the priest among animals?" Wynne asked, trying to recall the local beliefs. "Doesn't this spirit protect an animal against a hunter's weapon?"

Aja nodded. "If it is with the animal. The *mweo mfumu* are watcher animal gods. *Kakoba* is always with them. The *mweo mfumu* use the spirit and strength of the *kakoba* to protect all animals," he said, using a patient tone he reserved for his pupils.

"Does *mweo mfumu* take on lion flesh? Could the *mweo mfumu* be scimitars? Has this Bemba tribe been protecting them?"

"The legend says so."

"Have you seen them?"

Aja shrugged noncommittally. She understood Aja's reluctance to answer. Some things were off-limits to novices and outsiders, sacred animals being one of them. The jungle and everything in it was sacred to Aja. He would teach outsiders, like Wynne, to understand and survive the jungle to better preserve it, but he felt the jungle would give up its secrets only when a person was worthy of the stewardship of them.

"What does the legend say about *mweo mfumu?*" Wynne bent and petted Snow, who was rubbing against her leg.

"They have dark powers. If you do not have a pure heart and look upon them—" Aja smacked his hand violently against his thin bare thigh, dramatizing instant death.

Could this legend have kept the native people away from the cats and actually preserved their habitat? "Have you seen one?"

He stared up at the sky, seeing something only someone of his years and understanding could see. "I have seen many things."

So he wasn't going to tell her one way or the other. She tried again. "Okay, so let's assume the Bemba have been protecting these creatures from man—" Wynne still had a hard time believing the animals existed "—they obviously need the Bemba to keep them hidden. If Hellstrom is telling me the truth, he must have hired a guide from this tribe to take him to the creatures—"

"I doubt Hellstrom find tracker among Bemba. This tracker knows death will follow him."

"I have to be sure. I can't let Hellstrom kill the *mweo mfumu.*"

"What if Hellstrom told you this to lure you in jungle to rid himself of you—now that you see his real spirit?"

"This safari could be about getting rid of me and killing the *mweo mfumu,* or setting up alternate routes for poaching and moving the meat, maybe branching out." MacKay visualized in her mind. He might have something to do with expanding the poaching. "I just don't know. I have to find out if the *mweo mfumu* actually exist and quickly. Do you think the chief will see me?"

"You arrive with me, he will see you. We go at dawn, while *nkalamo yalubuka* sleeps from his night of hunting and prowling." Aja had used the Bemba term for maneater lion, *nkalamo yalubuka*.

He had nailed Hellstrom's personality perfectly. Maneater. And Wynne knew she was at the top of his prey list.

It had taken Wynne forty minutes to reach the base camp and secure the prisoners. She had noticed that Kaweki wasn't back yet and must have stayed at the party to watch Hellstrom.

Aja parted Wynne's company with a promise to meet her at dawn so they could visit the Bemba chief. Then he had headed off into the bush to sleep. She often thought of asking him to share her bungalow, but knew better. It would have been an insult to his warrior sensibilities. She had already embarrassed him twice today, by doubting his prowess in handling the poachers and by hugging him when she'd found him—or rather, he'd found her.

It was almost midnight and she was feeling the effects of the busy day. Her shoulder blades ached. Her stomach was growling. The last meal she'd eaten was supper, before she'd gone to stake out the river. The drinks she'd had at Hellstrom's weren't real food. She couldn't wait to get back to her hut and find a snack, but she had to check on Mehan.

Snow rode in the back of the Rover with Wynne, her warm panting breath on Wynne's shoulder a comfort as she traveled the extra two miles to the clinic. She had turned in the opposite direction of the clinic after leaving camp, then doubled back, turning off her headlights in case Hellstrom's men or another spy from base camp tried to follow her. She didn't believe Mehan was the only spy. How many of her coworkers were on Hellstrom's payroll?

The Rover bumped along toward the clinic. The rutty road conditions meant she couldn't get out of first gear, restricting her speed to ten miles an hour. Time felt as if it stood still. She prayed Mehan would be well enough to be moved to a safe location. He was their only witness. He had to live.

Wynne knew Eieb shared her concern, as well as something deeper. Earlier in the day, Eieb had returned the Rover to Wynne after he had dropped Mehan at the clinic. While they moved the poachers to Aja's camp, Eieb had seemed anxious to get back to the clinic and check on Mehan. Wynne had thought Eieb suffered from guilt at having shot a friend, despite the fact that Mehan had betrayed them all. But it wasn't until after they had made sure the prisoners were secure and in Aja's care and she had dropped Eieb back at the clinic that she had realized the real reason for Eieb's distress. Dr. Mukuka had been operating on Mehan, and the doctor had notified Mehan's wife, Kidaya. His wife had been at the clinic, and Wynne had seen the way Eieb had apologized to her, the heartfelt turmoil in his face. Wynne knew then that Mehan's wife and children were at the heart of Eieb's apprehension.

She pulled up next to the clinic. The sound of the Rover's engine flushed a small clan of bushbucks. They froze before darting off into the bush. The medium-size chestnut-brown antelopes kept the clinic's grassy yard mowed. Before the crackdown of poachers in the park, the animals wouldn't have come near man. But their fear had thinned over time. They spent their nights grazing in the safety of the clinic's yard rather than in the bush where they would be easy prey.

She thought of Bright Betsy's herd and the five elephants that had been killed. They had lost their fear, too, and paid dearly for it. That's what was so heartbreaking. While the animals' lack of fear helped tourism in the park, it made them easy marks for poachers, who didn't even have to hunt them.

Wynne ordered Snow to stay and exited the Rover. Against the moonlight, the yellow stone walls of the clinic looked massive, but the clinic was only thirty by fifty feet, hardly more than a small ranch house in America. Dim lights glowed behind the screened windows and cast a diseased gloom through the mosquito netting draped over the windows.

A crematorium was nestled fifty yards behind the building where all biohazard materials were burned, including unclaimed bodies. Luckily there were no fires tonight. Sometimes the stench reached for miles. Dr. Mukuka ran the AIDS clinic with funding from private American charities and the World Health Organization. The Zambian government's contribution couldn't cover the cost of bandages and syringes. The funding was never enough, and with one-point-two million Zambians with AIDS, the clinic was always overflowing, yet Dr. Mukuka never turned away a patient. He was a native Zambian and he loved the land and its people. If anyone ever needed proof that saints were alive and well on the planet, one had but to look in Africa.

Wynne remembered a package that had arrived that week in the mail and went back to the Rover to get it. She had wanted to give it to Dr. Mukuka but had forgotten it in all the commotion of Mehan's shooting.

She reached past the spare gasoline cans strapped in the cargo area—a necessity when she was working in the wild areas of the park. She found the brown package nestled between her tool kit and a survival kit. One quick grab, and she strode toward the entrance, Snow watching her through the windows.

A little bell heralded her arrival as she stepped inside the clinic. The smell of disinfectant, fever and disease hit her. AIDS patients filled two rows of beds in the sick ward, some coughing. Dr. Mukuka, a thin, willowy man, was bent over a patient listening to a woman's chest.

Wynne followed the sound of a woman sobbing to the end of the ward. Mehan's wife, Kidaya, stood in Eieb's arms. He was hugging her, supporting her limp weight, which wasn't much. She was a small, wiry girl of sixteen, barely more than a child. Young girls in tribes were sometimes married after their first menses and Wynne had grown accustomed to seeing teens with large families. She tried to put herself in Kidaya's place and see through her eyes, the hopelessness, the despair of being so young and losing a husband. How would the young mother feed her four children?

As if Eieb sensed Wynne, he looked at her, the weight of his guilt and misery pulling at his face. He shook his head at Wynne, and she nodded in understanding. Life's paradoxes struck Wynne. Here was Eieb, who had just been doing his job, comforting the wife of the man he'd shot.

Soon after her arrival in Zambia, Wynne had learned that death was a part of living in Africa. It was a place of harsh extremes. Drought and floods. Poverty and wealth. Predator and prey. The cycle of life moved at an incredible pace here. One split second of indecision could be the determining factor in life or death. Mehan could just as easily have shot Eieb. Like the native Africans, Wynne had hardened herself to the realities of life here, but she was realizing no amount of emotional armor would keep her from missing Mehan and feeling for Kidaya and his children.

Dr. Mukuka glanced at Wynne over the top of his black spectacles and walked toward her, his face solemn. "I see you've brought me a gift."

"I wish I had more," she said, her voice rough with emotion.

"We all do what we can." He patted her arm and took the package of *qinghaosu,* a Chinese extract from sweet wormwood, the newest cure for malaria. She knew no treatment was one hundred percent effective against malaria. The parasite injected into a human's bloodstream by mosquitoes continually adapted to the medicines used to inhibit and kill them. But *qinghaosu* seemed most effective. Unfortunately *qinghaosu* was expensive to make and dispense and the World Health Organization hadn't made it available to all Africans. Malaria cost Africa's economy an estimated twelve billion dollars a year to fight and the cheaper chloroquine was losing its potency. So Wynne shared her regular shipments from China with the clinic so they would always have it on hand.

"Have you had your dose?" he asked her.

"I have." While taking chloroquine, she had suffered two bouts with malaria, both in the hot rainy season from December to March. Thank goodness for the regular doses of *qinghaosu.*

He laid the box on a chair and said, "Come back to my office."

She followed him outside, watching the edge of his white lab coat brushing his calves. They paused outside the door. He'd long since given up his office space to patients. His shoulders were hunched in exhaustion, and he appeared older tonight than his fifty-seven years. He lit up a cigarette, took a few puffs and looked up at the moon and sighed. "There was nothing I could do. If we'd had better trauma equipment—"

"I know you did all you could."

They stood staring up at the moon for a moment, serenaded by the night insects. Wynne watched the moonlight gleaming off his glasses, the way it contorted the circle into elliptical splinters.

Dr. Mukuka broke the silence. "Do you know why he was shot?"

"Eieb didn't tell you?"

"No, and I gathered by the look on his face he didn't want to talk about it. And if you tell me, it will not be on the death report." He blew out a puff of smoke and said, "This is between friends. I liked Mehan. I delivered his children."

Wynne trusted Dr. Mukuka with her life, so she told him about Mehan being a spy. But she kept Hellstrom out of the mix. She ended with, "Who knows how many moles are in camp?"

"A bush meat ring. Right here." He shook his head. "And spies in your camp."

"Money can buy anything, including integrity and honor. Evidently there is a lot of money behind this ring."

"I'll keep my eyes open for you—especially on my rounds. The villagers might know something."

"Don't put yourself in danger, Dr. Mukuka," Wynne said. "They could hear of your inquiries and come after you."

"Don't worry, I may be an old doctor, but I'm not a foolish old doctor." He stepped on the cigarette and said, "One day I'll give these up."

"Right, you've been saying that since I met you."

"I've come to the realization everyone needs a vice or two to round out their life. You should find one."

For some reason she saw MacKay again in his black suit and cowboy boots, those mischievous dimples on his cheeks. He could become some woman's vice, all right. She frowned and said, "Please tell Aja I'll leave the Rover so he can give Kidaya a ride home. I'll walk back to camp."

"I shall." He grinned, then went back inside.

Wynne let Snow out of the Rover's cargo hold, then they headed back down the road on foot toward base camp, only moonlight and Snow's white fur to guide her. The day's humidity had congealed into the night's sticky dew, and it swirled in her lungs like Jell-O droplets.

Abruptly Snow paused in front of Wynne and glanced behind them. Wynne froze as she heard the rustle in the forest.

Chapter 6

Wynne hoped that it was one of the bushbucks she'd flushed near the clinic. But the sound was barely audible to her trained ear, not the steady plod of a deer. Had Hellstrom sent his henchmen?

Snow had heard the sound too, and was already crouched low, nostrils flaring, eyes beaming at something in the forest.

A snap of her hand, and Wynne palmed the slingshot. She loaded and spun the slingshot. It whined as she built rpm's.

The rustling in the forest came from the left and moved closer…closer.

Snow readied to spring.

Wynne gave her the hand signal to wait.

The rustling stopped ten feet away. Wynne felt her heart pounding. She sensed something or someone watching, waiting for the right moment….

A sleek large shadow sprang toward her. She fired. At first she thought it was a man, but she realized it was a cheetah when she hit its nose and the animal roared in pain. The big cat recovered and dove at her again.

Before Wynne could fire again, Snow lunged between Wynne and the cheetah. One whack of Snow's massive paw, and the cheetah tumbled to the ground and came up on its paws.

The big cats faced each other, hissing, snarling, and growling. Snow held her ground, letting the cat know she was determined to protect her territory, which included Wynne and the base camp. The cheetah finally retreated. It kept one wary eye on Snow as it crept off into the woods to stalk another meal.

Wynne felt her heart still racing from the encounter with the cheetah. A cheetah was the last animal she had expected to attack her. There were only twelve thousand left in the wild. They usually posed no threat to humans and feared them. The cat must have been one of several pairs recently released into the reserve for relocation and it was disoriented, or just plain hungry and not picky about its next meal.

She saw Snow pacing and sniffing the air, agitated by the attack. Wynne had never seen Snow defend her territory so aggressively. It must have something to do with Snow beginning to hunt at night. Soon she'd feel the call of the wild and she'd leave. Wynne had to ready her heart for it. Somehow.

At the thought of losing her, Wynne felt tightness in her chest. She bent and quieted Snow, running her hands over her coat. "You look okay, but don't go getting all feral-kitty on me. You hear?" She touched her nose to Snow's. "I'm not ready to lose you yet."

Snow rubbed her face against Wynne's neck.

"Let's go home." Wynne cast a wary glance into the forest. She was glad it wasn't Hellstrom's men, but they could turn up at anytime.

With all her senses still on alert, she walked the rest of the way into camp. The moon hung over the camp buildings like a globe, tranquil, yet watchful. The camp was laid out in a rectangular grid. The mess hall, male barracks and Kaweki's cottage bordered the northern side.

She passed headquarters, a sandstone square building that made up the camp's southern side, along with the LZCG operations center. Wynne thought about searching Hellstrom's desk there, but Kaweki always made sure a ranger manned both offices. The radio and expensive equipment inside both offices were easy marks for thieves. Solomon, a new recruit, was on duty tonight in the operations center, and Moke, an old veteran, was guarding headquarters. She'd have to find the right time to search it, maybe later.

She walked past the primitive dirt landing strip that cut a wide swath behind LZCG headquarters. The LZCG used it for their helicopter to spot poachers and for small planes bringing in supplies. At the end of the runway, she could see the Big Five Habitat, its cinderblocks painted in brightly colored zebras, giraffes, buffaloes, elephants: the children's artwork. Fenced cages jutted from the rear and sides of the Habitat building, filled with convalescing animals.

Her bungalow stood behind the Habitat, away from the male dormitory, at Kaweki's insistence. He hadn't wanted gender mixing and the problems that could arise from it. Neither did Wynne and she was happily situated near the Habitat. But it meant a longer walk to headquarters and the mess.

She spotted Dr. Leonard's jeep parked in front of the Habitat. He was the park's veterinarian and his office was in the Habitat. A light burned in his operating room. It looked as if he were busy with a sick animal tonight.

Wynne really wanted to go to her hut, but she couldn't go to sleep without telling Dr. Leonard about the cheetah attack. She headed for the Habitat. Snow followed her.

She gave Snow a hand signal to wait outside. The animals inside didn't enjoy having a potential predator nearby and they went a little crazy in their cages if they smelled the leopard.

Wynne stepped inside the Habitat. Her footsteps tapped across the tile floor. She gazed at the ceiling and walls decorated like a forest. Papier-mâché replicas of animals, created by the children, filled the jungle. She smiled, remembering how the children enjoyed decorating the foyer.

She passed the classroom on the right, where the children learned not only about animals but the three *R*'s. Next to the classroom stood a dormitory for the older male teens who were lucky enough to be chosen as assistants to Dr. Leonard. The girls went home to their parents every night—it kept the boys minds on their studies and away from temptation, so Dr. Leonard had said. The assistants also taught the younger children. The door was closed and it was quiet. She guessed the teens were asleep.

Across the hall, a room held juvenile or baby animals. Right now they had aardvarks, porcupines, hedgehogs, hyraxes and a litter of flying squirrels. All had either lost their parents by local hunters or had been displaced from a recent forest-clearing conducted by the government for collective farming.

Wynne came to Dr. Leonard's surgery. The door was closed but a ray of light beamed beneath it. She pressed her ear against the door and heard the Rolling Stones playing from inside. Mick Jagger belted out *Sympathy for the*

Devil. Dr. Leonard always operated to the Stones. She knocked.

"Enter," he shouted over the music.

Wynne stepped inside, the smell of antiseptic and animal thick in the air. The room had a concrete floor. The walls were painted an institutional white, and a tiny window sat near the ceiling. An autoclave, a portable X-ray machine and a cabinet filled with medical supplies were wedged along the walls. A fluorescent lamp hung from the ceiling. Dr. Leonard stood directly beneath the lamp, bent over a blue monkey.

Dr. Leonard was a tall, thin African with short-cropped graying stubble for hair. Wynne guessed he was about forty. Equal measures of kindness and intelligence graced his face. He had attended veterinary school in England and had grown up in Livingstone, a Zambian city near Victoria Falls made famous by the nineteenth-century missionary doctor and explorer, David Livingstone. When Henry Morton Stanley found Dr. Livingstone in the heart of Africa, the phrase, "Dr. Livingstone, I presume," became legendary. Dr. Leonard's first name was Livingstone, a touchy subject. It had caused him a lot of ribbing in vet school; its parents hadn't thought that one out very well. Woe to someone who called him anything but Dr. Leonard now. His tongue could be sharper than his scalpels.

For a moment he reminded Wynne of her father, standing there in his lab coat, bent over an animal on an operating table, the sterile veterinary scent wafting through the room. Many times her father had let her watch him operate on the zoo animals. She smiled at the memory.

Dr. Leonard didn't glance up. "Hello, Wynne."

Wynne always marveled at Dr. Leonard's peripheral vision. Sometimes it seemed as if he had eyes in the back of his head. "Operating this late?"

"Poor creature was attacked by wild dogs. I found him not far from here. I'm just stitching him up." He spoke with a proper English accent.

Wynne stepped closer, but stayed far enough to not break the sterile field. She looked down at the monkey. It lay faceup on a table, its head fallen to one side. Dr. Leonard was working on the animal's arm, where the blue-gray fur had been chewed away and the flesh torn open. Dr. Leonard had stitched half of it back in place.

"What brings you here so late?" Dr. Leonard asked as he carefully made another stitch.

"I just ran into a cheetah near the clinic and wanted to tell you."

"A cheetah, you say. That's wonderful news. The lads and I will get a tracking collar on him tomorrow." Dr. Leonard's stern operating expression lightened. "Maybe our project to introduce them into the park isn't doomed."

"Maybe not, but he might come here looking for a meal. Our caged animals could be easy pickings for him."

"I'll see that the cage doors are locked. And I don't plan to sleep tonight." Dr. Leonard's insomnia had bothered him since he lost his wife a year ago. "You up for a game of poker later?"

Wynne didn't suffer from insomnia, but Dr. Leonard thought she did. She just liked their poker nights. It was like spending time with her father. "I don't think so. You win every time. What do I owe you now?"

"Just a case of oranges, a jar of peanut butter, some Belgian chocolates—"

"See, that's why I don't like to play with you," she teased. "I'll have to rob a market to get all the stuff I owe you."

Dr. Leonard grinned like a Cheshire cat, obviously pleased with his skills in besting her. He tied another suture and said, "Is it my fault you're unlucky at cards?"

"One day I'll beat you." Not. But she could hope.

She listened to the music for a moment and thought his hands worked with the same precision as the Stones played, fluid and swift, not missing a beat. After a moment of silence, she said, "May I ask you something?"

"Ask away." He motioned to her with the scissors.

"This is all hypothetical of course."

"Of course," he said as if he knew full well that with Wynne there would be nothing hypothetical about it.

"Do you think an animal thought extinct can live undetected in today's world?"

"Where in today's world?"

"Here, Africa."

"I happen to believe Bigfoot, the Yeti, the Loch Ness monster and the chupacabra are all creatures that should have been extinct for thousands of years."

"You believe in those creatures?"

"I do," he said, sounding affronted. "Does it make me seem a little daft to have faith in the work of cryptozoologists?"

"Not at all."

"I also believe animals have ESP and gorillas and whales are smarter than we give them credit. The trouble with man is his arrogance. The earth is an amazing place, filled with mysteries we will never know about, and if we become blind to them because of narrow-mindedness, then more's the pity for us. Why do you ask? What have you discovered?" Dr. Leonard stopped sewing a moment and gave her his full attention.

Wynne didn't want to divulge what Hellstrom had said to her about the scimitar. If Dr. Leonard became involved, it could put his life in danger. "I just wondered what you thought."

"I'm afraid my opinion is just that, my opinion. It's not very beneficial or scientific. I'm sure I'd be laughed out of the Royal Academy of Science."

"On the contrary, I value your opinion. It matters a great deal to me."

"So this is all purely supposition?" Dr. Leonard wore a skeptical look as he began bandaging the monkey's arm.

"Yes." Their conversation lulled, and Wynne listened to the music as she watched him work.

Dr. Leonard broke the pause. "I heard about Mehan," he said, shooting her a look. "Itezhi lives in the same village with Mehan's family. When Eieb broke the news to Mehan's wife and gave her a lift to the clinic, the whole village knew what had happened—"

"And Itezhi told you after his parents told him."

"Pretty much." Dr. Leonard nodded.

Wynne guessed the good doctor had the counsel and friendship of all his assistants. They probably looked on him as a father and told him everything.

"How is it that Mehan became involved in poaching?" Dr. Leonard asked.

"I'm unsure." Wynne had already told Dr. Mukuka about the poaching but she was reluctant to involve Dr. Leonard and have to worry about his life, too. "I only know that there's a poaching ring somewhere near here and they could have more spies in our camp."

"In our camp?" Dr. Leonard frowned. "Surely not. People here have steady jobs, why ruin it by taking blood money?"

"Mehan is just one among many. You and I both know game guards and wildlife officials are corrupted all the time."

Dr. Leonard's brows met over his nose. "I hate to admit it, but you speak the truth. Kenge's arrest just last month proves the corruption even goes all the way to the top."

"I know." She recalled hearing about the Zambian Interior Minister being charged with granting illegal safari hunting licenses in the game-managed areas. It had distressed her as much as finding a bush meat poaching ring operating right under her nose. "Have you seen Mehan talking with anyone in camp lately? Anyone that looked suspicious?"

"No, no one. I'm kept so busy with the animals, I rarely see what goes on here in camp. I wish I could help. One thing is certain, I pray to God that you stop these poachers." His voice deepened with concern. "Their boldness will draw other poachers. We'll lose our animals."

"I know." Wynne echoed the same sentiment.

"Does Kaweki know about this?"

"Yes, I told him."

"He's a good man. He'll take care of it."

A knock on the door grabbed their attention.

"Enter," Dr. Leonard said, tying off the bandaging job on the monkey's arm. He bent and listened to the monkey's heartbeat with a stethoscope.

Mama Luwo, the camp cook, stepped into the operating room. She looked around sheepishly and spotted Wynne, her lazy eye seeming to go in a different direction. She wore a pink and yellow house dress given to her by the Baptist mission in Lusaka. Her chest heaved as if she'd run the whole way there.

She pursed her lips at Wynne, exposing her missing

front teeth. "Miss Wynne, I thought I'd find you here." When Mama Luwo pronounced Wynne's name it sounded like "Wind."

"Is something wrong?"

"No, I just wanted you to know I left a snack in your hut. I would have come sooner but *chizwango*—" She pointed to the door, her eyes widening with fear.

"It's just Snow. If you would make friends with her—"

"Make friends with a *chizwango?*" Mama Luwo said, using an abstract term used among locals for any animal capable of harming man. She shook her head at Wynne, years of superstition fueling her fear of the leopard.

"You could start by saying her name once in a while."

"Bad *juju* to address dangerous animal by name."

Wynne knew this was a local legend, too, and said, "I know, but Snow will not harm you."

"So *you* say." Mama Luwo blinked a dubious look at Wynne.

"Did you see Snow on your way inside?" Wynne asked, unable to keep the worry from her voice.

"She gone. Probably hunting where she should be. Tell her, Dr. Leonard. *Chizwango* make no good pets. No good." Mama Luwo shook her head.

"I think she knows that." Dr. Leonard eyed Wynne.

Was this some kind of combined leopard intervention? First Eieb reproaches her about Snow. Now Dr. Leonard and Mama Luwo. "I know," Wynne said, her tone defensive.

"She'll find a mister one day and be gone from here." Mama Luwo's fear melted and she seemed to sense Wynne's anxiety. She patted Wynne's arm. "You can find a nice dog for a pet—uh? Dogs make nice pets."

"Yes, they do," Wynne said, aware Mama Luwo meant well, but she could be hard to take sometimes. Wynne guessed the added attention Mama Luwo bestowed on her stemmed from the fact Wynne was the only woman ranger in camp, and Mama Luwo had raised ten daughters of her own. Her daughters now lived in other parts of Africa and she rarely saw them. So Wynne had somehow become the object of Mama Luwo's mothering. The trouble was Wynne wasn't used to being mothered. "I guess I should go then. 'Night, Dr. Leonard."

"You'll keep me informed of the progress?" He bent over the monkey and listened to its heartbeat with his stethoscope, while he gazed at Wynne.

They both knew he was speaking about the spy and poachers. "I will."

Mama Luwo had already torn out the front door. Wynne searched for Snow but didn't see her. She hoped Snow didn't run into the rogue cheetah again.

"Mama L, wait." Wynne jogged to catch the little woman.

"Did you hear about Mehan?" Wynne asked, running up to her side.

Mama Luwo wagged her head, then seemed preoccupied with keeping an eye out for Snow.

Wynne tried again. "Are there any other spies here in camp that you know of?"

Mama Luwo sped up, but she came up short when she reached Wynne's bungalow. She flapped her arms, flustered for a moment, then pointed inside. "You want anything else?"

"No, you really don't have to wait on me like this."

"I know, but I want to—oh, forgot to tell you a package came for you on mail truck today. I go now." She turned to flee.

Wynne grabbed her arm. "Mama L, you didn't answer my question."

"Uh, spies." She hesitated for half a second, before she said, "No spies, I know of."

Wynne was certain she was lying. "If you know something, please tell me."

Mama Luwo's good eye glistened with fear and she looked on the verge of tears. "I can't tell you, Miss Wynne. I want to live." Her voice was a hoarse whisper.

"Please…"

Mama Luwo jerked her arm free of Wynne's grasp and shot toward the mess hall like a bullet. Wynne wanted to run after her, but she knew Mama Luwo's fear ran too deep. How many other people knew of the spies and had been hiding it? How many people she believed were her friends in camp were working for Hellstrom? She didn't want to believe anyone capable of being bought, but Mehan had turned.

Wynne shoved aside the mosquito netting covering the door and stepped inside her stone hut. The earthy scent of the mud brick floor and thatch roof lingered in the air. Mama Luwo had made sure the mosquito netting covered the inside of the shuttered windows, and she had turned on a solar battery-powered light on the ceiling. It cast a warm glow in the small space.

Wynne spotted a wooden bowl and spoon sitting on her bamboo desk. The bowl held couscous and *n'shima,* a paste of boiled maize meal dipped in gravy made with beans. It was a food staple in camp, and it smelled wonderful. She heard her stomach growling.

She wolfed down the food and took off her clothes. She sponge-bathed in tepid water left in a pitcher and bowl. The camp didn't have running water, and when she needed a bath, she bathed in the Zambezi.

When she walked to the teakwood cabinet she used as

a dresser, she spotted Mehan's carved leopard. She ran her fingers over the statue. The cat was snarling, paw raised to strike. Every detail, from the teeth to the leopard's whiskers, was carved exactly in Snow's image. It was a beautiful work of art. She thought of Mehan's senseless loss of life, and she couldn't help the empty heaviness that slipped into her chest.

She set down the leopard and opened the cabinet. Out of habit she made a quick visual sweep for scorpions and snakes, then pulled out a *SpongeBob* nightshirt—Cody's gift to her last Christmas—and donned it. God! She wished she could somehow teleport Cody here for the night.

It was their shared laughter that she missed, Cody's bright smile that always won Wynne over and made her feel special. Wynne hadn't seen Cody since the last time she was back in the States, over two years ago. Wynne had hoped she'd come to Africa for a visit, but law school was taking up all of Cody's time and she couldn't get away.

One day Cody would fulfill the golden child political aspirations her mother had had for Wynne. First Cody would be partner in her mother's law firm. Next, the Senate. Then maybe she'd run against Hillary Clinton for president. If anyone could live up to her mother's aspirations, Cody could. Wynne had been nothing but a source of disillusionment for her mother. All she really wanted was her mother to accept her for who she was. But Wynne knew that would never happen.

She spotted the package Mama Luwo had mentioned. It was tucked in a corner, near an aluminum trunk she kept with all her camping gear and tools. Wynne picked up the heavy package and sniffed it, as if she might get a whiff of home. But it only smelled like the musty scent of her bungalow. She used her dagger, cut the twine and tore off the brown wrapping paper.

She opened the top and found the note Cody had scribbled on a piece of brown shopping bag. She was always in a hurry, grabbing anything to write on. Once Cody had written a message on an empty cardboard roll of toilet paper. Wynne had felt like a monk reading a thirteenth century Greek scroll. Now Wynne turned the scrap of paper right and left to make sense of Cody's cryptic scratching:

Yo Sister Innie,
Care package number 44, hot from Dee Cee. College is a bore. Bore. BORE. I wish Mom would let me stay in the dorm, but you know how she is. And I hate the thought of law school. I want to change my major. You think that'll cause World War III in the mother-daughter landscape?

Wynne shook her head, "You betcha. Mom will fight tooth and nail before another daughter disappoints her." So Cody had finally broken beneath the yoke of their mother's smothering control. Cody didn't like strife, and so she was easily led by their mother. Wynne didn't think her little sister would ever rebel. But it didn't surprise Wynne. Her mother suffocated everyone she loved. Wynne read on.

Anyway, the dresses are from Mom—can you tell? I found them lying over the box before I mailed it, so I threw them in—don't laugh. She just doesn't get it. We can only hope one day. I've cleaned out my closet, too—for your kids at the camp.
Anyway, the fudge is hot out of the pot—you're

lucky I didn't eat it all, and I bought all the old stand-bys I could find.

I had lunch with Dad and he sends his love. Keeps threatening to visit you, but we both know he'll never leave work long enough for that.

Till next time. Miss you.

> Loves, hugs and kissy-poos,
> Cody

Amid jars of peanut butter and boxes of Ritz crackers, she pulled out Cody's shorts, jeans and T-shirts with the latest logos: *Buffy the Vampire Slayer, Survivor,* more *SpongeBob,* Shrew And Proud of It. The kids who volunteered at the Habitat would have first crack at them. They were always asking Wynne if her sister had sent another package of clothes. Cody's closet cleanings were a big hit here.

She found the dresses her mother had sent. They were sequined cocktail dresses—her mother's way of protesting Wynne's values and career choice. Wynne envisioned some of the girls wearing the dresses while they worked at the Habitat and she smiled.

She tossed the dresses aside and picked up the tin. It smelled like a chocoholic's dream come true. Cody had a way with fudge that could make Hershey's envious. The recipe had been handed down to Cody from their Grandma Sperling, who passed away when Wynne was eighteen.

Wynne inhaled the scent of the fudge and it brought back fond memories of her grandmother's house. When she had cooked fudge, the whole house smelled like a chocolate bar. Wynne missed that smell, and her grandmother. She was the kindest woman Wynne had ever known.

Wynne set the tin aside. If she opened it now she knew she would gorge herself on it, and she wanted to share it with the kids at the habitat. It was a real treat for them. Wynne knew Grandma Sperling would be smiling somewhere when they ate it.

In the bottom of the box, she reached her weakness: four boxes of Twinkies. "Bless you, Cody," Wynne said, staring down at them. Good old American carbs. There was only so much *n'shima* a person could eat before their taste buds protested.

She'd share the fudge, but not these bad boys. She tore open a Twinkie and moaned as the white filling mingled with the sponge cake and tantalized her taste buds. A little piece of heaven right here in Africa.

A knock on the door ruined the moment. "Who's there?" she called.

"Me, darlin'. Open up."

At the sound of the Texas drawl Wynne felt every muscle in her body tighten. She swallowed the rest of the Twinkie whole as she wondered what the hell he was doing here?

Chapter 7

"It's really late." Wynne looked at her open windows and wondered how long MacKay had been standing out there. He could have been watching her through the mosquito netting over the windows.

"You didn't call." His voice sounded pitiful, like a male hyena whining outside the den of a female hyena in heat.

"Because it's late." Wynne opened the door only a crack and kept her foot braced behind it in case he tried something.

He looked heart-stopping handsome in the moonlight. He still wore his suit, minus the bolo tie. He'd unbuttoned his shirt down to the middle of his chest, exposing a gold St. Christopher's medal and a thatch of dark-blond chest hair. In one hand he held a serving tray he'd obviously pilfered from Hellstrom's party and in the other a bottle of champagne. A crooked grin tilted his mouth and deepened his dimples. Those long-lashed liquid blue eyes sparkled at her.

"I can't see you very well...." He leaned in closer to peer through the crack. "You gonna open up, or what?"

Wynne closed the door another inch and had to squint at him through the crack. "How did you get past the guard?"

"Told him I was visiting you. He laughed and pointed me to your hut."

Great. The guys would pull her chain about this for a week. Too bad MacKay hadn't met the cheetah on his way in.

"Guess you don't get too many male callers. But I'm here. You gonna open up, or what?"

"Why should I?"

"Come on, darlin', I come bearing gifts." He shoved the champagne bottle at her nose.

Wynne started to tell him where he could stuff his gifts, but if he had wanted to, he could have tried to force his way into her hut. Instead he'd shown up on her doorstep, bearing lures and begging to come inside like a stray dog. Obviously, violence wasn't on his mind. But what was? Hellstrom must have ordered MacKay to seduce her and discover her next move. Maybe she could turn it around and learn more about Hellstrom's operation through MacKay—or at least learn what Hellstrom had planned.

But she wasn't going to make it easy for him, so she said, "I can't be bought with champagne."

"Okay, can I tempt you with tea sandwiches? I think they're cucumber." He sniffed the tray and his handsome face wrinkled in a frown. "Yep, cucumber. I'm a rib man myself."

"How did I know that? You can only stay a minute."

Wynne opened the door.

MacKay stepped past her. All she could see were his broad shoulders, while she caught a whiff of alcohol on his breath, mingled with his spicy aftershave. He smelled better than a Twinkie, better than any man she'd smelled in a long time.

He swaggered into the room, his head almost reaching the bamboo rafters. He turned and shot her a look. An air of intimacy seemed to sizzle between them. His presence overpowered the small space. Wynne could have sworn the walls had shrunk inward by two feet. The air grew ten degrees hotter, too.

He set the tray and bottle down on her desk. "Mighty cozy place you got."

"Yeah, it's the Taj Mahal." She glimpsed his Magnum holstered beneath his jacket and didn't ask him to sit in the desk chair—the only chair she owned. He wouldn't be here that long. She opened her hand. "I'll take the gun."

"Haven't we done this before?"

"Yeah, and we'll continue to do it as long as you keep wearing your best buddy there." She motioned again to the cannon in his holster. "Now lose it."

"All right, but you're the most distrustful woman I've ever met." MacKay slipped his hand inside his black jacket. "You need to relax, darlin'."

Relax around him? Right. She kept her eyes on his hand and the gun.

He pulled it out and started to lay it on the desk.

"Uh-uh. I'll take it." She snatched it out of his grasp and put it into the desk drawer.

"You really don't trust me, do you?" He almost sounded hurt. "I told you I was a teddy bear—"

"Right, and I'm Goldilocks."

He lifted his hands and grinned at her. "You wanna search me for more weapons?" There was way too much eagerness in his voice.

"I'll trust you don't have anything else hidden anywhere."

"Nothing that will stay hidden long." He crossed his arms over his broad chest and began undressing her with his eyes.

Wynne realized she had invited this virgin-stealing Texan into her room and she was wearing only a nightshirt. One puny cotton nightshirt and underwear. The way his eyes were eating her alive stoked a fire that had been dormant in her for a long time. She envisioned his large hands sliding along her body as he pulled up her nightshirt, then his biting her panties and pulling them down with his teeth.

His gaze landed on *SpongeBob,* and his grin widened.

The vision dissolved. Wynne realized he was the enemy, and two years of celibacy was really getting to her. She stomped over to the cabinet and pulled on the thickest terry cloth robe she owned, then faced him.

"You amaze me, darlin'," he said with laughter in his voice. "I thought you'd sleep in chain mail."

Very funny. "The nightshirt was a gift from my sister."

"That your sister in the photo there?" He picked up a picture of her family from the desk.

"Yeah, about fifteen years ago. Cody was three. I was nine. That's a BTD photo."

"BTD?"

"Before the divorce."

"That explains it."

"What?"

He rubbed his thumb over her parents' faces. "The smile on their faces, like it was pasted there only for the photo."

Even then Wynne had felt the tension between her parents and had known their marriage was doomed. It was disconcerting that MacKay had sensed that just by looking at a picture for three seconds. She grabbed the photo from him and set it back down.

He still eyed it, his expression somber. "I always wanted parents and figured if I had some everything would be just dandy. But I guess that ain't always true."

"My parents just weren't compatible." The truth was her mother constantly put down her father for not opening his own practice and making more money as a veterinarian. Her father had realized he'd never live up to his wife's expectations and he had left her. Wynne never felt bitter about her father's exit. No one could live up to her mother's high standards.

An uncomfortable silence settled between them. MacKay seemed mesmerized by the photo and lost in his own thoughts. Wynne found herself sort of sorry for MacKay. At least she'd had two parents. He'd never even known his mother. She felt uncomfortable at the unbidden feeling and stepped in front of the photo, blocking his view.

They were a foot apart. He blinked down at her with those kiss-me blue eyes. She saw her own reflection filling them up, felt the life force of his body touching hers. She could almost feel his hands on her body.

He reached toward her upper lip. "You've got something right here…." His finger glided across the edge of her mouth.

Wynne felt his finger scorch her lips. A tremble started in her knees and worked its way up to her thighs.

He slowly licked the cream from his finger. "Hmmmm, not bad." His voice grew husky.

"What if that had been poison?" she asked, her lips still tingling from his touch.

"I don't think so." He pointed at the Twinkie wrapper on top of the package Cody had sent her.

He didn't miss a trick. "Okay, I think you've stayed your minute." She no longer cared about questioning him. She just wanted him out of her hut so she could think clearly.

"That's a Washington, D.C. minute, darlin'. Not a Texas minute. We haven't even opened the champagne yet." Before she could stop him, he'd popped the cork, cutting off her words of protest. Champagne spewed down over his hand and dripped on the floor.

"You must hold the record for bottle opening," she said. He'd probably done this so many times it was like breathing to him. Wynne threw him the towel she had used to dry off from her sponge bath. "You might need this."

"Thanks." He dried his hand and glanced around. "You wouldn't happen to have two wineglasses around here?"

"It just so happens I do." Wynne strode over to the teak cabinet and pulled out two crystal goblets.

"Now that's a surprise." He cocked a brow at her. "You entertain in your hut a lot?"

She understood the implication behind his words. "No, it's not what you think. A friend and I open a bottle of home-brewed wine whenever a lion cub or elephant calf is born." That friend was Eieb.

"You close to this friend?" He searched her eyes intently.

"I'm not dating him, if that's what you're asking."

"Glad to hear it." He looked amused or pleased. It was impossible to tell behind that enigmatic grin.

She wiped the inside of the glasses with the hem of her nightshirt to get out any dust, then handed them to him. "And are you dating anyone?"

"Not at the moment." He gave her a long assessing look, like she was the only woman in the world for him.

She saw through the expression, a look he reserved for every woman he was with. He probably had a stable of women who he'd lured into believing they were special. When it came to deceiving women, he had more tricks than a horny court jester. "You seemed kinda friendly with Jacqueline," she said, keeping her voice casual.

"Just met her a day ago when she arrived at Hellstrom's from London." He poured the champagne into the glasses.

"I thought you'd known her longer than that."

"She and I hit it off right away. Nice girl."

How long had it taken him to seduce her? She segued into a different subject. "I heard Hellstrom's planning a safari."

"Is that so?" He had the talent to look surprised.

"Yes. I thought you'd know about it since you were staying on the compound."

"I only know he scheduled one for me, but I didn't think he was planning on going along."

He was lying. It was in his eyes.

"Here you go." He handed her a glass.

His hand brushed hers and lingered. The warmth of it made her pull back. He grinned, knowing why she had flinched. She frowned down at the drink. "I told you I don't do champagne."

"Come on, try it." His dimples deepened in a grin that could coax a woman into drinking hemlock.

"You first." Wynne pointed to the glass.

"You don't trust anybody, do you? I didn't spike it with a date-rape drug—" He chugged the glass of champagne down. Then looked at her expectantly.

"Will you leave if I drink a glass?"

"You've got my word."

His word? The word of a lothario and a criminal. Comforting. She chugged it down in three gulps. "Okay, you can go now."

He shook his head, looking forlorn. "This hurts, darlin'. I had high hopes we could get to know each other better."

"Some other time." Wynne walked to the door and

opened it. Snow had been waiting at the door, and she leaped inside.

MacKay froze and eyed the leopard warily. "I'd heard you were packing a leopard."

So he'd been asking questions about her. Hellstrom had probably filled him in. "She won't hurt you—" Wynne grinned "—unless I order her to."

"Nice kitty." He bent slowly and held out his hand.

Snow, the furry defector, padded over to him like they were old friends. She rubbed her whiskers against his hand. When it came to judging a person's character, Snow was usually pretty good, better than Wynne sometimes. But in this case the cat had been taken in. MacKay's way with females didn't seem to stop with humans. It just proved that an animal's intuition could be flawed, too.

"You're a beauty, you are." His long fingers stroked the length of Snow's spine.

The cat arched her back as if it were the best thing she'd felt in her life.

"So you've made a pet out of a leopard?" He gazed over at Wynne.

"No, she comes and goes when she likes." Wynne lied just a little. She couldn't watch his large hands working their magic on Snow's back any longer, so she said, "Speaking of going." She pointed to the open door.

What seemed like real disappointment glistened in his eyes, then he straightened. "Sorry kitty, another time." He sidestepped Snow, then crossed the hut to the door. He paused in the doorway and asked, "When can I see you again?"

"I don't know."

"How about tomorrow? You can show me around the park."

So he could watch her every move and report back to Hellstrom? "My job keeps me busy."

He winked at her. "I won't stop trying, darlin'."

Wynne rolled her eyes.

He felt his empty holster and said, "I can't leave without J.D."

"Right, the Texas security blanket." She saw him grin as she walked over and pulled the gun out of the desk drawer. She plopped it in his hand, carefully so their hands wouldn't touch. "There you go." She pointed to the door. "No more excuses."

The leather on the holster whispered as he shoved the Magnum inside. "You sure know how to treat a guest," he said, giving her a kicked-puppy look as he stepped out the door. "I'll see you again sometime."

"And I'll still be busy," she tossed back at him. "Good night."

She closed the door, bolted it and sighed with relief. Tonight she had managed to maintain her distance. What about the next time she saw him? Okay, she had to admit, she'd felt a physical attraction for him—an intense attraction. But controllable. She was the queen of control. Hadn't she lived a celibate life for two years? But then, there hadn't been someone around like MacKay, Mr. Testosterone, scratching at her door at all hours. She had to be honest with herself; MacKay could possibly become more dangerous than Hellstrom—if she let him.

A knock on her door made her jump. MacKay just couldn't take no for an answer. For some reason her heart sped up and pounded against her ribs. She sucked in her breath as she flung open the door.

"What is it this time—" She clamped her mouth closed when she saw Eieb looking at her oddly.

* * *

"Sorry, it's only me." Eieb pointed behind him. "Were you expecting the guy I saw leaving here?"

"No." Wynne motioned him inside, then closed the door.

"Who was that? A *new* friend?" Eieb bent and petted Snow.

"He's nobody."

"He's somebody if he's coming out of your hut in the middle of the night."

"Okay, okay," she said, knowing he would badger her until she spilled the details. "His name's MacKay. He's somehow involved in the poaching ring. I just haven't found out how yet."

"What's he doing in your hut—" Eieb glanced at the sandwiches and bottle of champagne "—besides eating and drinking?" He picked up a sandwich and tasted it.

"Other than being a royal pain, I don't know. I think he's here to try and discover what our next move will be so he can report back to Hellstrom."

Eieb scowled as he finished off the sandwich. "Are you sure it's Hellstrom?"

Wynne quickly filled him in on finding MacKay at Sausage Tree Camp, attending the party, the shipping documents she'd found in Hellstrom's office, his finding her there and the safari he was planning with MacKay.

When she was done, Eieb asked, "Do you think Hellstrom is toying with you about the scimitar?"

"I don't know what to think."

"I've heard the legends as a child. I think you'll find it is all a hoax the chief uses to keep his people under his control." Eieb gripped the brim of his baseball cap, picked it up, then nervously settled it back on his head.

"I can't hardly believe an Ice Age mammal like that has

survived, but I still have to check," Wynne said. "Aja has agreed to take me to question the Bemba tribe tomorrow. I know Kaweki will have extra patrols in the park after I told him about the bush meat bust, but can you cover for me and keep an eye on my herds?"

"I can, but aren't you going to tell Kaweki?"

"No. What if they do exist? And word gets out—"

"You don't trust Kaweki?"

"I do, but all it takes is one slip of the tongue. Imagine the people all over the world who would scramble to profit off the scimitar. Not to mention the scientists who would want to study them. They would never be able to survive in peace. They might even end up in a zoo, or worse." Wynne grimaced. "For the sake of the animals, we have to keep this to ourselves."

"You're right, but what if Hellstrom tells someone?"

"He might have told MacKay, but I don't think he'll tell anyone else. He wants to exploit the animals for money. He came right out and admitted that to me. I don't think he'll want anyone finding them before he does."

"Let's hope he doesn't." Eieb picked up the bottle of champagne. "You mind?"

"It's yours." Wynne watched him take a long swallow and said, "I forgot to ask how Kidaya is doing."

At the mention of Kidaya, his face flooded with emotion. "She seemed to be okay when I took her home. She was upset, of course, but thankful." Eieb's voice trailed off and his grip tightened around the bottle. He paused, then said, "She doesn't blame me for, you know…"

"I know. No one can blame you for doing your job. Mehan was in the wrong."

"I know, but it still hurt me to see the pain on her face, knowing I'm partly responsible for putting it there."

"It will take a while for both of you to forget." Wynne touched his arm, but he didn't seem to notice.

"How will she survive? She's so young. I have to do something for her." Eieb set down the bottle on the desk.

"The children are in the Habitat program. We can feed them and take some of the burden off her."

"That's true. Her sister is watching the children for the night. I hated to leave her alone…." There was a restless depth of feeling in his voice that Wynne had never heard before.

"I'm sure she'll be okay."

He was silent a moment, his eyes tortured by a memory, then he said, "I asked her if she knew of anyone else taking bribes."

Wynne felt relieved she didn't have to question her. "What did she say?"

"She hasn't seen anyone else with Mehan, or anyone paying him."

"I guess that's good news. Maybe he is the only turncoat in camp." Wynne recalled her conversation with Mama Luwo and knew that was wishful thinking. Eieb had enough on his mind with Kidaya and Mehan's death, so she didn't tell him about Mama Luwo's fear.

"We can only hope," he said, sounding emotionally and physically exhausted. "I'm tired. I'd better go. I'll cover for you tomorrow. I hope you find out something definitive about the scimitar. And be careful. It might be a setup just to lure you into the jungle."

"I'll be careful." Wynne saw Eieb out, then felt the bite of uncertainty. What if it was a trap? Would MacKay be part of it? After he'd tried to seduce her with his sweet talk, dimples and grins. She almost welcomed meeting him in the bush. At least he wouldn't be hiding behind his duplicity. She was pretty sure in combat the teddy bear he claimed to be would be in shreds, and the ex-SEAL MacKay would resurface.

She thought of something she had to do and she dressed and left her hut.

Wynne saw the camp jeep parked out in front of Kaweki's bungalow. Kaweki and Colette had made it home from Hellstrom's party. It was late, but lights gleamed in the bedroom window. She gathered her courage and knocked on the front door.

She heard thumps, cursing, then Kaweki flung open the door. He wore an inside-out T-shirt and shorts. He was heaving as if he'd run a marathon. Sweat trickled down his brow, and smears of lipstick dotted his neck and cheeks. She had interrupted more than just his sleep. She turned and started to walk away, "Sorry, sir, I'll talk to you in the morn—"

"Oh, no you don't." He grabbed her by the arm and pulled her around. "I'm here now, Sperling. What the hell do you want?"

"I had to talk to you."

"Talk, then, but make it quick." He gripped the door as if she wasn't getting invited inside.

"Did you find out anything at Hellstrom's tonight?"

"Nothing."

"He didn't mention the safari?"

"No." He held her gaze too long.

She had a feeling he wasn't being completely honest with her. "But Hellstrom is going on a safari. I heard his servants talking about it. We can't let him go. It's probably a poaching expedition."

"He's in the safari business, and head of the LZCG. If he wants to go on a safari, how can I stop him? Unless we have proof that I can take to the magistrate and the board, we'll be made fools of."

"But we have to do something."

"Our hands are tied, unless we catch him red-handed with the evidence. And we won't be able to do that until we have more time and do more maneuvering. We'll get him, but not on this safari. Now forget it."

Colette called out from another part of the house, "George, who is that?"

"No one, love," he shouted back. "We'll talk about this later. Good night." He slammed the door in Wynne's face.

She stared at the door and understood Kaweki's reluctance. His job was at stake. The thing that bugged her was it felt like he'd just given her the brush-off.

She didn't like disobeying her superior, but she could go over his head to the powers that be. But that would take days and who could she trust? There was so much corruption in the government. And like Kaweki said, who would believe her without proof?

Wynne started to knock again and tell Kaweki about the scimitar, but would that change his mind? Would he believe her? Ice Age cats alive and well. What if she found proof tomorrow that scimitars existed? She couldn't let word of it get out. And she couldn't let Hellstrom exploit them, or worse, kill them. It was just another reason she had to follow him on this safari. It might be her only chance to arrest him with hard evidence. He hadn't been on a safari since he'd taken over the LZCG. This safari must be highly important to his poaching business. And it just so happened MacKay had arrived in time for it. She was certain this was no ordinary hunting trek into the bush.

* * *

The next day Wynne, Aja and Snow had slipped out of camp at dawn. She had made sure she wasn't being followed and had driven northeast, traveling along the Muchinga Escarpment that bordered the Luangwa Valley. The scarp hills had been created by two massive tectonic plates, drifting apart, and tearing Africa in half. And it had left a twisted, jagged, mountain range filled with deep gorges, sheer cliffs and steep hills as magnificent and unforgiving as Africa itself.

They had gone as far as they could in the Rover, but the *miombo* woodlands became too dense and the terrain too steep. They were forced to set out on foot. Now, they hiked along an elephant path that wound up a three thousand-foot scarp mountain. Tropical undergrowth and massive trees surrounded them. Steady drops of water hit her neck from the canopy of leaves overhead. The water mingled with the perspiration on her neck and felt good in the one hundred and twelve degree heat.

She glanced at Aja ahead of her and he hadn't broken a sweat. It was the end of the dry season, but the rains hadn't yet arrived and the mountain air had a suffocating feel to it. In the two years she'd been in Africa, her body had adjusted to the heat, but it wasn't like being born to the climate. The intense heat still sapped her energy. It didn't seem to bother Aja at all; his thin wiry legs kept a steady pace, uphill. Did he have ice in his veins? Snow didn't seem to mind the heat either and stayed at Aja's side.

Wynne paused and wiped the sweat trickling down over her eyelashes with the back of her hand. Her gaze swept the thick underbrush and trees for any signs of an ambush. Twenty yards away she saw the bushes moving near a fam-

ily of wild pigs searching for roots. A squirrel sprinted
along a tree bough overhead, irritating a family of monkeys. Nothing out of the ordinary.

She hadn't even found evidence of bush meat poachers
in the area. But it wasn't easy carrying tons of meat through
mountainous dense forests on foot, and they usually operated where there was easy access to a vehicle. Wynne saw
that Aja and Snow were getting ahead of her again and she
jogged to catch up to them.

They reached a clearing. A beautiful waterfall and an
oxbow lagoon opened up before them. The water was so
clear and blue she could see the multicolored pebbles on
the bottom. A herd of puku antelopes lay on the shore opposite them fifty yards downstream, taking refuge from the
heat. They seemed to sense the new intruders were of no
threat and they didn't move.

Aja didn't break his stride and began walking past the
water.

Wynne couldn't let this chance to cool off pass her by,
and she said, "Hey, wait a minute. Can we please stop?"
Okay, she was sounding like a whining child on a road trip,
but she couldn't go another step. She was already dropping
her backpack.

Aja gave her a disgusted grunt, then paused near the
edge of the lagoon.

"Is the village much farther?" Wynne staggered into
the water. The cool dampness felt like ice against her skin.
She moaned with pleasure.

Snow followed her, until the water reached her chest.
The leopard welcomed the coolness, too, and she pawed
at the water, dunking her muzzle.

Aja merely frowned at both of them, cupped his hands

and sipped water. "You, Wynne Sperling, never make good warrior, if you not get used to heat."

"I know, maybe one day." Wynne felt the cool water soaking her body and sighed in relief. "How far away is the village?"

"Not far now."

Not far in Aja's terms could mean miles. Wynne didn't press him. It was enough he trusted her to bring her to this tribe.

"It's beautiful here," Wynne said, feeling revived now that she was wet. She dunked her head and walked out of the river, dripping.

"This Hidden Valley."

"I've never heard of it."

"Not on maps. The heartbeat of Bembaland."

"Bembaland?" This was the first time she'd heard this term.

Aja nodded. "Zambia's northern province." He motioned to the lushness around them. "All this for miles, used to be Bembaland. Bembaland used to be filled with herds of every manner of animal, before greed visited the tribes and poachers sold the lives of animals for such a cheap price. Life simple then. Food abundant. Now we have starvation, poverty. Herds dwindling. Bembaland no longer belong to the Bemba but a testament to the ivory and bush meat trade." Aja sighed and his face grew solemn. "We go now and meet Chiti-Mukulu."

Wynne knew the highest chief of the Bemba bore the name Chiti-Mukulu. She looked forward to meeting him.

Aja began jogging along the river. Snow followed on his heels. Wynne brought up the rear, thinking he didn't move like any elderly man she had ever seen.

* * *

By the time they had finally reached the village, cumulus clouds had gathered. Their shadows arced across the hillside, covering the towering trees, tropical undergrowth and cleared patches of maize on the outskirts of the village. Wynne heard children laughing as they neared the huts.

Snow would frighten the villagers so Wynne ordered her to wait in the forest, then she followed Aja into the village.

They passed wattle-and-daub huts that formed a circle around the *n'saka,* a public area where all village business took place. Women and girls clad in multicolored *chitenges,* skirts made of strips of cloth wrapped around the waist, left their cooking *bomas* and ran toward Aja. Naked children followed. Warriors, dressed only in loincloths, sat around a communal clay pot of frothy *bwalwa bwamipashi,* beer made from sorghum flour. They sucked the brew through reed drinking straws. Wynne had seen many ceremonies among the Bemba that involved the use of beer. It was an integral part of their social structure.

The warriors were the last to rise and make their way to Aja. They called greetings, clapped and bowed, graciously humbled before Aja. He must have been highly regarded in this village.

Aja grasped their hands and wished them well. He turned to one man with no teeth and asked to see the chief.

He nodded at Wynne and said in Bemba, "She stays with the women."

Aja shook his head. "She is here with me to see Chiti-Mukulu."

The warrior gave her a wary glance, then motioned them to follow. He paused before a stone hut. Several women, most likely the chief's wives, rushed out to greet them.

Aja spoke to them, and they went inside to announce Aja's arrival.

Some of the children tugged at Wynne's slingshot, and she took it off and showed them how to use it. After a moment, the women returned and waved them inside.

The strong scent of burned mopani wood wafted through the air. A large reed mat lined the earthen floor. To her right, a tiny shrine of mounded stones held six teeth closely resembling Hellstrom's scimitar tooth. Blue and yellow lines circled them: *juju* to ward off evil. In a corner, on a dais of stones, the chief sat in the bench seat of an old truck. Two shy boys fanned the chief with huge banana leaves and wouldn't look at Wynne. The chief appeared about forty, wiry, with an intelligent face. He wore only a loincloth and munched on fried mopane worms.

He motioned for Aja to sit, then passed the bowl of worms to Aja.

Wynne remained standing, obviously not yet worth Chiti-Mukulu's notice.

Aja scooped up a handful of worms, nodded a thank-you and handed the bowl back. He chomped on them, then introduced her. Aja spoke to the chief in his own Bemba language.

The chief gave her the once-over, then invited her to sit with an airy wave of his hand. She claimed a spot next to Aja.

"Why you come here?" He addressed Aja, but looked askance at Wynne, his eyes studying her blond hair.

Aja explained about Hellstrom and the scimitar being in danger. The chief's expression turned grave.

Wynne finished with, "I come to see if the *mweo mfumu* exist." She addressed the chief in fluent Bemba. This seemed to please the chief and the severe lines in his brow relaxed a little.

"Just like a woman to doubt. Are you married?"

Wynne didn't know what difference that made and she shook her head no.

Aja said, "Married to animals."

The chief seemed to enjoy that and laughed. He passed the worms to her.

She had eaten them before. They weren't her favorite African food, but they were a good source of protein and she couldn't offend the chief. She grabbed a handful and chewed them, feeling the fried stringy bodies crunch between her teeth. She reached in her backpack and pulled out a Twinkie, opened the wrapper and handed it to the chief as a goodwill gesture.

He sniffed it, then licked it. Once he got a taste, he dove in, smiling and chewing. "Married to animals but know how to cook," he said. "You need a husband."

Wynne shook her head and for some reason MacKay's handsome face popped into her mind. She forced him out of her head and said, "Husbands have big heads. Animals only have big teeth."

Another round of laughter. The banter went on for twenty more minutes. When it died down, Wynne asked the chief, "Have you seen poachers on your hunting trips?"

"I see them on the edges of the valley. They take much game, and we have to go farther to hunt. Sometimes my people go hungry."

"Why don't you turn them in to the local rangers?"

"Others have done this and been killed. Poachers burn their villages and crops. We keep to ourselves here, in peace."

Wynne couldn't blame the chief for fearing poachers. They were infamous for terrorizing and burning villages; some even dealt in human contraband and kidnapped young girls to be sold into slavery. And until the government could hire enough rangers to assure that the villagers would be safe, they wouldn't come forward. It was a catch-22.

Wynne decided to take matters into her own hands and said, "I will pay for any information you might have. Please spread the word to other tribes. If they come to me with valid information, I will pay them."

He seemed torn for a moment, then shook his head. "I have nothing for you."

"But will you tell other chiefs?"

He nodded.

"Thank you." She knew he wasn't going to risk putting his tribe in danger and turned the conversation back to the scimitar. "I know of one of these bush meat poachers. A bad *bwana,* who claims to know where *mweo mfumu* live. How can he know, when Aja tells me you are the only Bemba tribe allowed to guard the *mweo mfumu?*"

"We had a warrior taken by *chibanda.*" The chief grimaced at the mention of the evil haunting spirit.

Hellstrom was probably *chibanda* in this case. "And did this *chibanda* have golden eyes like a lion?"

The chief nodded and looked amazed that she knew this. "He took the form of this golden-eyed *bwana.* He came bearing gifts of food and guns in exchange for the location of the *mweo mfumu.* I sent him away, seeing the *chibanda* hiding in this *bwana.* But one of our warriors was lured by the great wealth and agreed to be his guide. I try and stop him, but he escape. This warrior is dead to our village now. He will die from the *mweo mfumu juju.*"

"You sound so certain he will die."

"If he go to the *mweo mfumu* with evil in his heart, he die—if any man go to them with impure heart, they die."

"How do you know this?"

"Our ancestors watch over them for many centuries, and now we do. I know what they capable of doing." His eyes took on a grim, almost hypnotic glow, as if he were seeing horrible things.

"So these are the fangs of these gods?" Wynne motioned toward the teeth on the stone shrine.

The chief nodded.

"Do you have other evidence of them?" The teeth could be thousands of years old.

"You must see to believe. I would not show anyone else this, but since Aja bring you, I show you." The chief shot her a disapproving look, walked to a small pit covered by a bamboo top. It was painted with blue and yellow stripes. The chief said a prayer over the pit, then lifted out a lion skin. He held it up. "A *mweo mfumu* spirit die a week ago."

Wynne examined the pelt. It had the strong feral scent of lion and dried flesh. But the village could have recently killed a large lion. It proved nothing. "Thank you," Wynne said in Bemba. "Can you take us to the *mweo mfumu?*"

The chief shook his head and shared a knowing look with Aja. "We cannot take anyone."

"But this bad *bwana* will harm them." Wynne couldn't keep the frustration from her voice.

The chief's pupils dilated and he stared long and hard at her as if looking through her. He started to say something but Aja grabbed his arm and shook his head, his expression a warning.

"What?" Wynne's gaze shifted between the two men as she grew anxious. "Please tell me. I might need to know this."

The chief looked toward Aja.

Aja appeared torn, then he saw Wynne's anxiety and nodded his approval.

"You have bad *juju* following you," the chief said. "You should fear for your own life."

Thunder rolled overhead. Wynne felt the rumble in her chest, and it seemed as if the whole mountain was shaking. She didn't believe in voodoo. This chief had certainly put on a show for her. So why was she feeling those icy fingers crawling down her spine again?

Chapter 8

Two hours later, Wynne and Aja drove along a savanna that bordered the edge of Hidden Valley. Hints of sunlight peeked through dark scudding clouds. The savanna grasses had reached the end of their life cycle until the rains came, and patches of brown and red dotted the landscape. Only near the banks of the Mfungwa River was there enough moisture in the soil to keep it green. After the rains came, herds of elephant, wildebeest, zebra, impalas and puku would migrate here to feed on the thousands of acres of new grasses that emerged. Rains gave life. Drought took it away. Mother Nature choreographed the harsh balances in Africa.

Wynne's gaze swept the miles of open land, then along the river. All she saw were a few herons and a flock of buzzards who'd stopped to drink in the river. "Do you see any animals anywhere?"

"Not one." Aja frowned out the window at the river and huffed under his breath. "Strange. Should see one animal drinking. Hot season bring them to river. Only water nearby."

"Maybe the animals are frightened. This is on the edge of the valley, where the chief said the poachers had been."

"Still, need for water stronger than their fear. Should be few brave animals near river. No sign of any."

"You're right." Wynne grimaced and kept her eyes peeled for poachers or animals. Something wasn't right here.

She thought of her conversation with the chief. She still didn't have proof the scimitar existed, but she had learned about poachers being in the area. Still, she couldn't forget the chief's words or shake an uneasy feeling that had clung to her since they had left the village. She sensed that Aja felt it, too.

When she couldn't stand the silence any longer, she said, "Can I ask you something?"

He nodded.

"Back there at the village when the chief told me about the bad *juju*. Had you sensed it around me, too?"

"Yes." He glanced at her, his brow wrinkled with worry.

"When were you going to tell me about it?" Not that she gave credence to local erroneous beliefs or anything.

"Sometimes better not to know." Aja shot her a pointed look, a perceptive, almost frightening gleam in his dark eyes.

Wynne felt a prickling sensation go down her spine and she asked, "Is there anything else I should know?"

"Just be careful, Wynne Sperling." His words took on an ominous tone.

Snow sat up in the backseat at the mention of bad *juju*. She sniffed Wynne's shoulder as if to check and make sure she was okay.

Wynne reminded herself she didn't believe in magic, or voodoo, or bad luck following her. It was just local folklore.

Abruptly, she slammed on the brakes. Her breath caught in her throat as she stared at the sea of bones in front of them. Waves of heat streamed up from the baking ground, and for a moment Wynne thought she was seeing a mirage. Piles of skeletons stacked two and three feet high. She recognized elephant skulls, buffalo, zebra and kudu. Poachers had been here all right.

"Oh, my God!" She felt her heart breaking and gripped the steering wheel so hard her arms trembled. She had never seen Aja lose his composure, but he stared open mouthed at the killing ground, shocked, speechless.

She turned off the engine and got out. An eerie silence shrouded the area, the only sound the sigh of the dead grass.

Aja recovered from his shock, and emerged from the Rover. Snow followed him. He stopped, closed his eyes and raised his hands, then said a Bemba prayer over the bones. His voice had a mournful eerie quality that echoed in the silence as he appealed to the animal gods to bring the herds back.

She saw soda cans dropped carelessly near the remnants of a campfire. If they'd had a DNA lab, she could tag them for evidence. She scanned the ground for footprints, or tire tracks, but the ground was too dry and hard packed, like cement. With the rainy season coming in a few weeks, the whole area would be muddy, perfect for tracking. Something the poachers must have known.

Aja finished his prayer and bent near the campfire area and smelled it. "Poachers here two moons ago."

"Two months. We won't catch them now." Wynne grimaced at the dark droppings from buzzards splattered over the bones and on the ground. The vultures had picked the bones clean.

"Now we know why we see no animals." Aja waved a hand over the area. "This where they were."

"Yeah, right here." Wynne felt the loss of so many animals choking her. She swallowed hard and walked over to a meat rack, still standing. She touched the tiny strips of dried meat caught in between the leather thongs that held the sticks together. "I bet when Hellstrom visited the chief, his men were down here killing everything in sight." She lost her temper and kicked the meat rack.

It crashed to the ground with a heavy thud, and fell across a mound of bones.

"Don't let your anger rule you, Wynne Sperling," Aja said, his voice a warning.

Aja believed that was one of her major failings. She had to admit he was right. She'd had to struggle with controlling her anger since finding her first poacher.

The sound of a plane engine made Wynne glance up. A black and red biplane sailed overhead. It looked like a World War I relic. The plane passed them, then made a wide sweeping turn. Something about the plane didn't feel right. A knot of tension bit at her gut as she watched it dive lower and lower toward them.

"Take cover," Wynne yelled, just as shots rang out.

She darted out in front and zigzagged toward the Rover, hoping to lure the shooter away from Snow and Aja.

Bullets thumped all around her. She hit the ground and glimpsed two Africans in the cockpit as the plane zoomed past her. The passenger held an Uzi submachine gun, and he shook it at her and yelled something she couldn't understand.

The plane had to climb again.

Wynne saw that Aja and Snow had run toward the trees

that grew along the river. He had pulled off his slingshot already, whirling a rock.

Wynne took cover behind the Rover to confuse the shooter. He couldn't shoot at both of them if they split up.

The plane dived again, heading between the river and the Rover. Bullets whizzed around Wynne as she double loaded and got off two shots. Four. But she'd missed. The shooter had ducked, spraying bullets without aiming.

She dove beneath the Rover's front bumper to take cover. Bullets thudded into the Rover and around the ground where they'd been standing as the plane passed.

She rolled out and looked for Aja. He stepped out behind a tree and gave her the thumbs-up sign that he and Snow were okay. Relief washed over her.

He called out, "Wait until you see their faces. Focus on their eyes. I'll take pilot."

"I'll aim for the passenger." Wynne nodded, keeping her gaze on the plane as it swooped toward them again.

She took a deep calming breath, reloaded and concentrated, letting the slingshot become an extension of her arm. It was all about timing. When to snap her wrist. *Don't be afraid of the bullets. Find your target. Stare into his face.*

At that moment, Aja left the cover of the trees, a clean target. He was distracting them, whirling his own slingshot. She cleared her mind of her fear for Aja, of everything except the shooter's face. He pointed the gun at Aja and fired. Wynne had a clean shot of the side of his head and took it.

The shooter dropped the gun and slouched forward. At that moment, Aja hit the pilot. The African grabbed his head and barely managed to clear the tops of the trees and keep the plane steady.

Wynne knew Aja had spared the man's life. If he had wanted to he could have killed him instantly. When Aja had taught her how to use the slingshot, she had seen him pluck the wing feathers from a flying crane at one hundred yards without harming the bird. He had retrieved the feathers and told her that when she could do that, she would be proficient with the sling. Yeah, right. She could only dream of being that good.

She waited to see if the pilot would make another sweep, but the plane climbed higher and disappeared over the scarp hills.

Wynne realized she was shaking from the adrenaline rush.

Aja walked over to her, Snow following him. "*Nkalamo yalubuka* declare war."

"Yes, war." That's what it had become between them and Hellstrom.

That night before going back to camp, Wynne and Aja had stopped by most of the nearby villages and spread the word about the bush meat poachers being in the area. She wasn't sure if any of them would be brave enough to come forward, but she hoped that offering reward money might give them an incentive. She couldn't bear the thought of coming upon another poaching death camp like she'd found today. And it was one way to fight back against Hellstrom.

Aja had stayed in Chiawa village for the night, where he was good friends with the chief. Now she drove along the road to base camp with only Snow in the Rover. Antelope darted in the headlights and she swerved to avoid them. That's when she noticed headlights in her rearview mirror. They gleamed like two wolf eyes following her. She couldn't make out the driver behind the bright headlights. A memory flashed of the plane attack, and she veered right.

The vehicle followed, but didn't ride her bumper. It kept four car lengths between them.

She reached base camp and skidded to a halt near her hut. The vehicle followed her and pulled up beside her. In seconds she had her slingshot palmed and loaded. She hopped out, whirling it, as MacKay got out of a Land Cruiser.

Wynne frowned and stilled her weapon. She didn't want another repeat in her hut like last night. He'd made her feel defenseless, and she couldn't let her guard down around him. Not after today.

MacKay walked toward her and Snow. "How are you, darlin'?"

"Not in the mood." She strode past him and refastened her slingshot around her waist as he bent to pet Snow.

"Ah, now, that hurts."

Wynne heard MacKay pause behind her. She expected him to follow her and she turned to see what he was up to. He had his nose up, sniffing the air like an animal scenting a predator.

"You smell that?" he said. "Smells like fire."

She caught the faint scent of smoke. She tried to peer past the thick cover of trees on the other side of the landing field, but darkness veiled everything.

"Smell's getting stronger." MacKay followed her gaze. "Must be a couple of miles away."

Wynne hurried to the Rover's cargo hold and fished through a toolbox and grabbed the night-vision binoculars her father had given her as a gift last Christmas. The card had read: "Daddy Santa's contribution for catching poachers. Get the sombitches." Needless to say, unlike her mother, her father encouraged her work here in Africa. He had even put contribution boxes in the zoo's gift shops and sent the donations to the Big Five Habitat, along with his own sizeable checks.

Wynne scrambled up on the Rover's hood, then hopped on the roof. She scanned the area above the tree tops and spotted the huge plume of smoke billowing skyward. In the binoculars' green vision field it looked like a dragon opening its wings.

"Can you see it?" MacKay asked.

"In the east. About three kilometers away. My God, it's near Zambezi village."

"What can I do?" He actually sounded as if he were worried.

"Go wake Eieb and the men and tell them to turn on the siren," Wynne said.

MacKay hurried to the barracks, yelling, "Fire, fire." His deep voice boomed through camp. Why was he being so helpful?

Kaweki appeared as if he'd been waiting for her arrival. He came toward her, his brows furrowed. "You owe an explanation about where you've been today, Sperling."

"Yes, sir," she said, glad she wasn't getting the third degree now. She wanted to inform him about the airplane attack, but she couldn't tell him about her trip to the Bemba tribe.

"Where is the fire?"

"The village."

"You and Eieb pick up Dr. Mukuka. Mr. MacKay and I will bring the men." Kaweki hurried back toward headquarters.

Snow brushed up against Wynne's leg, spooked by the fire's scent. "It's all right, girl. I know you're afraid." Wynne led Snow to her hut and left her there where she'd feel safe.

Abruptly, the base camp siren screamed through the silence. It was a World War II air raid siren, loud enough that she felt it in her chest. It took thirty seconds to reach a high-pitched crescendo, and then it dropped to a low roar. It had a way of gripping people with fear, and Wynne was no exception. A bush fire could sweep through a village in minutes and destroy everything in its path.

Wynne and Eieb had picked up Dr. Mukuka, and he sat in the backseat, puffing nervously on a cigarette and blowing the smoke out the window. "These bush fires can spread so quickly," he said, breaking the taut silence in the Rover.

Wynne sped around a curve in the road and said, "I just hope we're not too late to save the village." Through a thick stand of banana trees growing along the roadside, she spotted plumes of flames licking the air. She knew they were too late.

"Dear God," Eieb said under his breath as he saw the flames.

The Rover rounded a curve, past the trees. Chaos met them. Smoke clouded the night sky. Flames leaped from one hut's grass-thatched roof to another. Families were running and screaming and crying, carrying what little possessions they owned and trying to control cattle and livestock.

Wynne pulled in behind MacKay and Kaweki. They had parked several hundred feet away, on the opposite side of the road, a natural firebreak. MacKay, Kaweki, Dr. Leonard and the rangers were grabbing children that were too scared to run and the elderly and carrying them into a field of maize growing behind the village. MacKay had two little toddlers draped over each shoulder.

Dr. Mukuka leaped out, his cigarette in his mouth, grabbing his black bag. Wynne and Eieb raced behind him toward the village.

Flames from the huts shot forty feet into the air, heat swelling in massive waves. Wynne felt the heat stinging her face and arms as she ran.

A little girl fell near Wynne's feet. Wynne grabbed the crying child and carried her to her mother, who had stopped for the little girl, but couldn't reach her because of the frantic villagers.

"Is everyone out of their huts?" Wynne yelled over the roar of the fire, setting the little girl in her mother's arms.

"I think so," the woman called over her shoulder as she took off running with her daughter.

Wynne made a sweep of the burning huts. An elderly man staggered from one, beating at the fire on his clothes. Wynne rushed toward him.

Heat from the flames took her breath away and she covered her face with her forearm, driving forward toward the man. She grabbed his right hand and threw him away from the inferno.

He lurched three…four…steps then stumbled to the ground. Wynne rolled him over and over, throwing dirt on his clothes, feeling her hands burning. When he was doused, Wynne dragged him a safe distance away from the fire.

Dr. Mukuka bent beside the man, took off his lab coat, and gently placed it over the burned villager. "This will keep you warm. You'll be okay," he said, picking up the man's wrist and checking his pulse.

The burned man caught Wynne's wrist in his hand. His voice was a raspy whisper, and she had to bend down to hear it over the roar of the fire. "My wife…in hut…my wife," his pleading words ended on a cough.

"I'll find her." Wynne made another dash toward the hut. The man's wife was in there. She had to help her.

"Wynne, stop!" Dr. Mukuka yelled at her back.

But before she could reach the burning hut, someone grabbed Wynne from behind and dragged her away from the towering flames.

"Let me go!" Wynne fought the person, but the arms were too strong, the chokehold on her waist and forearms too tight. "Let me go!" she yelled in frustration.

"You're not going in there, darlin'."

Not him again. "You don't understand," Wynne screamed. "There's a woman in that hut."

"You can't go in there. Take a look at it."

He paused when they had reached the maize field. Wynne saw the flames now, consuming the hut. Her eyes burned from the smoke and she felt ragged breaths of frustration against his steely arms clamped across her ribs and stomach. Most men couldn't have held her up like he was doing and she was almost impressed by his strength.

"You can put me down now," she said.

"If I have your word you'll stop trying to burn yourself a new hide."

"You have my word that I won't break your kneecaps."

"That's the ranger Wynne I know." He plopped her on the ground in front of him.

"You don't know me at all."

He hadn't dropped his arms. Wynne turned to break his grip, but he caught her and jerked her against his powerful chest. It felt like she'd come up against a brick wall. He gazed down in her eyes and said, "Don't worry, darlin', I'll keep trying." He winked, then dropped his grip on her.

Wynne stepped back as if she'd been bitten. "Just stay out of my way."

He saluted her, then helped an elderly woman shoo her chickens from a burning coop. Why was he acting like a stand-up guy? He was in the poaching business, a man who profited off of killing. He shouldn't care about the villagers.

Wynne scanned the village for survivors. No one. Nothing but flames shooting sixty feet into the air.

She heard an engine and glanced up. The LZCG helicopter materialized in the night sky. It flew straight for the village. A Bambi bucket, bulging with water, hung from its belly. When it came closer, she saw who was at the controls. Hellstrom. How did he get here so fast? Someone in base camp must have called him.

The rotors pounded the air, whirling dirt and flames below it. It dived. A wall of water fell with a thud over the village. She watched the helicopter zoom above the trees toward the Zambezi river to reload. The last report Wynne had heard about the LZCG helicopter, Hellstrom had grounded it, supposedly waiting for an engine part. The LZCG used it to scout out poacher trails from the air and to fight bush fires. But here was Hellstrom piloting it. Good Samaritan that he was.

The helicopter came in for another pass. Half of the flames had been extinguished. The rotor whacked the air, licking the flames upward. Wynne felt the rotors' thunderous beat inside her chest, throat, stealing her breath. The same sensation she'd felt next to MacKay a moment ago.

The Bambi bucket swung so low the flames reflected in its black underbelly as it dropped a deluge of water. Water met fire and sizzled. The villagers cheered the helicopter on.

Wynne scowled at the craft as it sailed over the treetops. She headed toward the row of rangers and village men who were throwing dirt on the edges of the fire with anything they could find. Fighting the fire with water was out of the question. Tributaries off the Zambezi turned to baked mud in the dry season and the village's only water source was a shrinking stream half a mile away, Hellstrom's water source at the moment.

Several rangers had commandeered the villagers' three shovels. Poor families couldn't afford shovels and buy food, too. Farming implements were communal property. The villagers themselves had resorted to using buckets, baskets, even their hands to scoop up the red dirt.

Wynne took off her combat boots and commenced scooping.

"Make room." It surprised her to see MacKay jump into the fray. He jerked off his right boot and filled it with dirt.

Were those gold toe kicks on the end of his Tony Lamas? How expensive were those boots? She looked at her own thirty-dollar pair of boots, then back at him. His dimples seemed to stretch from cheekbone to jaw.

She quickly glanced away. Her burned hands stung as she worked, but she was glad for the sensation. It kept her thoughts off the burned village. But then she glanced at the hut that belonged to the injured man. The thatch and mud-wattled walls fluttered into the sky, what was left of the man's life disintegrating into waves of ashes. She swallowed hard and glared up at Hellstrom as he made another sweep over the village.

How convenient his timing was, indeed.

Wynne gripped one edge of the stretcher, and MacKay had the other end as they strode toward the clinic door. MacKay had volunteered to help Dr. Mukuka and Wynne transport the severely burned man Wynne had saved, and she was once again stuck with the irritating Texan.

Dr. Mukuka held the door for them and MacKay glanced anxiously toward the clinic. MacKay hadn't been his normal obnoxiously charming self, probably because he hadn't spoken in the past fifteen minutes.

"Are you okay?" Wynne asked.

"You betcha, darlin'." His voice didn't have his usual confident twang. In fact, he sounded like he was sitting in a dentist's chair.

The burned man moaned as they stepped inside the clinic. Wynne saw only one nurse on duty, and she was helping a patient through a coughing fit.

"Put him in the empty bed on the end." Dr. Mukuka motioned to a cot that had been erected in the corner.

They set the stretcher down and Wynne bent to help Dr. Mukuka transfer the patient to the cot.

"Providence shined down on us tonight," Dr. Mukuka said. "This poor man was our only burned victim."

"I guess we were lucky." Wynne didn't think this man would feel that way.

MacKay began backing away from the bed as if he'd seen a ghost. He stared at the patients in the clinic, wearing a deer-in-the-headlights expression. "I need some air." He almost ran to the door.

She wondered what had happened to him.

"Nurse Muleya. We need your help," Dr. Mukuka's commanding voice cut across the clinic.

The nurse moved the spittle cup away from the patient, set it aside and ran toward them. She bent and helped them lift the burned man. He groaned as they gently laid him on the cot.

Wynne looked down at the man, his face contorted in pain. His eyes were so glazed with agony, so despondent, Wynne wished his wife could have been spared. "Will he be all right?" Wynne asked Dr. Mukuka.

"With a lot of tender loving care."

Wynne touched the man's hand—the only place he wasn't burned. "Feel better soon," she said, the words sounding empty even to her own ears. They left her feeling depleted as she headed outside.

She found MacKay sitting on a seat, carved from the trunk of a sausage tree, a present to Dr. Mukuka from a patient. Smoke and ashes had smudged MacKay's jeans and turned his white shirt charcoal-gray. His hair had turned dirty brown from smoke. His knees were akimbo, elbows propped on his thighs, head bent. And she heard him hyperventilating.

"Are you okay?" she asked.

"Can you rub my back? It helps."

Two options were before her. Rub his back. Or leave and let him pass out. He had helped in the village, and she found herself reaching for his back.

When she touched him, she grew painfully aware of her burned palms. His back was broad, the sinewy muscles like granite beneath her hands. She felt the heat of his body seeping through his cotton shirt.

"That's better," he said in between gasps.

"So what's going on with you? Are you afraid of the coats, the blood or just the clinic?"

"Coats?"

"You know, white coats."

"It's not the doctor. It's the smell. When I went in there…" He shook his head, the self-assurance in his voice nose diving. "It reminded me of the infirmary at the orphanage." His voice trailed off into short gasps.

"You had a bad experience there?"

"Almost died from an appendix attack once—well, thought I was dead. Wish I had been a few times. All I can remember about that god-awful experience is the smell of disinfectant and alcohol and Sister Nadia's garlicky breath." His breathing slowed, not sounding so much like a ceiling fan in need of oil. "It smelled like that clinic."

"Was she your nurse?"

"My tormentor, more like." He turned and looked up at her, as if she were Sister Nadia.

He held her gaze, and for a moment he looked boyish and vulnerable. Wynne felt a stab of sympathy for him. "Does this happen to you every time you go into hospitals?" she asked, her voice softening.

"Pretty much." He kept looking up at her with those lost puppy eyes.

Wynne focused on his lips, the way the moonlight hit them. Although he appeared vulnerable, his lips still had a sensual fullness. A memory flooded back to her, his finger brushing her mouth as he had wiped the Twinkie cream from her lips, the fantasy she'd had in the hut, his teeth pulling down her panties…

Wynne tried to clear her head. To think rationally. But her lips were actually starving to taste his mouth. She remembered how he had pulled her close in the village, the feeling of his body next to hers. They had fit perfectly. And if she cared to admit it, it had felt good to be held in his arms. Too good.

Thankfully, he turned around and her common sense took over.

She had to think of something to say, to get her mind off his nearness. "Then why did you volunteer to bring back the patient?" she asked, trying to sound nonchalant and not look at the short blond hair brushing his collar that called out to be stroked. She cleared her throat and said, "We could have gotten someone else to help."

"Thought I could handle it. Can you press a little harder, darlin', right there between the shoulder blades."

Was he beginning to enjoy this? "I think the boogie memories are all gone now." Wynne stepped away from him. "I need to get back to the village." She stepped around him to leave.

He stood up and blocked her way, looking well enough now to run a marathon. "I should thank you for taking care of me." He grabbed her hand then bent and kissed her palm.

Wynne felt the softness of his warm lips and roughness of his five-o'clock shadow. The sensation somehow soothed her burned palm, and she wondered what his lips would feel like all over her body. She felt flushed. He made her feel unsteady inside. It frightened her and thrilled her at the same time.

His lips moved up her wrist, warm and moist, and trailed a line up her arm. She felt his five o'clock shadow brushing the tender skin on her wrist, and the sensation sent a shiver through her.

Pull away. Think. Fight it. But she could feel him pushing up the sleeve of her shirt, his lips moving along the inside of her arm. And that friction of his coarse whiskers, abrasive, yet tormenting her senses. She envisioned his mouth on her breasts, her belly, moving up her thighs. Surely just one taste of his lips wouldn't hurt.

Wynne grabbed his hair and pulled his head up to her mouth for a kiss. She clamped her arms around his neck, forced his body against hers and devoured his mouth.

Chapter 9

Months of loneliness poured out of Wynne as she felt a kind of strange white-hot release in his arms.

He groaned as his tongue dipped in her mouth, urging and hungry, while his hands slid down her sides and pulled her hips against his.

"Darlin', I want you," he whispered against her mouth, then he moved one hand up to cup her breast.

Wynne grabbed his powerful shoulders and arched against him. Her body didn't feel like it belonged to her any longer. It was all his, hot and needy, ready to be molded by his touch.

At the sound of a voice clearing, Wynne and MacKay broke apart.

Wynne, breathless and weak-kneed from unspent desire, glanced over at Dr. Mukuka. A huge grin covered his face.

He puffed on a cigarette, then said, "I thought Mr. MacKay might need help, but I see he has all he needs—"

"It—it's not what you think," Wynne said, her voice still ragged with lust.

"It damn well is." MacKay tried to grab her again, but she jumped back and took up a *tantui* defensive stance.

"It isn't." Wynne stared at him, defiant.

Dr. Mukuka said, "Carry on, children." After a loud chuckle, he strode back inside the clinic.

Great. That went well. Could she ever look Dr. Mukuka in the face again? Wynne headed for the Rover, ran really. She could feel her body still purring from MacKay's kisses. "If you want a ride back, better get it in gear," she said over her shoulder.

"Oh, I want a ride, all right," he said, disappointed. "And you do, too, but you're afraid to relax long enough to enjoy it."

"This is Africa. You relax and you get killed."

He snorted derisively behind her. "Africa's an excuse for you, darlin'."

"Don't bet on it." She got into the Rover and slammed the door.

He hopped in on the passenger side and said, "Oh, I know it."

"Oh, really, how is that?"

"I know women."

"I'm sure you do. How many Saturday nights did you have to spend in a honky-tonk to glean this knowledge?" She started the engine.

"I lost count a long time ago." He let out a long, self-satisfied breath.

"That's too bad."

"No, it just makes me an expert." He grinned, a soft curl of his lips. His face glowed green from the dashboard lights. He looked like a handsome satyr in Day-Glo makeup.

She didn't like his expression. He'd never know her, carnally or otherwise.

At her silence, he said, "You should let the doctor bandage those hands."

"No time for that," she said, scowling and shifting the truck into reverse.

She popped the clutch and their heads hit the seat. The *Simpsons* clacked in unison.

"The fire is out, darlin'. Why you driving like a bat outta hell?"

The fire wasn't out. It was just beginning.

Ten minutes later, Wynne reached the village and hopped out of the truck before MacKay could, glad to escape the stifling suffocated feeling inside the Rover. MacKay hadn't spoken to her after she'd almost given him whiplash. He'd just cracked his knuckles and shot her long curious glances, sometimes grinning. The more he grinned and cracked, the more determined she had been not to initiate another conversation with him.

She sorely regretted letting her guard down with him at the clinic. She tried not to recall the feel of his lips singeing hers, the way his body had pressed hard against hers. She felt flushed and tingly again in all the wrong places and she forced the memory away.

She strode past the village men and women making temporary livestock paddocks with sticks and goat-hide thongs. The older children had huddled together in a group, corralling their families' cows, chickens and goats. Dr. Leonard was helping them. Wynne noticed Eieb and the other rangers were putting out the last of the smoldering embers. Hellstrom had landed the helicopter in a field, and he stood beside Kaweki, lethally debonair as ever in a white shirt and khakis. He wore a tan fedora pushed slightly back on his forehead and he looked like he'd just stepped off the set of an *Indiana Jones* movie.

She paused and watched MacKay join their little group. She noticed Hellstrom try to hide his annoyance that MacKay had been with her behind a tactful nod. Then he shot Wynne a speculative glance.

She gave nothing away in her expression.

Kaweki turned and addressed the villagers. "I believe we all owe Mr. Hellstrom a debt of gratitude for containing the fire and saving your crops."

The villagers applauded. Even Dr. Leonard smiled and clapped, taken in by Hellstrom.

Kaweki slapped Hellstrom on the back. "I don't know what we would have done without your prompt help, Mr. Hellstrom. There are no words to thank you."

"It was my pleasure. The least I could do."

Memories flashed in Wynne's mind, Kidaya comforted by Eieb, the burned man losing his wife, finding the bush meat graveyard, the guys in the plane trying to kill her and Aja. Wynne fisted her hands and dug her nails into the burns on her palms, marshaling her self-control. She wanted to expose Hellstrom for the murderer he was, but she couldn't. Not yet.

She walked over to stand beside Eieb. Smoke and soot covered him. His eyes were bloodshot and he looked tired. He leaned close and whispered, "What's down with Kaweki? He's fawning all over Hellstrom."

"I know."

"I have been thinking about this fire." Eieb rubbed the soot from his eyelashes. "I'm willing to bet it is the work of poachers. They must have somehow learned that one of the villagers tipped Aja about the poachers and helped set up the sting for us."

"Yes, but no one knew that but us." Wynne paused, and she felt the blood drain from her face. "Oh, my God!"

"What's wrong?"

"At Hellstrom's party, I told Kaweki about the tip from the village. He's the only one who knew." She paused and made a face. "He seemed nervous at the party when he quizzed me about the sting. I didn't think anything of it at the time."

"But it all makes sense now. Kaweki told Hellstrom and he ordered his men to set the fire in retaliation?"

Wynne hated to think the man she had trusted for two years, who she'd given her loyalty to, had betrayed all of them. But she remembered the brush-off he'd given her last night when she'd asked for help in stopping Hellstrom, and now here he was acting like Hellstrom's puppet. It wasn't like Kaweki to pay court to anyone.

"I'll be back." Wynne walked over to where Kaweki and Hellstrom stood. She faced the villagers and spoke. "Can anyone tell us what happened? How the fire started?"

Frightened faces stared back at her.

"Anyone? Please? Was it poachers?"

Not a word, only the crying of tired young infants and toddlers.

One of the men who was tying sticks together, spoke up, "We saw nothing. Nothing. It just started."

Wynne saw terror in his face, heard the intimidated undertone in his voice. She had seen the same expression earlier on Chief Chiti-Mukulu's face.

Kaweki grabbed her arm and whispered, "They just lost their homes. Stop browbeating them."

"But its obvious poachers did this." Wynne pulled away from his grasp and saw the anxiety in Kaweki's eyes, the nervous twitch in his cheek, and she recognized the weakness in him. He wasn't the same man she'd known. He had fooled everyone as Hellstrom had.

Hellstrom said, "Poachers so close? The chaps must have a death wish. Surely you don't think it was poachers?" He blinked innocently at Wynne.

"Of course it was. Why else would they be so afraid?" Wynne swept a hand toward the people.

"Perhaps the chaps are worried about their lodgings." Hellstrom raised his voice. "I'd like to extend an invitation to all the displaced to stay temporarily at my compound. I'll send transport for them."

A titter of admiration went through the villagers. They didn't know they were appreciative of the devil's kindness. It was all Wynne could do to swallow her indignation and watch Hellstrom play Man of the Year.

"Now that's true generosity." Kaweki motioned for the villagers to clap again.

She waited until Hellstrom's glee club had quieted, then she addressed the villagers again. "I know all of you are afraid. If anyone wants to talk to me, I'll be in camp. I promise you'll be safe."

"If this is the work of poachers, we will all catch the criminals responsible." Hellstrom grinned his four hundred-watt public smile.

She knew what really lay beneath the grin—murder, intimidation, narcissistic ruthless mentality. "Of course, that's what I meant," Wynne said, keeping the contempt from her voice.

"ZWA and the LZCG make a great team, don't you think?"

"Yes." She ground out the word and noticed that MacKay's usual grin had slipped. She smiled politely at Hellstrom. "If you'll excuse me."

He blocked her way and looked her squarely in the eyes. "How was your day, Wynne?"

Wynne saw the triumphant sparkle in his golden eyes, the victorious grin, and the subtext beneath the words was evident—How did she like his little air expressed gift? "Just great," she said, nonchalantly. "But probably not better than yours."

Hellstrom chuckled. Wynne noticed that MacKay was watching them and he was cracking his knuckles.

Kaweki grabbed Wynne's arm and said, "Follow me. I need to talk to you and Eieb."

He motioned for Eieb to follow them. She and Eieb trailed Kaweki into the field, away from everyone. She felt Hellstrom's and MacKay's eyes following her.

Kaweki paused, the nervous tic in his cheek becoming more pronounced. "I interrogated one of your prisoners and found out there is a poaching camp along the Zambezi. And I'm going there tomorrow to arrest them. I want you both with me." And he added as an afterthought, "You're the best rangers I have."

"Yes, sir," Wynne said, sharing a quick look with Eieb.

Kaweki turned to Eieb. "And don't think I didn't know you covered for her today." He shook a finger at Wynne. "Where were you today?"

"Looking for poachers and spreading the word to the nearby villages."

"From now on, you don't make a move without me knowing. You know how dangerous it is in the bush, especially with these poachers so close. No one goes out alone. Got that?"

"Copy that, sir." Wynne shared another knowing look with Eieb.

"And I'm working on a background check on the

MacKay fellow and the other board members of the LZCG. I don't know who is involved with Hellstrom and who isn't."

"A good idea." Wynne kept the disgust out of her voice.

"You just make sure you both are at headquarters at 0800."

"Yes, sir." She saw Kaweki's twitch had moved to a corner of his mouth.

"Now, it's been a long day for you two. Go back to camp. Get some rest. I'll clean up here. Give some of the men a ride back."

"Yes, sir."

Wynne watched Kaweki rejoin Hellstrom and MacKay. Kaweki managed to keep his stiff-backed, proud walk, but she felt the last of her respect for him drain away.

Twenty minutes later, Wynne, Eieb and three rangers, Chileya, Zhieka and Duwisib, rode back to camp, the *Simpson* dolls clacking along with the road noise. The rest of the crew and Dr. Leonard were either catching a ride with Kaweki, or helping Hellstrom's men move the villagers to his compound. Wynne didn't fear for the locals, since she knew this was just P.R. for Hellstrom. He would never harm them on his own property. He had already intimidated them into silence by orchestrating the burning of the village. Now he would take credit for being their savior and everyone would continue to worship at his feet.

"I'm tired." Chileya, sardined in the backseat between Duwisib and Zhieka, broke the silence. He spoke English, blended with a hint of Lozi accent. He was one of the smallest rangers, but the most vocal. He had a pixie-like face and bucked teeth and reminded Wynne of a mongoose. "I hate fires. It could have been avoided if they'd put out their cook fire. That's probably what caused it. Carelessness."

"The villagers know to be careful during the dry season," Eieb said.

"They can make mistakes," Chileya fired back.

"We know who caused the fire." Eieb's gaze met Wynne's for a second.

"You were wrong about poachers. The only poachers I've seen are the ones you arrested," Chileya chattered on.

Duwisib, the wise guy in the group, said, "That's because you never leave the mess hall."

"That's a lie. I work like everyone else."

"Sure you do," Duwisib teased.

"I do. And I would never have taken this job if I had known firefighting was part of our job description—"

"Then why didn't you stay at camp, no one asked you to come," this from Zhieka, the opposite of Chileya. He was beefy, barrel-chested and always wore a scowl.

Duwisib managed a dig. "Poor Chileya, afraid of everything, but not *n'shima.*"

Chileya was famous in the mess for hording food in his clothes, which made him an easy target for Duwisib's ribbing.

As Wynne pulled up into camp, five side-striped jackals darted across the headlights and disappeared into the bush as Wynne parked near headquarters.

Chileya spoke up, "Did you see those beasts? I bet they are after someone's boots."

"Only yours," Duwisib said, getting out of the Rover.

Chileya sneered at Duwisib's back, his little rodent teeth showing. Last week Chileya had left a pair of leather boots outside the barracks and jackals had stolen them.

"I'm for bed," Zhieka said, piling out of the Rover's back seat.

Wynne and Eieb hung back from the other three as they walked toward the barracks. Eieb stared at their backs and said, "I wonder if they can be trusted."

"I don't know." It had taken her almost a year of battling their culturally biased chauvinism before she gained their respect and acceptance, and she had considered them friends. Now they seemed like strangers to her.

"I never thought Kaweki would turn."

"I didn't either." Wynne thought of Colette, Kaweki's wife. She would be another casualty in all of this. She loved Kaweki with all her heart.

"Did you see the way he looked directly into our eyes and tried to set us up?" A fierce expression contorted Eieb's normally composed face. "It was all I could do not to strangle him."

"Kaweki will find out in the morning when we don't show up for duty that his scheme to set us up didn't work." Was MacKay part of the plan? She had managed to avoid him before she left. She hoped he'd finally realized his little seduction plan wasn't going to work on her.

"I'd like to see Kaweki's face when he finds out."

"We can use Kaweki to get to Hellstrom," she said. "If he's been dealing with Hellstrom face-to-face, he can testify against him."

"And we will make sure he does." Eieb's expression turned darker. "How far do you think the corruption goes with this bush meat ring?"

"I don't know. Hellstrom is chummy with the minister of ZWA. He could have connections all the way to the cabinet as far as we know. We can't trust anyone." It hit Wynne that they were basically standing alone in a massive hive of killer bees.

"But you know of someone?"

"I can write the American embassy in case…" Wynne paused, unable to voice what she was thinking.

"We don't come out of the bush," Eieb finished for her.

"We will." She tried to sound upbeat while hiding her growing uncertainty. "Now get some rest. I'll see you before dawn," she said.

"Don't sleep too soundly."

"I won't."

Eieb looked concerned for her, but turned to head for the barracks. Wynne knew Eieb wouldn't rest easy, worrying about her safety. The day's heat and humidity lingered in the midnight air along with traces of the village fire as Wynne made her way to her hut. Insects chattered their nightly croon, humming until she stepped too close to them.

As she passed the LZCG's door, she remembered seeing Solomon, the ranger on LZCG duty tonight, helping move the villagers. No one was manning the office.

She slipped inside. A solar light cast a sallow glow into the office. Posters of wanted poachers hung on the walls. Wynne glanced at them. One was missing. Hellstrom, himself.

A red light beamed from the antique radio receiver that sat on a small desk to her left. A computer sat next to it. Hellstrom's office here was nothing more than a space in a corner, partitioned by two bamboo screens. This office was quite different than his home office. His small pine desk looked like a yard sale find. Wynne flipped through the papers on his desk and found several advertisements for his safari business and those of the LZCG board members.

She opened the drawers. There were no locks to contend with. In the last drawer she found several interesting things, a map of all the Zambian Wildlife Authority parks glued to a foam backing and a ranger duty roster. Colored-coated pins were stuck in different sites on the map, as if he had a grid of where every ranger was at every minute of the day. To anyone who didn't know what Hellstrom was up to, it looked as if he was just keeping up with his job. The commander of the LZCG station had to know where the rangers were in case poachers were found. But she knew exactly what it was, a poaching chart so his men could move easily through the parks.

She opened another drawer and found the check register for the LZCG and flipped through it. Hellstrom had written a two hundred pound check to the Zambian Wildlife Authority every month going back three months, since he began as chairman. But Wynne had never heard of them receiving the money. Was Kaweki pocketing it?

Muffled voices drifted through the window. Wynne jumped and pressed her back against the wall. The voices came closer:

"I need money now." It was a woman's voice.

"It'll be mailed to you, woman."

Was that Zhieka speaking?

"If you know the big chief, you'd better tell him I don't like the payments being late. Got to live on something."

"You'll get your money, but I wouldn't make waves."

"Without my eyes, he'll know nothing that goes on."

"I said, you'll get your money."

"I'd better or no eyes."

Footsteps. Closer. They strode past the window.

Wynne shoved the checkbook back into the drawer, then crept to the door and cracked it enough to see the silhouette of a man and woman. Nurse Muleya? Even in the darkness, there was no mistaking her white uniform...or Zhieka's barrel-chested, tall, muscular build.

Nurse Muleya must have told Zhieka about Mehan being brought into the clinic, and Hellstrom must have figured out since Wynne hadn't arrested his men right away that she had learned about the rendezvous at Sausage Tree Camp. He was always one step ahead of her.

Wynne waited until their voices died away, then slipped out of the office. She reached her hut and saw the solar battery-powered light casting a dim glow through the windows. Everything was as she had left it before the fire, except...

She froze and her blood ran cold. It was the red dress she'd worn at Hellstrom's, the one he'd admonished her for taking off. It was hanging on the door to taunt her, Hellstrom's way of taking credit for the fire in the village. It was also a warning that he could manipulate her any way he wanted. He was the predator and she was nothing more than his quarry.

A moment of panic gripped her. Would Snow be waiting for her inside? Would one of Hellstrom's men? Wynne slid the dagger from her ankle and quietly picked up the hanger and dress and slid it onto the ground. Then she kicked open the door.

Chapter 10

At the sound of the crash, Snow leaped up where she was sleeping near Wynne's floor mat. The leopard stared at her with alert eyes.

Wynne glanced around, saw the hut was empty, then said, "Don't worry, girl, it's only me." Wynne crouched down and gave Snow the hand signal to come.

The leopard sprang up on Wynne's shoulders and licked a greeting across Wynne's cheek.

"I missed you, too," Wynne said, realizing she needed Snow more than Snow needed her. She was the one thing in Wynne's life at the moment that was unwavering and secure.

They greeted each other with licks and rubs and growls of welcome. Snow leaped down from her shoulders and scented the air pouring in through the open door. The night called her, and she prowled through the doorway before Wynne could close it.

Wynne went to the door and called after the cat, "All right, have your fun, but don't go far and come home. Do you hear me? Come back." She sounded like a nagging mother talking to her teenage daughter. What was happening to her? She was turning into her mother.

She picked up the dress and watched Snow's figure, grayed by the night, slip off into the bush. She started to call her back, but paused. Eieb, Dr. Leonard and Mama Luwo had been right. Snow deserved a normal life in the bush, a Mr. Claws to sweep her off her kitty feet, and make her forget about her domesticated life. She should never have grown so attached to Snow in the first place, but how can you control who or what you love? She pulled back the mosquito netting and closed the door, locking it.

She looked at the dress, the red chiffon glowing like blood in the dim light. Her first instinct was to burn it, and leave it ablaze in front of Hellstrom's house. But since he'd gone to so much trouble to taunt her with it; it obviously was a bone of contention for him. It had been the first instance where she had openly defied him by not wearing it. And it must have stuck in his craw. She might be able to use it against him somehow, and she needed all the ammo she could find.

She thrust the dress inside her backpack, then went to an aluminum trunk where she stored camping gear. Beneath a box of medicines and herbs, she found a stash of firecrackers. She dropped them in the backpack's outside pouch, then found a leather satchel that she had sewn herself. Gingerly, she packed it on top, within easy reach.

She sat at her desk, pulled out several sheets of writing paper, and composed a letter to the American embassy and addressed it, sticking her passport and work visa in the envelope.

She reached for a second sheet and paused, her pen over the paper. Why was writing this second letter so hard? Her mother wasn't the best nurturer in all the kingdom of motherhood, and she might be calculating and vindictive when it came to getting her way, but she was the strongest woman Wynne knew. When it came to legal matters and getting strings pulled, her mother hobnobbed with the most powerful U.S. senators and had even been invited to White House gatherings. If anyone could see Hellstrom prosecuted, Maria Van Warren-Sperling could. Unleashed, she was a legal tornado.

Writing to her mother was the hardest thing Wynne had ever done in her life. It was like admitting her mother had been right, that Wynne had failed and needed her support. But it was either eat crow or let Hellstrom get off scot-free, so she forced the words down on the paper.

Hi Mom,
If you're reading this that probably means I'm no longer alive, but I still need your help. I hate to ask this of you, but I pray you will do one thing for me.

Wynne explained about Hellstrom and all that he was responsible for, and she ended with,

I don't regret having worked here in Africa. I think I made a difference, no matter how small. And I'd do it again, given another chance. But I do regret our estrangement.

Love,
Your daughter,
Wynne

Did her mother care enough to see Hellstrom punished? She addressed the letter and stuck it inside the envelope to the embassy with forwarding instruction in case of her death. Then she left the hut and headed for the Habitat so she could stick the envelope in the mailbag.

She gripped the envelope in her hand and realized she had never really been frightened in Africa until now. She faced death every day in her job, but facing death and not knowing when it would strike was quite different than seeing it on the horizon and looking into its face. And the face she saw was Hellstrom's.

Bang. Bang. Bang.

"Miss Wynne, are you there?"

Wynne jerked awake. Her groggy mind registered the knocking coming from her door.

"Miss Wynne! I need you."

Wynne recognized Mama Luwo's voice. She opened the door and found Mama Luwo rocking back and forth, her expression filled with whatever had terrified her.

"Mama L, what is wrong?" Wynne asked, grabbing the elderly woman's shoulders.

"Inside…horrible, inside, inside…" She thrust a trembling finger toward headquarters.

"Stay here and calm down." Wynne closed the door, so Snow wouldn't frighten Mama Luwo further, then headed for headquarters.

She noticed a wash of purple just lightening the horizon. It was almost dawn. She dreaded what she would find, but she could already guess.

Inside headquarters, Kaweki's desk stood off to the right. A radio transmitter and receiver had its own table beside his desk, so Kaweki could listen to all ranger reports out in the field. It looked similar to the one the LZCG owned, but ten years older.

To the left was the brig, a small iron-barred cell. The door was open, the cell empty, save for a sleeping mat and chamber pot. The imprisoned poachers were gone. Several feet away Monday Son, a new ranger on the force, lay supine on the floor, a knife through his heart.

Wynne felt the knife somehow in her own chest as she looked down at Monday Son. His face was bruised and puffy. His right arm bent back, obviously broken. Death had frozen a frightened expression on his face. His attackers had worked him over. He was only eighteen. Two years younger than Cody. The sight of him ripped something deadly loose in her. She knew in that moment she would go to any lengths to stop these killers, to stop Hellstrom. The power of the emotion frightened her.

Mama Luwo had followed Wynne and peered in the door with huge eyes. "What to do, Miss Wynne? What to do?"

"Did you see anyone?"

"No, no. I just came in to give Monday Son breakfast. I found him, found him like this." Mama Luwo shook her head, tears streaming down her face.

Wynne shot her a pointed stare. "Do you know of anyone else beside Kaweki and Zhieka who work for the poachers?" Which one of them had helped the poachers escape and murdered Monday Son?

Mama Luwo hesitated for a moment, battling with her conscience, then she nodded. "They the only ones. What to do?"

"I want you to wait until Eieb and I leave, then go to *Bwana* Kaweki and don't tell him you came to me first." Wynne knew Kaweki would have to report the murder to the police so he wouldn't come under suspicion.

Mama Luwo nodded and wiped at the tears on her cheeks with the back of her hand, then she left.

Wynne followed her out and saw Eieb. His rifle was slung over his shoulder, a huge machete hung clipped to his belt. He wore camouflage fatigues and his baseball cap was turned backward, the brim touching his collar.

"What is down?" he asked.

Wynne nodded toward headquarters. "Monday Son is dead. The poachers are free. We need to get going before Kaweki wakes up. I've got to get my backpack from my hut. I'll meet you at the Rover."

Wynne hurried to her hut, glad no one in camp rose before dawn. Snow had come back from her nightly prowl, and Wynne found her pacing near the hut. She looked agitated, sniffing the air, her eyes watchful. From helping her father and working with animals in Africa, Wynne knew all animals possessed an innate sense of danger, but Snow's insight always amazed Wynne. Was Snow sensing the danger that lay ahead of them?

Wynne grabbed her backpack, then she and Snow left the hut. She heard Aja's distinctive whistle. He appeared out of the darkness like an apparition and fell in beside her. "There was trouble?"

"How did you know?"

"Always trouble when *Nkalamo yalubuka* near."

Wynne didn't want to put Aja in harm's way, but she knew he would demand to go with them.

Aja patted the leather satchel hanging on his hip. "You bring juju bag?"

"I did. It's here." Wynne gently touched her backpack where she had stashed her own satchel; similar to the one Aja was wearing. Hellstrom thought he was so clever, that he was so in control. But she had a few surprises of her own for him.

Chapter 11

Rain beat against the windshield and sounded like fists hitting the glass. The rainy season had rumbled into Zambia. The whole afternoon it stormed, and Wynne had been forced to drive the Rover through axle-high mud.

She listened to the *Simpsons* dolls clacking and rocking, their symphony keeping time with the pounding rain. In the rearview mirror she saw Aja napping. Snow had curled up beside him. Eieb hadn't spoken in the last hour and looked deep in thought.

She recalled staking out Hellstrom's compound, waiting for the safari caravan to leave. When she had spotted MacKay driving one of the two trucks, a Land Cruiser, she knew he had lied about having any knowledge of the safari. Her suspicions about him had been confirmed. It still irritated her that she'd let down her defenses and kissed him. The part that annoyed her most was that she'd liked it. That she'd liked him and half-believed he was a good guy.

She'd reproached herself a zillion times as she had followed Hellstrom and the turncoat Texan north, through the Munyamadzi game-managed area. They had driven along the scarp mountains and were now heading into the North Luangwa reserve.

She fought the wheel and said to Eieb, "I hope we don't get stuck again."

Several times the mud had ground them to a halt, and once they had almost taken a nose dive down a steep mountainside.

"They gotta make camp soon. It's getting dark." Eieb looked out his window, squinting through the driving rain at the sky. He shifted in his seat and nervously fingered the brim of his Garfield cap.

"I've never seen you so antsy. What's wrong?" she asked, gripping the wheel as the front end of the Rover hit a log. It slid three feet before the tires found traction again.

"I've been thinking about..." His words trailed off.

"What?"

He hesitated, then the word seemed pried out of him. "Marriage."

"Marriage?" Wynne almost lost her grip on the steering wheel. "Did I hear you correctly?"

"I've been thinking about it all day. If I should..." He couldn't say what he was thinking and he started again, "If we should, you know—"

"We're going to stop Hellstrom. He's not going to win." Wynne filled her words with more bravado that she felt.

"But if we don't."

"We will."

"Okay, we will." He didn't sound convinced.

"Jeez, you're the last person I thought would be thinking about marriage," Wynne said. "Was that you, who swore to me after Simalikiti chewed up your heart and spit it out, you would never marry? Or had an alien inhabited your body?" She knew Eieb had left his village and become a ranger to forget his childhood sweetheart. How could he be talking about marriage again?

"A man can change his gig." His voice took on a defensive tone and he adjusted his hat again.

"Okay, so a man changes his mind. Who is he thinking of marrying?"

"No one."

Wynne tried to recall who Eieb had dated. For the two years she'd known him, he'd lived pretty much for his job. Like she had. She thought a moment and said, "I know who it is."

"You do not."

"Kidaya."

His silence spoke louder than words.

"You're feeling guilty about what happened to Mehan. I wouldn't make any rash decisions."

"It's not guilt or a rash decision. I can't live like you with only a leopard for company."

"I've had dates."

"When was your last date?"

Wynne considered this, her burned palms beginning to itch as she recalled MacKay's lips and the feeling of his stubbly beard on her skin. The mind-blowing kiss. "I've dated," she said again, adding too much emphasis to her voice.

"Name one person here."

Wynne couldn't and said, "Hey, I dated a lot in college."

"Name a name."

"Okay, George. George Blechman." He'd been her lab partner. They'd been working late and he took her virginity in the back of the zoology lab, next to Howie, the teaching ape skeleton, and jars of pig fetuses cooking in formaldehyde. Admittedly, it wasn't such a pleasant memory. But it had gotten the job done. Wynne had made a pact with herself that she'd lose her virginity before the end of her freshman year and she had.

"Make up another name."

"I'm telling you the truth. George is real."

"But you didn't get involved."

After that night, she couldn't see him without smelling formaldehyde. "He had a girlfriend," she lied.

"Anyone else?"

"Jason Berger. Met him in *tantui* class." She had liked him a lot, and the sex was hot, but when he'd started finding fault in the way she practiced the discipline, she gave him the old heave-ho.

"Let me guess, it didn't last." Eieb's voice dropped to a critical tone.

"It wasn't meant to. He wanted a bath mat for a girlfriend. Or a doormat, he never could decide."

"You could have compromised. See, you push everyone away. If I can consider marrying, you can at least consider dating someone."

"Fine, you go right ahead. But marriage doesn't cure guilt or loneliness. My parents lived together for twenty years. They were the two loneliest people I know. No, thanks."

"Ha, see, you just admitted you're lonely."

"Did not. I'm happy with my life. Animals give you unconditional love and they don't try to run your life."

"Who tried to run your life?"

"Never mind." Wynne didn't want to talk about her mother.

The rain began to let up as quickly as it had started, and it trickled into a fine drizzle hitting the windshield.

Eieb pressed his nose to the passenger side glass, gazing through the misty shadows setting over the forest. "Maybe we should check to make sure they haven't set up camp yet."

"A good idea." She stopped the Rover and grabbed the binoculars from the console, then hopped out, glad to be out of the confines of the truck.

She walked through the rocky sloping mopane woodland that blanketed the mountainside, until she reached a clearing. The mountain dropped sharply away, and she had a clear view of the valley below.

She spotted the taillights of Hellstrom's three vehicles, winking as they bounced over the rough terrain of a gorge.

Eieb stepped up beside her and asked, "Are they still moving?"

"Yes, but—" Her words drifted off as her gaze swept the clearing in front of the trucks. "They're heading toward an established camp. I can see about forty men sitting around a cook fire." She moved the binoculars to the west and grimaced. "Wait a minute."

"What?"

"Two more camps. East of here." Wynne panned the bush and saw a huge herd of dark tiny bodies through the infrared lenses. "Looks like buffalo grazing about two miles from the camps. Could be poaching camps." Wynne thought of the conservation project that had cleared the North Luwanga Game Preserve of poachers. The Frankfurt Zoological Society in Germany had maintained it and financed it, and elephant herds were finally on the rise. Left unchecked, Hellstrom's group could wipe out ten years of conservation in a few days.

"Hellstrom's men must be operating in the area, establishing a new killing ground," Eieb said, his voice taut with worry.

She again saw in her mind the piles of bones his men had left behind on the edge of Hidden Valley. A sickening feeling rose inside her. "This may be our only chance to arrest Hellstrom with the evidence. We can't let him out of our sights.

"I know, but he's got an army of men. We're definitely going to need backup with this many camps."

"Got any ideas where we might get this backup?" Wynne lowered the binoculars long enough to glance at Eieb.

He grinned and said, "It just so happens I do. I have a friend at the Anti-Crime Commission, and I contacted him last night."

"Can you trust him?" Wynne had heard of the Anti-Crime Commission. The Zambian government had established it five years ago to investigate official corruption related to poaching. Their small staff of officers supposedly investigated government officials who collaborated with poachers. But the corruption was still unbridled, even inside the Commission itself.

"We went to college together," Eieb said. "He seemed honest enough then."

"Will he help us?" Wynne asked, hopeful.

"He said when we discovered where the poaching camps were to contact him. He'd have to clear it with his supervisor, but he said he'd send all the officers he could to help us."

"Does he know Hellstrom's involved?" Wynne asked, looking through the binoculars again. The taillights of Hellstrom's truck looked like two glaring red eyes staring back at her.

"I didn't give out any names. I just told him it was a suspect who we believed was running a large poaching ring."

"Good. It might be better he doesn't know it's Hellstrom. He probably has friends in the Commission, too."

"I'll call Chimza and let him know our position and where the camps are."

She watched the truck pull into the camp, while Eieb made the call. He had a bad connection and had to talk loudly into the receiver. She half listened to his end of the conversation, while she closely scanned the camp. It looked as if she had underestimated. She counted at least fifty-seven men now.

Eieb hung up and didn't look too happy.

"What is it?" Wynne asked.

"He said he couldn't have his officers here until tomorrow at the earliest."

"Let's just hope Hellstrom doesn't leave here until then."

"We'll have to make sure of it." Eieb walked back toward the Rover, his whole body stiff with tension.

Wynne followed him, gripping the binoculars in her hand and unable to control the uneasiness stirring insider her.

At the pace Aja was setting, they would reach Hellstrom's camp in thirty minutes. Night had darkened the mountains and they looked like a chain of massive sentinels. The drizzle had turned to thickening humidity, their damp footsteps braided with the cacophony of insects and the ever-present peals of animal calls. A deep roar echoed through the mountains like thunder.

"A lion," Eieb whispered aloud. "There must be a pride nearby." He was in charge of monitoring the lion prides within the Lower Zambezi reserve. And every time a new pride settled in the area, they opened a bottle of homemade wine that Eieb brewed. There would be no cork popping again until Hellstrom was behind bars.

An image of MacKay popping the champagne cork in her hut flashed, that sensual grin on his face. Why did her thoughts keep straying back to that two-faced jerk?

"I hope the poachers don't get to them before we can stop them," Eieb said.

"We'll see they don't." Wynne kept her voice optimistic, but Chief Chiti-Mukulu's words rushed back to her, *You have bad juju following you. You should fear for your own life.*

Snow paused, looked into the forest, and answered it with a low growl.

"She's feeling the call," Eieb said, jogging past the leopard.

"I know. She goes out prowling at night now." Wynne touched Snow's neck and caught the big cat's attention.

Snow fell in beside Wynne. Aja had moved twenty feet ahead of them, his form slipping between the night shadows almost unnoticed. She had to squint to keep her eyes on him.

"This would be a good place for her to live," Eieb whispered.

"She's free to choose." Wynne swallowed hard, reminding herself she had to let Snow go.

They lapsed into silence. For a moment, discussing the trivial aspects of their lives had made the danger facing them seem distant. Now, in the silence, it ricocheted back to them full force. Wynne felt the tension of battle building inside her.

Several minutes later they heard voices. Aja crouched behind the craggy rocks jutting from the top of a three hundred-foot gorge. Wynne and Eieb moved up beside him. She gave Snow a hand signal to sit, then peeked over the side.

Fires from Hellstrom's camp burned below them on the ravine's floor, dancing shadows over the more than fifty bearers—those employed to carry the animal carcasses—

gathered around them. The huge fires had been built on circular foundations of stones that kept the heat concentrated and insulated from ground moisture. They were eating *n'shima* and chunks of meat from a warthog roasting on a spit. The hog fat hit the fire like bullets, sizzling and spitting. Off to the side was a hippo corpse, slaughtered, massive chunks of pink meat hanging on a rack. Wynne knew they'd use this to bait lions and cheetahs.

A bullfrog-faced hunting scout, dressed in sneakers, jeans and T-shirt, and his helpers sat away from the bearers in their own little clique. Hunting scouts considered themselves above the bearers in the safari party and they rarely socialized with them.

The two Land Cruisers were parked next to a third jeep. Hellstrom and MacKay sat on the hood of a Land Cruiser, eating. Tungana stood off to the side, anticipating Hellstrom's every want.

Her gaze moved back to MacKay. His hair was wet from the rain, and his damp safari clothes clung to his well-defined body. He hadn't shaved and the dark shadow of whiskers only added to his ruggedly handsome face. A chest holster held his .44 Magnum near his right arm. Despite her aversion to him, she had to admit he was hot.

Hellstrom wore tan fatigues. A Glock hung from a holster near his hip. His clothes looked dry as if he'd changed for dinner. The English. They adhered to strict standards even out in the bush. He looked perfect as ever, not a black hair out of place. He glanced around as if he expected trouble, his yellow eyes glowing like a wary lion's in the firelight. She moved closer and strained to hear their conversation:

"Your first safari. What do you think so far?"

"I got to tell you, pal, having a tracker find the animals and tell you where and when to shoot ain't my idea of hunting."

"That's how it's done here, old chap." Hellstrom spit out a bone from the meat he was chewing.

"Well, it ain't sporting in my book. Half the excitement of hunting is tracking the animal yourself."

"This isn't America, old chap. One wrong move and you could easily take it on the chin. Why, I've had experienced men killed by elephants and buffalo. Let the scouts take the risk for you. You just need to aim and shoot. You can do that now, can't you, old boy?" Hellstrom said, his tone sarcastic.

"Sure, I can do that, old buddy." MacKay parroted his last words, adding a touch of good-humored derision to them. He set aside his plate as if losing his appetite.

"So how long are we supposed to hunt out here?"

"Until you fulfill your permits. Don't you have a puku and lion and zebra permit? It could take some time to track the lion and puku."

"When am I going to see this operation you've been talking about? From what I've seen so far, I gotta tell you, I ain't impressed. The buyers I'm working for are big-time. I mean big-time. They require a lot of meat and ivory. Before I throw in air support to arrange pickup, I gotta know you can deliver. And getting illegal permits to fly in here won't be cheap, so before I invest any more money and energy into this deal, I gotta see something."

"I can supply the meat, and I'll show you the first shipment." Hellstrom looked pleased with himself.

Wynne's fingernails dug into her burned palms and she gritted her teeth. Now she knew exactly what MacKay had been lying about.

"And what about that little girl ranger? I don't like her hanging around. She could ruin the whole operation."

Wynne's fingers tightened into fists. Little girl. She'd show him what a little girl was capable of.

"You needn't worry about her."

"She on your payroll, too?" MacKay offered a cigar to Hellstrom, then he extracted one from the box in his shirt pocket. He bit the end off, then lit it. He eyed the burning tip and waited for Hellstrom's answer.

"I own all of her, including her life. She'll realize that soon enough." Hellstrom's voice turned possessive. He shot MacKay a male territorial look, then stuck the cigar in his mouth.

Instantly, Tungana leaped forward with a lighter.

"You've had her then?" MacKay took a long draw on the cigar.

Wynne made a face. They were talking about her as if she were the soup du jour.

"We've been intimate, if that's what you're asking."

Wynne's eyes widened. Intimate? Trying to kill her was intimate?

Something stirred behind MacKay's poker face, then the relaxed grin was back. "I'll say one thing about her, she ain't bad to look at, but she's not my type. Too bossy, and a damned cold fish. Gotta be Rambo's sister to live like she does out in the bush. I like my women warm, soft and giving. Know what I mean?"

Wynne gritted her teeth until they ached. Rambo's sister? She'd give him Rambo's sister. To think she'd rubbed his back. She should have kicked him in the backside. It was all she could do to sit quietly and not use her slingshot on his head.

Hellstrom waved the servant away and took a drag off

his cigar. He blew a smoke ring up over his head. "There's something to be said for women with spirit. It's all about persistence, old chap."

"Good luck to you." MacKay puffed on his cigar. "I'd rather fight a rabid badger with a toothpick. So when am I going to see this storehouse?"

"Right now. Why do you think I brought you here to hunt?" Hellstrom leaped off the hood.

Hellstrom was playing it safe. If GMA scouts moved in on the poachers and they questioned Hellstrom about being so close, he could just say he's on a hunting expedition with MacKay.

"Fine by me." MacKay jumped down, too.

"Tungana," Hellstrom said. "You stay here. I'm entrusting you to be the chief-in-charge while I'm gone."

Tungana puffed out his chest, pleased as a kid getting his first crack at hall monitoring. "Thank you, *BaK para.* Thank you." The little man ran to a bearer and ordered him to clean the plates. Hellstrom really knew how to control Tungana with empty praise.

Wynne pointed to Eieb and Aja, giving a silent motion that they would tag along. Wynne wanted to bust Hellstrom so badly she could taste it. And as far as MacKay, tying him on a meat rack and leaving him to fight off the vultures with a toothpick seemed too lenient for him.

Eieb slipped on a patch of rock and all hell broke loose. The wet ground gave way beneath his feet. Mud and rock tumbled down the mountainside. Wynne saw Eieb falling toward the cliff's edge and she dove for his hands. Then she lost her footing and they were both falling.

Chapter 12

Out of the corner of her eye, Wynne saw Snow and Aja leap onto a ledge above them, then rocks and mud pummeled Wynne's face and body, and she lost sight of them. She clung to Eieb's hands as they tumbled toward the cliff's edge. She tried to anchor her body on something, but Eieb's momentum and the crumbling rocks and mud made it impossible.

Eieb reached the edge first. They were about to go over when they collided with a patch of briars jutting from the rim of the ledge. The impact knocked the breath out of her, but she still held tight to Eieb's hands.

Men screamed and chaos erupted as the landslide crashed to the ground below them.

She struggled to catch her breath and to hold onto Eieb's hands. She had landed perpendicular to the ledge, twisted around several shrubs. Briars gouged her face and body.

All she could see was Eieb's arms and the top of his head and chest. The rest of his body dangled from the cliff. The barrel of his gun had wedged between his neck and the ledge's edge. A lone bush had caught and twisted into the back of his shirt; it and Wynne's grip on his hands were the only two things holding him. One wrong move and they'd both be history. It was a sheer sixty foot drop to the bottom of the gorge.

Wynne heard the bush holding Eieb crack, the sound of roots being torn from their rocky purchase.

"This bush can't hold much longer," Eieb said in a ragged whisper.

Wynne felt his muddy hands slipping and looked into Eieb's terrified eyes. "I'm secure, and I've got you. Just hold on," she whispered back.

Every muscle in her upper body strained as she held tight to Eieb with one hand and used her other hand to rip off her slingshot. In seconds she had a slip knot around his wrist and firm grip on the slingshot. "If we go, we go together," she whispered.

"That's comforting to know." Eieb's shirt tore as the bush began to give way.

Wynne felt the tug of his weight as she carefully straightened, lying on her belly. She dug her toes in between slippery rocks and began inching backward, slowly pulling Eieb up onto the ledge. He grimaced as thorns dug into his back and the gun barrel butted his chin.

Deafening silence from below. Then a flashlight moved along the cliff. Wynne held her breath and froze.

The light swept closer...closer.

It passed just below Eieb's legs. Any second they'd be discovered.

The light moved along the hillside, roving, then flicked off.

Hellstrom barked, "Damned mudslides. Happens all the time in the rainy season. Half the continent turns to mud. Stop gawking. Clean this mess up before we get back."

Wynne let out the breath she'd been holding and waited until Hellstrom and MacKay's voice drifted off into the night. Snow and Aja leaped down to their outcropping. Aja grabbed Eieb's sleeve, while Wynne pulled on the slingshot. Together they eased Eieb back on the rock face.

"That was close," Eieb whispered, lying on his back and panting up at the sky, relieved to be alive.

"Are you okay?" Wynne kept her voice low, unwrapping the slingshot from his wrist.

"Besides the thorns in my butt, I think my ankle is broken."

Aja bent and examined Eieb's ankle. When Aja moved it, Eieb growled in pain. "Broken." Aja nodded.

"We'll take you back to camp," Wynne said.

"No, you will not. Follow those bastards. Arrest them for me. I'll make it back myself, and I'll keep an eye on those other two poaching camps we saw."

"Don't try to take them alone."

"I won't."

Wynne hesitated, and Eieb said, "Go on, get away with you."

Wynne couldn't leave without hugging Eieb. He whispered in her ear, "Remember to tell Kidaya."

"I will, but you can tell her yourself."

"Tell her." He looked at her in earnest, pleading in his eyes.

His gaze went straight to Wynne's heart, and she nodded, wondering about her own message. She had no one. She had distanced herself from basically everyone. There was her father and Cody, but they knew she loved them. Her mother probably didn't care if Wynne left her a message or not. Their estrangement was her one regret. Right now she wished she could ask Eieb to deliver a message to a soon-to-be-fiancé or lover.

Eieb pulled on her ponytail. "Godspeed, my friend."

"Stay safe." Wynne yanked softly on his dreadlocks, then she hurried to catch up to Aja and Snow. They headed gingerly over the muddy rocks. She didn't have a good feeling and she glanced back at Eieb. He was struggling to stand, leaning on his rifle. She hated to leave him. But worse, she had an innate fear she'd never see him again.

Wynne and Aja stayed behind the two men and kept them within eyesight. They were traveling on foot. All Wynne and Aja really had to do was follow the scent of MacKay's Corona cigar. The acrid trail of it was like a flare in the night.

Hellstrom and MacKay were moving along a poaching trail, recently cleared, the moldy vegetation and small trees left to rot along the edges of the path. A Cape turtledove called in the distance, while tiny hyraxes, small rodents, scampered through the brush near her feet. The nightly shrieks and groans of animals drowned out her footsteps.

Snow stayed behind Wynne and Aja, scenting the hyraxes and the male humans ahead of them.

The path led into a *dambo,* a small valley that remained waterlogged. The trees gave way to small shrubs, thick grass and orchids.

"Did you hear that?" MacKay's voice echoed through the vale as he looked in Wynne's direction.

Wynne and Aja dove beneath the shoulder-high grasses. She held her breath and gripped Snow's neck tight to her chest. She prayed they hadn't been seen.

"It could have been an animal, or snake."

"I'm sure I heard human footsteps."

"If you're going to jump at every sound, old chap, it's going to take half the night to get to the operations area."

"I know what I heard, *old pal.*"

"I don't doubt you heard something. It takes a while to get accustomed to the sounds of the bush—walk carefully up ahead, my men have snares out."

"Snares?" MacKay spit the word out like it left a bad taste in his mouth.

"This area is a rich grazing land through the dry season, plenty of game comes here. It's an easy kill. Part and parcel of making the quota, old chap. You can't run a business without a product."

Wynne and Aja frowned at each other. Snares were the most inhumane form of poaching. The barbed wire nooses rarely killed the animal, only maimed the poor things. The harder they struggled to free themselves the worse the damage. They could suffer agonizing torture for weeks before they succumbed to death. If she found them in time, Wynne always tried to take snared animals back to the Habitat to be saved, but if the damage was too extensive, the animal too close to death, she had to put it down. It was a part of her job that she would never feel comfortable doing, though if it ended an animal's suffering she would do it.

"Just stay close," Hellstrom said.

Wynne wondered if Hellstrom knew MacKay was an ex-SEAL. The way MacKay was keeping quiet and letting Hellstrom lead, she doubted it. Why hadn't MacKay told him? Maybe that was something he only told women to impress them.

The sound of Hellstrom's and MacKay's footsteps faded across the *dambo* as they followed the trail to the base of another hill.

"Let's find those snares near the trail."

Aja nodded.

They searched twenty feet along the trail. She found the first snare not three feet off the trail. It was a spring pole snare, the most popular kind. Poachers used them to kill everything from birds to buffalo. A bent sapling or branch provided the spring. The trigger consisted of three small sticks barely secured into the ground and attached by a rope to the sapling and a wire noose. The animal stepped onto the sticks and the bent branch snapped the noose around the animals' neck or leg.

She took pleasure in springing the traps with her slingshot. The wire hissed like a snake in protest, then Aja pulled up the whole maiming weapon. They had done this many times before, and they settled into an effortless rhythm, making little or no noise. All counted, they had found six.

"I wonder how many more are out here."

"Many more. We come back and search the whole area," Aja said as he buried the snares deep in the marshy grass so they couldn't be found.

They hurried to catch up to Hellstrom and MacKay. Snow lagged behind them and sniffed at the snares.

"Machine ahead." Aja cocked his head to listen, an affectation of his.

"Sounds like a gas generator." She pulled her night-vision binoculars from her backpack and found Hellstrom and MacKay heading toward a cave.

A dim light beamed out from the opening. Moths, mosquitoes and flies formed a writhing mass of bodies at the entrance. Meat racks were set up in front of the cave. Six men worked on the carcasses of two buffalo, tossing the freshly butchered meat into dry ice crates. Four men carried a filled crate of meat into the cave. There were at least thirty workers. Fifteen guards stood along the perimeter.

Wynne shifted the binoculars to an east pathway. Ten bearers and a hunter were bringing in two more dead buffalo. She scoped out the north side.

"My God…" Wynne said.

"What?"

"They're clearing an area for a landing pad near the cave, probably for choppers to load up and fly away. It's central supply for bush meat."

"May I?" Aja held his hand out for the binoculars like a child wanting a toy. Every time he used them he marveled at the infrared technology.

She handed them over.

Aja looked through them, his lips parting ever so slightly in awe as he swept in the landing pad and camp. Once. Twice. "If local rangers patrolled above, the caves would be good cover for the lion's den." Aja handed her back the binoculars.

"He's thought of everything."

"He *mipashi ya chialo.*" Aja used the term for spiritual lions, believed sent by a sorcerer to kill or maim. Aja believed Hellstrom was possessed by evil *juju,* thus a more formidable enemy than a mere man-eating lion. Maybe Hellstrom was the evil the chief had warned her of.

Wynne heard something and turned to see Snow padding up behind them. "There you are," Wynne said. "Back I see."

Snow greeted Wynne by rubbing against her legs, then Snow walked over to Aja.

He stroked Snow's muzzle. "What we do now?" he asked, his voice not impatient, just curious.

"We wait and keep an eye on *mipashi ya chialo.*"

Aja untied his *juju* bag from his waist and kissed it. "I wait with these."

Wynne pulled out her bag from her backpack. She opened the drawstring and extracted a hollow bamboo pipe and a leather belt. Fifty thorn darts were woven into the leather on the outside. Tiny wads of cotton were glued on the ends for a ballast, then she had tainted the points with a latex made from the giant milkweed plant, a widely utilized source for arrow poisons in Africa. The trick was to use just enough to stun your enemies, not kill them. She carefully fastened the belt around her waist, below the slingshot. She noticed Aja going through the same routine he had taught her. It never hurt to be prepared.

When she pulled out two cigarette lighters and twenty cherry bombs from the *juju* bag and stuffed some of them in her pockets, Aja grimaced. "What's that?"

"My own *juju*. Here, just in case we need them." She thrust the lighter and a handful of bombs at Aja.

He scowled at them.

"Light them and throw them. They make thunder and fire. Good if we need a diversion."

"You always were difficult student, Wynne Sperling." He narrowed his eyes at her.

"And that's why you've taught me for so long," she teased.

He wagged a finger at her. "This *juju* not as good as mine."

"Oh, I know. But it's louder."

"Louder not better." He grunted indignantly under his breath.

Wynne picked up the binoculars again and saw Hellstrom striding out of the cave toward a group of guards eating their dinner. They sat beneath a tree, fifty yards away from the cave.

Hellstrom cupped his hands and yelled, "Lemeck." The bark carried over the workers' voices and the generator.

Lemeck was a stocky man with a thick short Afro. He leaped to attention, dropping his food.

The two guards sitting with him, set down their plates, and double timed it back to their posts.

Hellstrom walked toward Lemeck.

She couldn't hear what Hellstrom was telling him. She whispered to Aja, "I'm going to try and hear what he's saying."

Aja nodded as if he'd heard her.

Wynne gave Snow the stay and wait command, then snaked along the base of the hill, forced to climb over rock piles that had been cleared away from the cave. She crept close enough to hear their voices.

"The last drill," Hellstrom said. "How quickly was the pack up?"

"An hour, sir."

"Get them to within thirty minutes. We have to be able to wrap up operations and move out on a moment's notice."

"When will we move?"

"It's only a precautionary measure. It appears to me that your men are getting lax." Hellstrom pointed to the two men who'd been talking. "Kill them."

Lemeck nodded.

Hellstrom leveled his golden eyes at Lemeck, and the guard stiffened. "And don't forget the order, those workers who have seen my face, die too. I know I can count on you." Hellstrom's lips parted in an indifferent grin and he patted Lemeck's shoulder.

Lemeck saluted. "Yes, sir."

Wynne bit down on her lower lip. That meant all the local bearers hired would be killed. My God! It could be a hundred men. How could Hellstrom give such an order in a laid-back manner, like he was asking the guard to take an afternoon stroll?

She watched Hellstrom walk back to MacKay, who stood examining the butchering process.

Hellstrom's assassin, Lemeck, now barked at his men in Chibemba. After a few minutes of castigation, they paced an imaginary boundary, their eyes narrowed off into the shadows, their rifles at the ready to shoot anything that moved.

Wynne started back to rejoin Aja. A sixth sense for danger made her glance upward. Eight guards were charging down the gorge toward Aja. They must have been staked out on the top of the gorge, watching them the whole time. Had Hellstrom known they'd been following him and lured them into this trap?

The guards yelled, "Intruders! Intruders! Kill them!"

"Aja, above you," Wynne screamed.

Aja had seen the men before she had, and his slingshot whirled at his side. He hit one guard so hard he was knocked backwards. Aja used the blow darts on two more. Snow attacked a guard and sent him running in the opposite direction. One guard lifted his rifle to shoot Snow.

Wynne already had her slingshot loaded and in motion. She fired. The guard dropped the rifle and fell. The men Aja had darted crumbled in a heap.

Wynne lit a cherry bomb and sailed it at the last few guards. The guards screamed and dove for cover. It exploded in a burst of thunder, white flames, and smoke. Wynne saw Snow running from the bombs, terrified.

"Run, girl, stay alive," Wynne yelled and hoped Snow heard the command.

She lit more cherry bombs and hurled two toward the

cave. The guards and workers shouted and separated, diving behind crates and scurrying for cover inside the cave.

She spotted MacKay. He had his Magnum out and was heading for her. Wynne lit a bomb and hurled it at him. A "Howdy, there" from Little Girl Ranger.

The bomb landed near his feet. He let out a loud curse. Then he fled in the opposite direction, shoving men down like a linebacker and yelling for them to run.

"Coward," Wynne said under her breath as she torpedoed another bomb at his back. It just missed his head as he dove inside the cave.

She made a mad dash to help Aja. He was lighting his cherry bombs, and it looked like the Fourth of July on the side of the ravine. He was grinning like a child on Christmas morning. Gunpowder from the bombs burned her nostrils as she hurried to close the distance between them. Maybe they could get away.

Before Wynne could reach him, ten other guards materialized out of the smoke. Lemeck led them. They were closing fast, from the opposite direction. Aja hadn't seen them. Wynne hadn't either, until it was too late.

She watched in horror as Lemeck aimed his rifle at Aja and pulled the trigger. The muzzle flashed in the dark. Aja's body buckled. He staggered several steps, then fell backward.

"No," she screamed, feeling as if someone had reached inside her chest, crushing her heart.

Lemeck turned his rifle in her direction.

Wynne didn't have time to deal with her raw emotions. Her instinct to survive took over. She whirled her slingshot and fired at Lemeck. The rock hit its mark, Lemeck's temple. He fell face forward on the ground, his gun beneath him.

The guards clambered over him and shot at her. Bullets

whizzed past her and she ducked behind a rock. She reloaded and grabbed her dagger. But before she could fire again, she sensed a more imminent threat behind her. She turned to see Hellstrom.

He had the Glock pointed at her.

Suddenly time froze and stretched out before her like a slow-motion nightmare. She threw the dagger. It seemed to take forever before it struck his shoulder. He staggered a moment, his face a mask of agony. But he kept his grip on the gun. His hand trembled so much he couldn't aim. A crazed inner force seemed to drive him, and he grabbed the gun with both hands. Anger bloated his face blood-red, the *mipashi ya chialo* had surfaced. His eyes were predatory and sharp. An arrogant smile turned up the corners of his mouth, then he fired at her.

She felt her own blood splatter across her face, before she felt the bullet enter her side. Her body jackknifed. Pain gouged at her with agonizingly slow white-hot fingers. She felt it all the way to her spine. Bit by bit, the pain sucked the breath from her chest. An overwhelming current of sadness pulled her under…and she had no message for anyone. No message. It was her last thought before blackness consumed her.

Chapter 13

Wynne woke to a buzzing in her ears, a pain in her right side and the memory of Hellstrom's golden eyes glaring at her. Just before he'd shot her.

The air around her felt stifling hot. Perspiration covered her body. Her mouth was so dry it felt like she'd swallowed a mouthful of sand. Flies buzzed around her. Had she been left for dead? She heard male voices and the sound of the generator.

She opened her eyes and saw the inside of a tent. It was daylight, the sun beating down on the roof. Someone had taken off her clothes and she was only wearing her bra and panties. A sheet covered her.

She reached to lift the sheet and realized her wrists were bound with leather thongs. She used both hands, caught the edge of the sheet, and raised it enough to peer at a bandage wound around her middle. Blood had seeped through an area over her left lower ribs. She sat up and winced from the pain in her side. Her world spun and her head felt like it weighed a thousand pounds.

After a moment, her equilibrium cleared. Where were her clothes? Her weapons? She glanced around the tent and found only a wooden basin filled with bloody water and a sponge floating in it.

How long had she been out? Was Aja alive? She could still see him getting shot. He had to be okay. He just had to be. Did Eieb make it back to camp? Would he send help? So many questions and no answers.

She could hear voices outside. She wound the sheet around her, grabbed the tent's center pole with her bound hands, and pulled herself up. Black dots swam before her eyes from the pain. She clung to the pole, forcing herself to breathe, and waited for her vision to clear.

She staggered to the tent opening, pushed the flap up, and peeked out. The cave entrance was a hundred feet from the tent. Men worked steadily on the bush meat. She recognized some of the men she'd darted last night.

Hellstrom and MacKay were walking toward the tent. Hellstrom didn't look at all wounded, but his eyes had taken on a hard glazed look.

Wynne dropped the tent opening and listened to their voices:

"How's the little girl warden?" MacKay asked.

"Alive."

MacKay chuckled. "Gotta give her credit, she put on a mighty fine show last night."

"Not good enough," Hellstrom said without amusement.

"What you gonna do with her?"

"I don't know yet, but my bloody father always said to me, 'Son, keep your enemies close and your friends at a distance. If your friends stab you in the back, you'll have time to react. And if your enemies try it, you'll be prepared.'"

Their footsteps paused near the tent entrance. "Sound advice, but why not just get rid of her now?" MacKay asked.

Wynne twisted her bound wrists until the leather bit into her skin. MacKay obviously didn't care anything about her, lying, womanizing, poaching pond-scum that he was.

"Because—" Hellstrom hesitated, and Wynne envisioned his lips stretching in a slow calculating grin "—I'm not done with her yet. There's an inordinate amount of enjoyment to be had breaking a beautiful strong-willed woman like her. But I think you know that—"

"Enjoyment?" MacKay snorted, a sound halfway between a snicker and a croak. "Your idea of enjoyment is not even in the same ballpark as mine."

"Come now, she turns you on. Admit it, old chap."

"About as much as finding a female rattler in my sleeping bag. And I can't see you breaking Sister Cherry Bomb in there."

Wynne ground her teeth.

"She might be too much woman for you, old chap, but not for me," Hellstrom said, mixing his words with a note of superiority.

Wynne had studied Psychology 101 and deviant behavior in college, and she knew the real reason Hellstrom kept her alive. He needed to feel power over her and derive pleasure from it in his own twisted way, a compulsion fueled by a physically abusive father and mentally ill mother. He must have never felt in control as a child.

"Now, I must see how my patient is doing," Hellstrom said.

Wynne moved to the side of the tent opening. A holster held Hellstrom's Glock on his hip. If she could get it…

Hellstrom stepped through the tent flap.

While he was leaning over, Wynne kicked him in the face and dove for the gun. The pain in her side was so intense, she missed the gun.

He staggered back and fell against the tent, her kick hardly having any power behind it.

She reeled on her feet, trying to keep her balance. The sheet fell from her body.

Hellstrom rubbed his bleeding lower lip. His nostrils quivered and his pupils turned to pinpoints as his eyes roved over her body in a clinical and detached way.

Wynne felt exposed and vulnerable. Though the pain in her side was excruciating, she took up a defensive stance, her bound hands out in front of her.

His eyes shifted between her feet and her hands. "You think I'm going to fight you, when you can hardly stand up?"

"You're such a gentleman." Wynne kept her hands in a battle stance. "Is Aja alive?"

"You'll have to find out." He wasted a brilliant smile on her.

Wynne wanted to ask again, but Hellstrom was toying with her. He knew Wynne cared about Aja, and he was using that. So she said nothing, bent and swept up the sheet at her feet. The movement hurt like crazy, pain stabbing her middle. With her bound hands, she tossed the sheet over her shoulder and draped it across the front of her body.

He grinned, his white teeth flashing, his straight black hair falling beside his temples. He looked handsome and deadly. "I was quite disappointed in you last night. Stabbing me. It hurt my feelings terribly."

"I'm really sorry I did that." She didn't sound at all repentant. "Is that why you killed Aja? To get back at me?"

"I should tell you, I'm not vindictive, unless pushed."

His gaze scoured her body again, seeming to look past the sheet, then he stepped closer.

Wynne held her ground. The gun was within her reach again. She had to keep him talking. "I guess money is the only thing that pushes your buttons."

"Until I met you." His golden eyes glinted with a hunger to overpower her. He reached out and pushed the strands of hair that escaped her ponytail behind her right ear.

His touch caused the hairs on the back of her neck to rise. He deliberately let his hand brush her cheek. "Who else knows about my little business venture, besides your friends?"

"No one, except Kaweki. And he's your man."

Hellstrom seemed pleased by her detective work, and let his hand move along the base of her jaw. "That one was easy. Kaweki loves his wife too much and wants to give her more than his meager salary can afford, so I help him out and he helps me."

"Kaweki is a fool. He already has Colette's love. It doesn't matter to her how she lives as long as she's with him."

Hellstrom's hand paused at the base of her chin. "It's a matter of pride with Kaweki. You know that."

"And I guess Zhieka and nurse Ratchett were easy buy-offs too."

"Everyone has a price in a poor country like Zambia." He ran his thumb over her jawline, and he scrutinized the lines of her face as a lion would study the size of its prey.

It was all she could do not to knock his hand away. "So who else on the LZCG board have you bought?"

"None so far, but give me time. I've only been the chairman for four months. All I need is time to find out who is weak."

"You like preying on people's weaknesses."

"I've yet to find your weakness." He let his hand trail down her neck. He gazed directly at her, a hypnotic deep golden hue in eyes that consumed anything in his vision.

"Don't hold your breath," she said.

"You're making me terribly glad you're still a problem. We have a lot to discover about each other." His fingers reached for the edge of the sheet and curled around the base of her neck.

"If you don't mind, I'd rather do it with my clothes on."

"You look fetching in the sheet."

Wynne went for the gun. This time she caught it with her bound hands and aimed it between his eyes. "Move back."

He took a step back and held up his hands.

"Now, get moving. We're going to walk out of here."

"No, we're not." He refused to move.

"We are." She didn't like the patient, superior look on his face or how relaxed he seemed.

"You'll have to shoot me."

"I've never shot a man at point-blank range before, but I *will* shoot you." Her hands trembled; the gun felt like it weighed a hundred pounds. She had never wanted to kill another person before this moment.

"Are you having a touch of conscience?"

"Don't you wish." Her finger itched to press down on the trigger.

"Then shoot me." He dropped the hospitable pretense from his voice. "Shoot the bloody thing!"

"Don't make me do it."

"You can't, can you?"

She aimed the gun at his knee cap and fired.

Click. Nothing happened.

Click. Click. Click. The clip was empty.

He reached for the Glock.

Wynne whipped the gun toward his face, but he grabbed her wrist, then drove his fist into her wound.

Her knees buckled. An explosion of pain made her see stars.

Hellstrom caught her and shoved her back against the tent. He grabbed her ponytail and forced her to look into his eyes. She felt his heavy breath on her face and smelled the odor of peppermint toothpaste. She glared back at him in defiance.

"Do you think I'd come in here with a loaded gun?" His expression turned venomous.

Wynne couldn't answer him. It was all she could do to breathe and not scream. Each breath felt like a saw blade in her side. She wouldn't cry out for him. He'd enjoy it too much.

"How're things in here?" MacKay's voice made them both look at him. He had poked his head inside the tent, as if he'd been standing outside the entrance, listening. His gaze found her and every vestige of expression slipped from his face.

"Everything is just peachy keen." Hellstrom enunciated each word as he supported Wynne against him.

Wynne couldn't pull away and fight the agony, too. She tried to manage a glare for MacKay, but she knew the pain on her face masked it.

"Things don't look so good to me." MacKay spoke without taking his eyes from her. He stepped all the way inside. "You okay, darlin'?"

MacKay was the last person she wanted to come to her rescue, or to see her so defenseless. She managed to gasp out, "Leave."

"See, everything is fine." Hellstrom's arms tightened around her waist.

"Well, I know when I'm not wanted. Hey, when are we going hunting? The morning's wasting."

"As soon as I'm done here."

"I'll get ready." MacKay left.

Hellstrom whispered to her, "I know you're distraught at the moment, so I'll leave you to think about my generosity in not wrapping my hands around your beautiful neck and strangling you right now. Maybe the next time I come in here, you'll appreciate me quite a bit more. Now, let's get you to bed."

"Go to hell." Wynne managed to pull away. Without his support, she fell to the ground.

He looked down his nose at her. "You look rather charming on your knees."

Wynne gave him the most defiant stare she could manage and held her side. Blood oozed through the bandage and dripped through her fingers.

A malicious smile turned up the corners of his mouth, then he began to leave. But he paused and said, "By the way, MacKay has a permit to kill a leopard. And I'm sure it will take the trackers only a few hours to find your pet."

Wynne forced the words out, "If you think killing her will hurt me, think again. I'm attached to no…one."

"*Au contraire,* my dear, you and I are attached." His face lit with bitter triumph, then he left.

She knew he was right. They were connected in the worst way, inseparable enemies, yoked together by opposite ends. Wynne gritted her teeth and put pressure against her wound. Blood trailed down her arm now. Her only hope was that Snow had been frightened by the cherry bombs and headed for the hills. Above the pounding in her head, she heard Hellstrom bark orders at Tungana to attend her.

Tungana ducked into the tent. He was so short he only had to dip his head. He was carrying a small bowl of white liquid. Once he saw her crumpled on the ground, the blood on her hand and arm, his eyes widened. "To bed. To bed," he said, bending and setting down the bowl.

She let him lead her back to the straw mat. She was so weak and hurting she couldn't resist.

When she was lying down she could speak better. "My clothes, where are they?" Her voice sounded raspy and feeble.

Defiance cloaked his face and he refused to answer her while he straightened the sheet over her.

"I want them back."

"*BaK para* must order it." He picked up the bowl and brought it close to her face. "You drink."

She turned her head away and said, "My friend Aja, is he all right?"

He refused to answer her and nudged her cheek with the edge of the bowl. "Swallow."

She shook her head and asked, "Did you heal *BaK para,* too?"

"I made him well." Tungana stuck out his chin proudly.

She'd finally found the magic string to pull that would make Tungana talk—his pride. "Like my friend?" she asked. "Did you heal him as well as you healed *BaK para?*"

He opened his mouth to answer her, then he clammed up. His chin snapped up to a superior level again. "You try and trick me." He thrust the bowl at her, sloshing a little on her neck. "Drink now."

"What is it?"

"For pain."

If he was going to kill her, he would have done it by now. She drank the chalky bitter liquid, probably a poppy extract.

"Get more bandages. Be back." Tungana stood, then his footsteps padded out of the tent.

Wynne laid on the cot in a fetal position. It somehow

helped the flaming claws digging in her side. She thought of Aja and saw his body double over as he'd been shot. God, she needed to know if he was still alive. And Snow. And Eieb. *Please let them be all right.*

She heard her mother's voice, "You'll fail at this like you failed at being my daughter," and Wynne felt the negative whispers, skipping through her heart and leaving tracks of doubt in their wake. Had her mother been correct?

Wynne felt someone shaking her and started awake. Tungana was bent over her, holding a solar-powered lantern. Its muted glow bathed the inside of the tent. She noticed a guard standing by the door, his rifle pointed at her. Large ears set off his mule-looking face. He didn't look happy to be guarding her.

"How long have I slept?" she asked, still groggy.

"All day. Dark now. Get up. *BaK para* wants you up. Dress." He held her clothes. They'd been washed and folded.

What degrading thing did Hellstrom have in store for her now?

Tungana had changed her bandage and the wound had stopped bleeding. The magic white analgesic Tungana had given her dulled the ache, but her side still throbbed. It also made her feel woozy.

"You can leave now. I can dress myself."

"*BaK para* say not to leave you alone. I'll help with the bindings." Tungana gave her a speculative glance and reached for her hands.

Wynne snapped a glance at Mule-face. He was watching her every move. "How about some privacy here?" she said.

"No privacy. *BaK*—"

"I know, I know. *BaK para* ordered it." It was worth a

try. She obediently held out her hands and allowed Tungana to untie her. "I don't even have the strength of a kitten. I'm not going to escape. You could send him out." Wynne motioned with her head toward Mule-face, giving it another shot.

"He stays. *BaK para* say watch you closely."

"Okay, okay." She gave up and dressed in front of both men. Tungana was all business about it, keeping his eyes on her hands in case she tried to overpower him. His size was deceptive. Pygmies were quick and adept at combat; they had to be to live in the jungle.

Mule-face received an eye-full, his Buckingham Guard expression never wavering.

Wynne forgot about the guard as her thoughts strayed to Aja and Snow. Was Aja still alive? Had Snow been able to elude Hellstrom's trackers? She bit her lip as Tungana helped her pull on her shirt. She saw the bullet hole in the side of the shirt. A small circle of blood surrounded it. Every movement clawed at her side. He helped her stand and put on her pants, but Wynne turned away and pulled up her zipper. It was demeaning enough having to rely on his help in dressing. Worse, Mule-face's alert, prying eyes hadn't left her once.

Tungana held out the thongs. "Retie your hands now."

She looked around the tent and said, "What about my boots?"

"*BaK para* say no boots."

Another tactic to degrade her, humbled and barefoot in front of His Majesty. She'd rather be an alligator's dinner.

"We go now."

Mule-face gave her a wide berth as she stepped toward the entrance. At least the humiliation of changing in front him hadn't dulled his unease around her. She shot him an icy stare, then stepped outside. Mule-face fell in behind her.

She blew the strands of hair that had escaped her pony-tail out of her eyes and knew she probably looked like the walking dead.

Tungana motioned for her to follow him. "This way."

Mule-face shoved her into motion with the end of his AK-47. *"Endesha. Endesha,"* he ordered.

"All right, I'm moving." Wynne walked ahead of him. Was she being led to her death?

As they passed the edge of camp, she noticed the lights near the cave. Winged moths, the size of birds, vied for the brightness among a whirling blur of flies and mosquitoes. She could see men steadily working on the meat. Ten buffalo and five puku were piled next to the butchering rack. The guards were back on duty, except there were only four, Lemeck noticeably absent. The bush meat operation was back in business, going strong. The gas-powered generator whined next to the cave. Wynne searched the carcasses for Snow's white fur, her heart pounding....

No white leopard. Her shoulders slumped with relief.

She scanned the camp for Aja.

No sign of him. Right now, she'd rather not see them and know their fate. It was better to hope.

Tungana led her away from camp along a recently cut path. They came to a cleared area, and Wynne picked up on Hellstrom and MacKay's muffled voices. As she moved closer, their conversation drifted toward her.

"It looks like we've got a deal," MacKay said. "I think you can supply my buyers. I'll take this order. I'll be back by the end of the month for more."

"We've got a deal, then." Hellstrom held out his hand and they shook on it; a contract between two devils.

Tungana, Wynne and the guard, stepped into the clearing. Hellstrom and MacKay sat in canvas folding chairs near a fire, puffing on cigars. Behind them stood a massive tent. This must be where Hellstrom conducted his business, away from camp and the prying eyes of his men.

MacKay spotted her first. For a split second he lost his self-possession and pity wrinkled his brow. Then the moment passed, and he stiffened in his chair and flicked ashes off the end of his cigar.

That couldn't have been raw emotion she had seen on his face. He was no different than Hellstrom, just in a more tolerable package. He lacked the narcissistic sociopathic qualities of Hellstrom, but he was still driven by greed and his impulsive sexual appetite. He wouldn't know a heartfelt emotion if it hit him in the heart.

When Hellstrom saw her, the yellow in his eyes deepened and glowed like amber. "Ah, there she is, and she's looking better," he said with insincere cheerfulness.

"Have you really been that worried?" Wynne fired back with the same glibness.

"I had actually, because I need to make a monumental decision." Hellstrom blew a smoke ring.

Was this where he told her he was killing her and he was such a gentleman he'd let her choose the method?

"MacKay is ending his safari, and I can't persuade him to go on with me to track the elusive scimitar."

"I'm surprised he doesn't want to get off the first shot." Wynne glowered at MacKay.

MacKay's face remained grave, unsmiling. He stubbed out his cigar. "Got to arrange for transport. I'm a busy man."

"I bet you are."

"But you haven't asked me about this decision." Hellstrom sounded like an irritated child trying to get his mother's attention.

Were they playing her? Okay, she'd bite. "So what about it?"

"You'll see." Hellstrom motioned to Tungana, who stood beside her.

He ran over behind the tent and clapped his hand. Two guards appeared, supporting Aja. He was alive. Alive! He wore nothing but a loin cloth. Blood oozed from a bullet hole in his shoulder that hadn't been bandaged. He was barely conscious. His head lolled forward on his thin neck.

She wanted to run to him, but that would show weakness before Hellstrom. She kept her expression indifferent. "So, what's he got to do with your decision?"

"You both do," Hellstrom said. "I'm giving you the choice to take MacKay's place on my little safari, or you can both be disposed of now."

He would kill them anyway; he liked playing God. But it could buy them some time. "I'll go, but I have a request."

He seemed placated that she was being so conciliatory, but also suspicious. "What is that?"

"That you allow Tungana to tend Aja's wound."

"And what will you give me in return?" Hellstrom asked, his tone calculating.

A proper burial, she was thinking, but she had to play the game. "Anything you want—within reason," she added.

MacKay shifted in his chair again, and he'd smoked the cigar down to the tip. He scowled at it, then dropped it and crushed it with his boot.

Hellstrom's gaze flicked over her body. "I do have something in mind." He nodded to Tungana.

The servant took her arm. "Wait a minute. First I watch while Tungana helps Aja."

"So distrustful. Very well, you can watch." He ordered Tungana to help Aja, then he motioned to Mule-face.

"Keep a close eye on her, Kanopi. If she escapes, I won't be happy."

Kanopi's mule-face seemed to elongate with fear. He nodded and bowed, "Yes, *bwana*."

"Don't worry, I'm not going to run away from you." Wynne's expression promised she'd do a lot worse things to him. She issued a challenge with a thin smile.

Hellstrom arched a brow at her, then he brightened with a new kind of eagerness. "Be quick about it, Tungana."

"Yes, *BaK para*."

Wynne knew this favor might cost her much more than she was willing to pay.

Chapter 14

Wynne had convinced Tungana that he could tend them both much easier in one tent, so he ordered the men to place Aja into her tent. Kanopi watched them from the entrance.

She sat beside Aja now, shooing away flies from the wound with her bound hands, while Tungana extracted the bullet. The Pygmy was using his fingers and a knife and digging into Aja's shoulder. Thankfully the white liquid Tungana had given Aja had sedated him. Wynne was feeling just a little light-headed herself, watching Tungana work his fingers into Aja's flesh.

"Ah, found it." Tungana pulled out a bullet and held it up for her to see like it was the biggest prize he'd ever won.

All she saw were his hands covered in Aja's blood. Had he dug his hands into her like that to extract the bullet? No wonder her side ached. She was relieved when he bent over a wooden bowl, dropped the bullet and rinsed his hands in water. He dried them on his tunic.

"Now, we clean wound." He had a little wooden box and he opened it up and pulled out a thick sticky substance in a vial. It smelled like turpentine, or something close to it. He poured it into the wound, then massaged the flesh around the area.

Even in Aja's sleep he jerked. He would have been in agony if he had been awake.

"What is that?"

"Sting, sting. Keep evil from wound."

Evil was infection. Wynne sniffed the paste. It smelled like tea tree oil, a natural antiseptic.

Abruptly a guard stepped halfway inside the tent. He had a haggard, raw-boned face and owlish eyes, wide, round and alert. He looked warily at Wynne, then turned to Kanopi and said in Bemba, "*Bwana* wants the woman."

Kanopi motioned for her to get up.

Hellstrom hadn't wasted any time in collecting his payment. Wynne squeezed Aja's hand as best she could with her bound wrists and said, "You'll be okay."

She thought she felt him squeeze her hand.

Kanopi jabbed the barrel of his AK-47 into her back. "Let's go."

"All right." Wynne rose awkwardly with her hands tied in front of her. Before operating on Aja, Tungana had given her another dose of the white magic, but it still felt like a knife was turning in her wound.

Kanopi trailed her outside. He motioned toward the owl-eyed guard and said, "Follow, Chikoko."

Wynne fell in behind Chikoko. They passed five guards standing nearby, their faces as hard as honed steel, their eyes full of contempt for her. Workers continued with their slaughtering process near the cave, the murmur of their voices as incessant as the steady drone of the generator. The odor of rotting carcasses, blood and butchered flesh wafted through the air, mingling with the suffocating humidity that blanketed the night air. The sight and smell sickened her and she glanced up and swallowed hard. Clouds rolled in front of the moon, building into heavy billowing masses. Another storm was brewing.

Chikoko led them down the small path she had used earlier. She searched for MacKay but didn't see him. After Hellstrom was done with her, would he hand her over to MacKay? A perk for becoming Hellstrom's new business partner? She'd rather die first. She tugged on the leather thongs holding her wrists, but Tungana had tied them in a slip knot that tightened the more she struggled to get free. Kanopi seemed to realize what she was doing and he punched her in the back with his rifle.

She glared at him, but continued to walk. The bark of hyenas drifted in the night, their song a gloomy dirge. Damp leaves and sticks crunched under her bare feet and felt like thorns. They came into view of Hellstrom's tent.

Chikoko paused near the tent and pointed inside with his rifle. "Enter, enter," he said, waving his hand.

The memory of Hellstrom's fist driving into her wound rushed back to her. She had never experienced that kind of pain before. What would he have in mind now? A cold knot of fear twisted in her gut.

Kanopi nudged her from behind. "Go!"

She glared at both guards, took a deep breath, then forced herself to step inside.

An oil lamp burned on a small fold-up camping table and Beethoven's *Moonlight* Sonata, played from a CD player. Mosquito netting covered a grass mat. Hellstrom sat in the corner, the red dress draped over his lap. His manicured fingers stroked the gown. The sequins glinted like Hellstrom's eyes, and the diaphanous silk had the sheen of fresh blood.

He'd found the dress in her backpack. His sexual fantasy of her wearing it must have saved her life—for the moment. Her heart pounded against her chest as she scanned the room for a weapon. A wine bottle. The glasses. Her gaze shifted to a set of maps covering the top of an aluminum trunk. A rock the size of her fist weighed down the maps. Hellstrom wasn't wearing his sidearm. He wore only safari pants, shirt and hiking socks and boots.

"Please sit." He motioned to a lawn chair near him. "Wine?" he asked, as if they were sitting in a drawing room at Windsor Castle.

Wynne saw several packages of Twinkies, two crystal goblets and a bottle of wine on a small table by his chair. God knows what he'd put in the wine.

"I see that look. You needn't fear I drugged it." He bent over and poured himself a glass and sipped it. "Sanctus St. Emilion Grand Cru. Bordeaux wines are the best."

"I'll take your glass," she said, sitting in the lawn chair beside his.

He forced a laugh, then handed her his goblet. He noticed her bound hands and said, "I apologize for the bindings."

"But you won't take them off."

"Why make it hard on both of us." He filled his own glass with wine.

"I think you're afraid of me." She tried to sound condescending while she listened to the thunder of her own blood pounding in her ears.

His white teeth flashed. "I see what you're doing, but reverse psychology has never worked on me."

"It was worth a try." Wynne chugged the wine. What would work on a predator like him?

Wynne managed to keep her hand steady as she handed him the glass. "I'll have another."

He poured carefully so as not to spill the wine on the dress. "Would you like one of these?" He pointed to a Twinkie. "I found them in your backpack. I didn't know you had a sweet tooth." He handed her the full goblet.

"Some people eat chocolate. I do Twinkies. It's my drug of choice."

"Please, take one." He handed her a Twinkie.

She shook her head and almost laughed at the absurdity of Hellstrom offering it to her. "I'm really not in the mood for one tonight." For the first time in her life, Wynne didn't have an appetite for her favorite food. Maybe it was the bullet wound in her side, or maybe eating one with him would ruin the pleasure of it for forever.

"Very well." He set it down, then stood, carefully arranging the gown on the chair. He walked to the trunk, placed the maps and rock on the ground, and pulled out a hairbrush. "You've got beautiful hair. I'd like to brush it."

Here comes the kinky stuff. She saw that he'd inadvertently moved the rock closer to her foot. "It tends to get in the way when I'm in the bush," she said. She should have cut it long ago, but it was the one remnant of feminine vanity she couldn't let go. Now she wished she had.

She didn't like that he stood behind her where she couldn't see his hands or his eyes.

"Relax, I'm not going to hurt you." He pulled the rubber band out of her hair.

"I bet you say that to all your prisoners." Or victims.

Her thick blond hair fell down her back. He ran his

hands through her hair, spreading it, and said, "You may not believe this but you're the only woman I've ever hurt."

"I bet a woman has never challenged you before," she said nonchalantly, trying to mask the panic coiling in the pit of her stomach. She fought the urge to squirm. "You can be pretty persuasive and charming when you want to be." He'd probably never had a woman see through his charismatic veneer. Jackie certainly hadn't.

"Come to think on it, I haven't. I've never met any woman who posed any sort of challenge. Perhaps that's why I've kept you alive." He bent close to her neck, his breath warm on her skin.

His lips moved an inch from her skin, and he murmured, "You bring out something uncivilized in me." He kissed her neck, then softly nipped her with his teeth.

The sensation didn't hurt. In fact the sexual bite might have turned on another woman. But for Wynne, she visualized lions mating, the male grabbing the female by the neck, the violence of subjugating her. The nip left a prickling greasy feeling on her neck, and she fought the desire to shove him away.

"I think I could easily fall in love with you."

Love her? Great. A greedy maniacal killer could love her. How did he treat women he disliked? She doubted that he'd ever had a normal relationship in his life. "Have you ever loved anyone before?"

"Sadly, no one but my mother. She was strong-willed like you."

"Your mother must have taken a lot of abuse from your father."

Hellstrom's breathing slowed as he grew pensive. He ran his fingers over the brush bristles, then said, "We both did. She more than I. It's his fault she ended up in an institution."

"What happened?" Maybe she could get him to drop his guard.

"He threw her against a wall, cracked her skull. She was never the same after that."

Wynne couldn't imagine the violence Hellstrom must have witnessed. It almost made her sympathize with him. Almost. "I'm sorry," she said.

Hellstrom squeezed Wynne's shoulder blade and she felt him looking down on her. "I've never told anyone that before," he said, sounding almost vulnerable.

"Sometimes it's good to get stuff like that off your chest. It's not an easy thing to live with."

"How well I know that. There's not a night that goes by that I don't have a violent nightmare about my father. And when he died I was glad he was gone. Does that make me a monster?"

The irony was he was already a monster and didn't realize it. "It's a lot of baggage to carry."

"I knew you'd understand."

He raised the brush, then the bristles drove into her hair as he dragged the brush through it.

She wanted to tell him he was sick and delusional and needed help, but she held her tongue.

"I used to love to brush my mother's hair. I still do when I visit her."

"Do you brush Jacqueline's hair?"

"I must admit I do. Does that make you jealous?"

Jealous? Was he kidding? "No," she said.

He laughed. "I can count on your honesty, if nothing else." He laid the brush aside and handed her the dress. "Put it on, please."

"I can't." Wynne leaned forward in the lawn chair and thrust out her bound hands at him.

He hesitated only a moment, then reached over and untied her wrists. "If you try anything, you should know I've instructed Kanopi to shoot you on sight if he hears one sound in here that isn't," Hellstrom cleared his throat, "intimate."

"Where's the fun in that?"

"Just a precaution where you're concerned." He slipped the leather bindings in the pocket of his shorts. "Now put on the dress."

"Turn around first."

"Turn my back on you? I don't think so." A chill slipped into his tone. "I already did that once and paid for it."

He crossed his arms and stared down at her as if he were waiting for a stage play to begin. Humiliation seemed an integral part of his whole domination plan. She downed the rest of her wine, then tossed the dress back at him. "I'm not putting on the dress," she said, sensing if he got his way he'd grow bored and kill her and Aja.

"You said you'd give me anything." Golden fire burned in his eyes. "Keep your end of the bargain."

"Anything else but that." The one thing he wanted. If she put on that dress it would be a sign she'd caved beneath his omnipotence and that he'd won.

He stood and jerked her up. As Wynne came up she grabbed the rock.

Several things happened at once. Kanopi appeared at the door, but someone jerked him back from behind. A loud thump, then he went down. Wynne threw the rock at Hellstrom. He ducked in time and caught her arm.

She swung at him.

He grabbed her other free arm. She tried to kick him and felt pain rip through her wounded side.

"Bitch, you'll learn," he growled, throwing all his weight at her.

He rammed her wound with his shoulder. Pain exploded as she felt the impact and fell backward onto a canvas chair. Hellstrom landed on top of her. The chair crashed to the ground beneath them. He knocked the breath out of her, and for a moment spots swam in her eyes. She blinked them away and saw MacKay grab Hellstrom from behind and throw him across the tent. Hellstrom tumbled on the mat. His face swollen with rage. He jumped up and growled as he charged MacKay.

Wynne grabbed a broken section of the chair and crawled to a corner. She held her side and watched the two men butt heads. Her wound began bleeding from the tussle with Hellstrom, and she felt it soaking the bandage.

In seconds MacKay had Hellstrom pinned to the ground, his massive forearm across Hellstrom's neck. Hellstrom wore the surprised expression of a lion who found himself the hunted rather than the hunter.

"Listen up, old buddy." MacKay stressed his last two words as if they were detestable to him. "Raping wounded women might be on your agenda, but it ain't on mine. Either you keep your hands off her, or the deal's off. So which is it gonna be?"

Hellstrom's intense and cornered gaze flitted between Wynne and MacKay as if trying to decide between her or financial gain. "All right, the deal," he said, his voice raspy from the pressure of MacKay's hand wrapped around his vocal cords.

MacKay leaped to his feet. He moved with the agility and speed of a much smaller man. He kept his eyes on Hellstrom as he walked toward Wynne.

"Don't come near me." Wynne brandished the broken wood piece of the chair, but it was a feeble attempt. She couldn't raise it past her waist.

"You ain't gonna try that, now are you, darlin'?" He snatched it out of her hand, then threw it aside. It hit the rock with a loud thunk. "Come on, now." He wore an I'm-here-to-rescue-you expression.

It galled her, but she let him put his arm around her waist and help her walk. She hated being at his mercy. But at the same time she had to admit it felt good to be supported by his brawny arms.

Hellstrom stood and glowered at her. "We're not done yet, Wynne."

"You are tonight," MacKay said as they left the tent.

Wynne stepped over Kanopi's crumpled body by the tent entrance and said, "You shouldn't leave your trash lying around."

"Yeah, you're right." MacKay's arm tightened around her waist. "I'll be more careful next time."

"Why did you do that back there? You probably just signed your death warrant."

"I don't think so. We're talking a multimillion dollar deal. Hellstrom may want you, darlin', but you're not ranking above the demands of his pocketbook, sorry to say."

For a moment, Wynne had forgotten what MacKay was. They lapsed into silence. Wynne caught movement out of the corner of her eye and saw Snow, crouched in the bushes.

MacKay spotted her, too.

"You won't tell him." Wynne heard the desperation in her voice and hated it. "He'll kill her to get at me."

"He wanted to hunt her down today, but I told him I wasn't interested in killing a lady's pet."

"Go away, Snow. Away." Wynne gave her a hand signal but her voice lacked command.

Snow didn't budge, her eyes gleaming at Wynne.

"Go on, you mangy creature. Go away." Wynne bent and tried to pick up a rock. Pain burned in her side. She stumbled and grabbed her waist.

"Here." MacKay swept up the rock and plopped it in her hand.

It was a compassionate gesture. Kindness was the last thing she wanted from him. She should have thanked him, instead, she flung the rock as hard as she could at Snow. "Go on. Go live your own life."

The big cat turned and slunk back into the forest.

Wynne felt as if someone had grabbed her heart in her chest and wouldn't let go. It made her breathing ragged and a lump formed in her throat. She hadn't wanted to say goodbye this way.

"I don't think she'll be back." MacKay swept Wynne up in his arms.

"I can walk." Wynne managed to get the words past the emotion tightening her throat.

"Sure you can. You're already stumbling around like a Sunday drunk."

She wished she was drunk and he wasn't carrying her. Most men couldn't pick her up like she weighed nothing. In fact it was the first time since she was a child and her father hefted her on his shoulders that any man had carried her. She had always carried herself.

It felt okay. The world didn't end. So she settled into his arms and laid her head on his broad shoulder. Somehow she knew he'd keep his word about Snow. He wasn't all rotten. He'd proven that. Some of the moral principles the orphanage nuns had driven into him must still be embedded in his core. They were just buried beneath his greed.

He reached Wynne's tent and gently laid her down on

the mat next to Aja, who slept. Tungana had bandaged his wound and covered him with a sleeping bag.

A lone gas lantern danced shadows along the canvas walls. For a moment MacKay knelt beside her, his eyes drinking her in.

He looked so handsome, the dim light flitting through his sandy blond hair. He wore tight jeans and a collared camouflage shirt, the short sleeves hugging his thick biceps. The buttons of his shirt were open at the top, exposing the golden hair on his broad chest and the St. Christopher medal. His five o'clock shadow had turned into a caramel-colored beard. Wynne remembered how his beard had felt on her palms and found herself wanting to touch it.

"You'll be okay now," he whispered. His gaze dropped to her lips.

"Right," she said, staring back at his mouth. Okay? She wasn't at all okay. She was remembering their kiss, and so was he. The pitiful thing was if MacKay had asked her to wear that god-awful dress she might have. And she might have willingly taken it off for him, too. If circumstances were different, but they weren't. He was an ex-SEAL, womanizing Texas cowboy crook, and who knew what else? He was the enemy.

"You needn't be afraid of sleeping tonight," he said, his voice husky with tenderness. "I'll be right outside." His gaze moved to her shirt and his brows met over his eyes. "Looks like you're bleeding again. I'll send Tungana in."

Wynne looked down at her shirt and saw a growing spot of blood on the left side. For a moment she'd forgotten about the wound. Now the ache moved up into her solar plexus.

He started to leave, but Wynne grabbed his sleeve.

"Why are you doing this?"

He cupped her chin with his large hand and ran his

thumb over her lower lip and said, "Because, darlin', any woman who kisses like you deserves better than Hellstrom." His expression turned aloof as he pressed a chaste kiss on her forehead, then left.

Such grave resolve on his face. He would keep them safe tonight, thanks to his skewed sense of honor. Tomorrow might be a different story. MacKay had told Hellstrom he was leaving to arrange pickup for the shipment of bush meat. Of course, he'd leave. He wouldn't want to hang around and watch Wynne's and Aja's execution. His moral turpitude was such that he liked to reap the benefits of lawbreaking and murder, but he didn't like to get his hands dirty while doing it. And if he did one moral deed like helping Wynne tonight, then he could justify leaving camp in the morning with a clean conscience.

She felt her forehead still tingling from his kiss and the scratchy sensation his beard had left on her skin…if things were different, but they were not. Not. Not! She felt the pain move up into her throat.

Thunder woke Wynne. It was dark in her tent, but it wasn't nighttime. It must be dawn or close to it. The air was so laden with humidity that she felt bathed by it. She heard male voices outside and running footsteps as if they were scurrying to and fro. She moved her hand and noticed that her hands and feet were manacled. Tungana must have done it during the night at Hellstrom's insistence and MacKay had let him.

She glanced over at Aja. For a moment, she couldn't see his chest moving, and he was as still as a mannequin. Panic grabbed her as she reached toward him.

He moved when she touched his arm, and she let out the breath she'd been holding.

"Wynne Sperling?" He blinked at her and didn't seem able to focus at first. The wrinkles on his forehead deepened.

"It's me."

"The time?"

"Dawn, I think."

"Why *mipashi ya chialo* hasn't struck his killing blow?" He raised his hands and looked at the iron manacles and chain connecting them. It was the kind used in prisons. His wrists were so thin, the shackles hung down on the top of his hands.

Wynne thought of the red dress and MacKay, and said, "He'll get around to it, I'm sure."

Aja glanced about the tent. "Any weapons?"

"I haven't found one yet."

Tungana came in bearing a tray with two bowls of steaming oatmeal, wooden spoons and her boots and socks. He looked at Aja and said, "Hmmm, better today. Eat." He set down the tray and her boots with a plop. "Eat, then dress. We're leaving. Thirty minutes."

"Where're we going?" Wynne asked.

"Safari."

"Where is MacKay?"

"Left early this morning." Tungana scampered out like a busy little mouse.

It didn't surprise her. Hit the highway before things got nasty. She had pegged him perfectly. That didn't stop her from feeling just a little betrayed.

"Why you ask after big one?" Aja grimaced as he sat up and reached over and picked up his bowl. His chains rattled and the bowl wobbled in his shaking hands.

"I had hoped he was our ticket out—"

"But?" Aja's keen eyes stayed on her as he sniffed the oatmeal.

"It was wishful thinking. I expected too much from a criminal."

"You like this big one, don't you?"

"No." She realized she'd almost snarled out the word.

Aja shook his head as if disgusted by her lie, then tipped the bowl so that the oatmeal slid into his mouth. His hands shook and he had a hard time holding the bowl to his lips.

She had no desire for food, but she knew she had to maintain her strength. She slowly sat up and felt something beneath her shirt, pressing against her stomach. Had a snake crawled up next to her to keep warm?

Gingerly she lifted the tail of her shirt. Tungana had wrapped a bandage all the way around her torso, and she saw MacKay had stuffed a man's watch in the folds. She pulled out the waterproof Timex and frowned at it.

"Looks like big one not disappoint you entirely." Aja lowered the bowl and glanced at the timepiece.

"He left me a watch. A watch. A freakin' watch. He could have left me a gun, but no he left me a man's watch. This is one of his jokes. I bet he laughed all the way out of camp."

"He could have left you with nothing."

"True, but if he had any integrity he would have helped us escape and stopped Hellstrom."

She started to toss the watch, but decided she might be able to use it somehow, so she slid it back inside the bandage fold, then picked up the oatmeal as best she could with her chained wrists.

After a moment, Kanopi stepped inside, and pointed his rifle at her, then at Aja. "Up. *Bwana* waiting."

Wynne shoved her feet inside her boots and tied them as best she could, not an easy feat with manacles cutting into her wrists and ankles.

Aja set aside his bowl and tried to stand. Wynne saw him teetering and grabbed his arm.

"Move, hurry." Kanopi jabbed her arm with his rifle.

"Thank you." Aja gave her hand a look that could fry it.

Wynne realized she'd embarrassed him by helping. She dropped his arm and they shuffled forward, their chains rattling in unison.

Thunder rolled again as Wynne and Aja stepped outside the tent. Dark ominous clouds churned in the west.

Hellstrom stood waiting for her, along with ten men, five of whom carried rifles. Kanopi was among the ranks. All the men were burdened by Hellstrom's rifle cases, crates of food, his chair and trunks. Hellstrom wore a fedora, tan walking shorts and shirt. His pistol hung from his hip. He carried her backpack. She noticed he'd left a corner of the red dress hanging out of the top to intimidate her.

She wouldn't let it work. She paused before him with more attitude than she felt at the moment. He looked like a predator who'd found his next meal and he couldn't decide whether to amuse himself with it or make the kill.

"I hope you both slept well." His voice had a saccharine note.

"Just lovely," Wynne said, wondering what malevolence lay behind his good cheer.

"I trust you're both ready to go on this safari."

"What if we said no?"

"I have to admire your sense of humor, Wynne." His gaze dropped to the irons on her hands and feet. "But you don't have a choice."

"I guess I don't."

He fed off the verbal sparring like it was crumpets and clotted cream, his need to dominate glowing in his face. He motioned to the guards, "Let's move out before the rain starts."

They set out on the path that led to the first camp where the mud slide had taken place. Wynne noticed an absence of animal chatter. Either they were leery from the poaching in the area, or something else had frightened them.

Wynne scanned the hills for Snow, but didn't see her. She prayed Snow had stayed away. She thought of Eieb. Had help arrived from the Anti-Crime Commission? Maybe they were just waiting for the right moment to rescue her and Aja? She hoped that was the case.

They followed along the path. When they reached the *dambo,* a flock of doves and lilac-breasted rollers flushed. The whisper of their wings fluttered overhead.

"Be careful here." Hellstrom sounded like the perfect host. "We have snares. Wouldn't want your chains getting in them."

Aja and Wynne shared a meaningful look.

When they reached the second camp, the first thing Wynne took in was her Rover, parked next to one of Hellstrom's Land Cruisers. Hellstrom had found their camp. Had he found Eieb?

Aja noticed it, too. The leathery wrinkles on his brow deepened.

A commotion made Wynne and Aja glance behind them. The poachers they had captured during the undercover sting walked into camp. They still wore camouflage fatigues, and an ivory earring still dangled from the leader's pierced nose and ear.

The poachers saw Aja first and glared at him as if they were remembering he had set them up, then their gaze shifted to Wynne. They had saved all their razor-sharp loathing for her, and if their eyes could shoot bullets, she would be dead. She leveled her most fierce stare back at them for killing Monday Son and escaping camp.

Her gaze shifted to an African, bringing up the rear. He was a tall, lean man with buck teeth. He wore a cap, a loin cloth, and bright colored beads around his neck, wrists, and ankles. When his gaze met Aja's, his eyes widened and he looked as if he'd seen a ghost.

At the sight of the man, Aja's face hardened. He spat on the ground and called the man, "a coward," in Bemba. It was the worst insult one warrior could call another. Aja wasn't done yet, and he cursed the man in an ancient Bemba tongue.

"Shut up, old man." A guard grabbed the chains on Aja's wrist and yanked on them, cutting off Aja's words.

Aja stumbled, but kept his footing, the intense look never leaving his eyes as he kept them fixed on Bucktooth.

Bucktooth shifted nervously from one foot to the other and lowered his gaze. He was visibly trembling now and didn't seem able to look at Aja or anyone else in camp.

Wynne had never seen Aja lose his temper and curse another person. This was a first. Then she put two and two together. Could Bucktooth be the tracker from Chief Chiti-Makulu's tribe? The one Hellstrom had bribed to take him to the scimitar? She saw a brand new Remington Bolt Action rifle hanging from a strap on Bucktooth's shoulder—one of Hellstrom's bribes, no doubt. It would account for Aja's reaction.

Aja glanced at Wynne now and nodded, as if he'd read her mind. Then he motioned with his eyes for her to look closely at Bucktooth.

That's when she noticed his baseball cap—Eieb's Garfield cap. The one she had given him for his birthday. She felt like she'd just nose-dived into a well and left her heart at the top.

Chapter 15

The poachers hurried toward Hellstrom. The leader obviously had lied to Wynne when she'd questioned him. He knew Hellstrom and knew him well if the smile on his face was any indication.

"Well, did you find him?"

The leader spoke first, out of breath. "We found him."

"Where?"

"Several miles away. He didn't get far on that ankle. It was almost too easy." He smiled, his small yellow teeth showing.

"Very good, old chap." Hellstrom pounded him on the back. Then he glanced at Wynne to feed off the hurt and agony that losing a friend had caused her.

Wynne channeled all of her mental powers to keep her expression blank, while inside she screamed. She saw herself hugging Eieb goodbye, feeling him tug on her ponytail, the almost pleading look in his face as he'd asked her to remember to tell Kidaya that he was going to marry her.

"Which one of you killed Monday Son?" She asked, using her best interrogating voice.

"None of us." The leader taunted her with a grin. "Your own man did it."

"Who?"

"Zhieka."

"That is enough discussion." Hellstrom stepped between them. "You." He pointed to the leader. "As soon as the shipment is picked up tomorrow, you dismantle this camp." His gaze grew intense, driving into the leader's eyes. "You understand?"

The leader nodded.

Wynne understood also. The workers in camp would be killed, their payment a bullet.

Hellstrom ordered the men to stow the gear in the Rover and Land Cruiser. Then he grabbed Wynne's arm. "You ride with me."

The moment Wynne felt his hand on her arm, the ache of losing Eieb turned into something alive and writhing. Something horrible was being born in her, clawing, snarling and hating. The *chibanda?* Though she didn't accept Bemba folklore, she imagined this was how evil felt when the *chibanda* entered a person. It urged her to wrap the chains holding her wrists together around Hellstrom's neck and snap it like a twig. Wounded or not, she might have used the last of her strength to do it. But that would mean certain death for Aja. She fought to control her anger. She wouldn't let it take over. If she gave into the feeling, Hellstrom would own a piece of her. She'd be no better than he was. She couldn't let that happen.

Thunder boomed, then the rain pelted them.

Hellstrom jerked her forward toward the Rover. Wynne's fists tightened as she lashed down the urge to strike back.

Rain pelted the Rover as they slowly crept along a trail on the scarp hills, toward Hidden Valley, the same area Aja had taken Wynne to only a few days ago. Hellstrom drove her Rover, while Bucktooth, the guide, showed him the way in the front seat. Kanopi sat in the back seat, his rifle pointed at her, his eyes wary. He sported a black eye and swollen lip, courtesy of MacKay.

She listened to the clicking of the *Simpsons* dolls. At any other time they would have been soothing to her; now they sounded like bones clacking.

She glanced out the window. Below them, along the scarp's rolling foothills, herds of sable antelope and zebra peppered the banks of the Mwaleshi River.

Out of the corner of her eye, she saw the Land Cruiser following them. Aja rode in the backseat, along with three guards. A guard drove while the bearers rode in the cargo hold.

"You needn't keep up the farce of this safari," Wynne said, watching Kanopi's hands tighten around the rifle as he kept an eye on her.

Hellstrom glanced at her in the rearview mirror. "It's not a farce, Wynne. Like I told you, the scimitar exist."

"I hope you're not falling for that Bemba chief's routine. He could make Sir Anthony Hopkins look like a bad actor."

"I grant you the chief is prone to theatrics and the teeth weren't that impressive, but it was the folklore and the carbon dating that actually convinced me. I thought it would convince you, too." He paused and his eyes narrowed slightly. "I'm glad you found the Bemba tribe so quickly, but I anticipated you would. I knew you cared too much about animals not to investigate my claims. And you're nothing if not resourceful."

"By the way, how're your flying buddies?"

"Sadly, they paid the price for bungling the job. But I'm beginning to regret my haste in killing them. Having you as my prisoner has given me an inordinate amount of pleasure."

"I'm so glad I'm here to entertain you." She feigned a smile. "But getting back to the scimitar. I still don't believe these creatures exist. And you can't trust this guy." Wynne glanced at Bucktooth, the Bemba guide. Her eyes went to Eieb's cap and the muscles over her heart clenched. "He'd probably sell his mother for a candy bar."

Bucktooth smiled back at Wynne, unable to understand English.

"He's not so bad. He'll take me to the cats so I can bag one and discover their location."

"And I'm along as part of the cheering squad? That it?"

"I want to see your lovely face when I shoot one just for you."

He wanted to feed off her frustration and anger so he could feel superior. "Don't go out of your way for me."

"I have hopes for you yet." A cynical sneer exposed his teeth.

Wynne decided to take a different tactic in dealing with him. "Don't hope too hard." She kept a question in her voice.

"What do you mean?"

"Your new procurer, that's what I mean."

His golden eyes narrowed a micron. "Please don't tell me you have feelings for that fool."

"I don't know. He kinda grows on you. I like his accent."

"He destroys the English language."

"His words come out pretty syrupy, don't they?"

"Syrupy?" Hellstrom's sangfroid slipped a tad.

"Well, more like poured honey. That must be part of his sex appeal. Yeah, that's it, sex appeal. He's sexy."

"If you like rubes, perhaps."

"If they were all built like MacKay, then it's easy to overlook a little lack of sophistication, don't you think?"

"No bloody excuse for it in my opinion." Hellstrom straightened in the seat, throwing back his shoulders.

"Huh." Wynne shrugged casually, but knew she was chipping away at Hellstrom's confidence. "I guess when you first meet him, he's hard to take, but once you get to know him, he kinda grows on you. And those Brad Pitt eyes. They really are beautiful."

"I hadn't noticed," Hellstrom said softly, his voice barely audible.

"You remember that party of yours. All those ladies flocking around him. He does have a way with the ladies. He really knows how to charm them."

"It's a performance."

"Oh, I know that. But deep down I truly believe he loves the ladies. Some men just love women—"

"He enjoys the gratification he receives from the woman he's with at the moment, perhaps."

"I don't know. You've got to admit his warmth attracts women."

"All women are easily led." He eyed her in the mirror as if he'd lost faith in her, too.

"Jackie must be. I distinctly remember seeing her in MacKay's fan club crowd."

"Jacqueline thought he was a mere curiosity. She'd never met a Texan before."

Wynne forced a smile and kept pouring it on. She was almost believing some of this b.s. herself. "Well, probably not one as smooth as MacKay. I've met politicians that could take lessons from him. And you have to admit he's quick on his feet."

She could see Hellstrom's brow furrow and knew he was remembering MacKay throwing him to the ground.

"I have to admire him. He doesn't sit back and do nothing when a woman is beaten. He jumps right into the fray and stops it." Then he got out of Dodge.

Wynne saw the words hit Hellstrom and knew he was remembering last night. His jaw muscles tightened. The cords in his neck stretched. His knuckles turned white as he gripped the steering wheel. He no longer looked at her in the rearview mirror. Was that humiliation on his face? The lion had been reduced to a cub.

She noticed Eieb's baseball cap sitting at a jaunty angle on Bucktooth's head, and she wanted Hellstrom to feel more than just shame. A lot more.

The Rover's wheels churned and spun. Limbs and leaves made up the primitive road along the scarp hills. The rain had washed most of the debris away, the trail nothing but sludge and the roots of trees clinging to the hill. It rained so hard Wynne could hardly see out of the window. She felt the Rover's back axle grinding in the mud and rocking. They were sitting on a forested hill, almost at a forty-five degree angle. Below them the Mwaleshi River raged, swollen from the rains. Whole trees pulled up by the roots floated like canoes on the surface. Hellstrom gripped the wheel, his jaw set at a determined angle. His mood had darkened since their last conversation, and he'd been taking out his frustration on the Rover.

Bucktooth said, "*Bwana,* stop. Go on foot from here."

"No, we'll make it." Hellstrom floored it.

Kanopi kept glancing out the window at the river, his eyes wide, his hands trembling as he held the rifle. He looked ready to open the door and bolt at any moment.

Wynne glanced at the ravine below them and watched as the angry river ripped off a chunk of the bank. Trees and earth splashed into the water, swallowed by the churning, turbulent swell, then were swept downstream.

"The rain wash out road. Too dangerous."

"We can make it."

"Please stop, *Bwana,*" Kanopi begged, his eyes as big as saucers now.

"Stop your bellyaching."

Wynne spoke over the sound of the rain's drumming, "My Rover digs in, but she can't do miracles in this mud. She's up to her axle now. Park her and we'll walk."

"Quiet!" Hellstrom glared at her in the mirror.

Bucktooth said, "Please. Stop now. I get out."

"Let me out, too," Kanopi said, his voice cracking with fear.

"You're all staying, goddammit!" Hellstrom pushed the accelerator all the way to the floor.

The Rover's engine growled. The *Simpsons* dolls clattered. Then the whole back end fishtailed. Trees cracked as the truck slid down the embankment and lost the last of its footing. Then they were tumbling over and over. Wynne grabbed the seat belt strap and hung on.

Chapter 16

Metal crunched. The Rover rolled over and over like an amusement park ride. Wynne clung to the seatbelt, feeling her body beaten against the roof, the seat. She collided with Kanopi. Several trunks in the cargo hold smashed into her body.

A tree limb burst through her window. She ducked. Glass flew. Branches scratched her face and arms. She lost her hold on the strap and her back crashed against the roof.

The Rover shuddered to an abrupt stop. It landed upside down, Wynne pinned between the roof and one of the trunks.

She could hear the roar of the river and glanced out the rear window. The Rover had landed six feet from the edge of the riverbank, lodged against the trunk of a huge brachystegia tree. The tree was leaning over the riverbank, barely supporting the Rover.

Wynne saw Hellstrom. His cheek was bleeding, but he seemed unharmed. He grabbed his backpack that had fallen next to him on the roof, then kicked out his window. He couldn't get out fast enough and scrambled through the opening like a rat trying to escape a trap. Bucktooth shimmied after him, looking bruised but in one piece. Rain and mud poured in through the broken windows.

Kanopi was beside her, his leg twisted at a broken angle. He seemed half-conscious. Wynne saw his rifle had landed beside her right leg. She reached out, but couldn't get her fingers on it.

It took all of Wynne's strength to shove the trunk off her legs. The trunk hit the roof with a loud thud. She felt the iron manacles cutting into her wrists. The wound in her side didn't feel half as bad now compared to the beating she'd taken in the Rover.

The truck groaned and creaked as it began to slip from the tree.

"Oh, no!" She grabbed the rifle and turned enough to shake Kanopi. "Wake up."

She could have left him, but enemy lines blur when a life was at stake. He probably had a wife and kids. Somebody somewhere loved him. The moment she began to look on human life as cheap would be the moment she would truly bond with Hellstrom. She slapped Kanopi's face a few times.

He roused and looked at her.

"Come on. Can you make it out?"

"My leg."

"Drag yourself. Hurry, this thing is going into the river."

Wynne crawled toward the window on all fours, the chains on her hands and feet making it impossible to move quickly. She wanted to reach for the rifle, but Kanopi wasn't moving fast enough, so she grabbed his shirt collar and pulled him with her.

Screeeeech. The Rover shivered. The *Simpsons* dolls clacked.

She felt the Rover sliding past the tree trunk. A few more inches and the front bumper would be free.

Wynne saw Eieb's baseball cap stuck in a corner of the windshield. She shoved it in her pocket, then slipped out the driver's side window. She turned to help Kanopi but lost her footing in the mud. She grabbed a tree limb to keep from tumbling in the river. It raged so close to them that she could feel the rumble of the rapids in her chest. Rain pelted her face and body.

She squinted and saw Hellstrom and Bucktooth climbing back up the ravine by holding onto tree limbs. They didn't even look back.

Kanopi was just sticking his head through the window, when the Rover shifted.

"Catch my hand," she yelled over the water's roar and the rain. She strained toward Kanopi.

He reached for her hand. Too much distance separated their fingers. The chains...the damn chains. She couldn't let go of the tree or she'd slide into the river.

She watched the Rover break free and jettison into the water.

The river grabbed it and consumed it. Kanopi's face went under, his eyes terrified, his mouth open in a scream. Then the current swept the truck downriver on its side, along with anything else in its path.

She saw Tungana and the guards at the top of the ravine, throwing a rope down to her. They had attached it to the Land Cruiser's winch. Hellstrom sat near a large tree, his legs covered in mud, his chest heaving, his face unreadable.

He seemed unable to glance away from her, as if he were seeing a shadow of himself in the dark and it frightened him.

She grabbed the rope and let the winch pull her up. Her side ached now. Her arms and face were bleeding, and her body felt as if she'd been on the spin cycle in a washing machine for a couple of days. When she reached the top, she collapsed near the Cruiser and let the rain wash over her face and body.

Hellstrom barked, "We'll move out on foot."

Two guards jerked her up.

The other guards pulled Aja out of the Cruiser. The worry on his face dissolved when he looked into her eyes.

She nodded as if to say, "I'm okay."

He motioned back and almost looked proud of her. Then a guard shoved him forward. Four bearers pulled out the safari gear in the cargo hold, divided it among them, then fell in line.

Wynne trudged behind Bucktooth and Hellstrom, fighting the sheets of rain stinging her face. He hadn't looked at anyone, just kept his head down, plowing through the rain.

She realized she was witnessing another side to Hellstrom, the boy sniveling behind his mother's skirt, the man hiding behind the cover of the LZCG so he could build a poaching empire. He was always hiding behind something. Having men killed to protect his identity, letting a man drown that he could have saved but he'd been too worried about his own hide. He'd ordered Eieb killed when he was vulnerable and couldn't protect himself. Deep down Hellstrom was a cowardly lion. He'd hidden it well behind his greed and narcissism, and she hadn't seen it.

The rain had stopped. A thick cover of darkness blanketed the valley. The storm had given way to a brilliant clear sky. Masses of stars winked around a full moon. They had set up camp in a meadow on the edge of Hidden Valley, north of where the airplane had attacked her and Aja. The Lubonga River had crested not far from them, then receded after the rains. Wynne listened to the whisper of waist-high elephant grass as it swayed in the night breeze, shaking off the last bit of moisture. The discordant clank of two puku sparring across the river echoed toward camp.

This setting might have been perfect, if she wasn't sopping wet, in irons and Hellstrom's prisoner. She sat next to Aja on the ground, feeling Eieb's cap pressing against her damp pocket. The sensation was somehow comforting, as if she could look over and see Eieb's grinning face looking at her. God, she would miss him, miss his poor attempts at slang, miss the way he read her so well. He was really the only person she could talk to. Wynne hadn't let herself feel the pain, but now it burned her throat and brought tears to her eyes.

And Snow. She worried about hunters, but Snow had worked alongside Wynne since she was a cub and she'd been shot at more than once by poachers. She knew how to dodge a bullet. Wynne just hadn't wanted to admit that to herself. Still, it didn't keep her from worrying or from feeling that Snow, along with Eieb's death, had somehow taken part of her with them.

Wynne blinked back tears and recalled her promise to Eieb. Would she keep that promise? She didn't know why but her hand felt for the watch. Her wound had started bleeding again, but she hoped Tungana hadn't noticed. The watch was starting to feel like a thorn in her side, reminding her of failure so far. She wanted to fling it into the fire, but the vision of handing it back to MacKay when she arrested him was too overpowering. Nope, she'd keep it. It gave her hope.

She'd taken off her socks and boots to let them dry and dug her toes into the damp grass. She noticed Bucktooth watching her across the fire. She quickly bent and looked engrossed in rubbing her ankles where the iron manacles had pulled away the skin, even though she'd been wearing long pants and socks. The chains on her wrists clunked against the leg irons and sounded like surgical instruments hitting the ground. Her wrists were in no better shape than her ankles, chafed raw. Scrapes and gouges covered her arms, neck and face. But she was glad to still be alive.

Aja had taken off the bandage Tungana had put on his shoulder and he had applied his own form of medicine, the gel from a wild aloe plant. The bullet wound was red, but there was no swelling.

Bucktooth sat away from the guards and bearers, who were huddled on the opposite side of the fire, finishing their meals. Since the river accident she had detected a split in the ranks. The guards and bearers were giving Bucktooth the cold shoulder. Every now and then they'd whisper and look at each other, then glance at her and Aja. Something was amiss.

Only one tent had been left in the Cruiser, the others had been strapped to the Rover's roof and taken a ride down the river with Kanopi. Hellstrom was holed up in the tent now, twenty feet away. Tungana was inside waiting on him. The light inside the tent illuminated his shadow, and she could see him darting around, doing Hellstrom's bidding.

On a safari it was expected that the *bwana* would shoot the meat for the camp's meal, but Hellstrom and Bucktooth hadn't been able to track or kill one animal. And Wynne couldn't have been happier. It only meant Hellstrom was suffering a little reality check, that he wasn't master of the universe.

Wynne saw Tungana hold up the red dress, the outline of it on the canvass made her gut clench. She had wondered what Hellstrom had in mind for retaliation. Now she knew.

One of the guards left the fire and walked toward Wynne. He was of medium height with a bald head. Three earrings hung from his nose. He handed Wynne and Aja several pieces of *nsemwa,* dried sweet potato and two small cans of beans.

He whispered in Bemba, "We saw what you did for Kanopi."

Hellstrom hadn't ordered that she or Aja be fed. Her stomach was so empty it ached, but she had refused to beg for food. Hellstrom would enjoy that too much. But here was this guard, breaking ranks to share his meal. "What is your name?" she asked with genuine warmth in her voice.

"Akid."

"Well, thank you, Akid."

He nodded then backed away from her. She saw that the other guards nodded at her, too.

She acknowledged them.

Aja bit the sweet potato, and said, "You have stolen some of *nkalamo ya musidi's* roar, Wynne Sperling." His dark wrinkled skin glowed bronze in the firelight.

"I doubt that. He still has us in irons. We're still his prisoners. We didn't arrest him with the evidence. He's still going to sell that shipment to MacKay and God knows how many other shipments." Wynne bit off a chunk of sweet potato. She glanced back at the tent and saw the dress hanging against the canvas. Was that a ploy to intimidate her? She swallowed the potato. It stuck in her throat like leather.

"The *mipashi* with us." *Mipashi* were good and benevolent spirits, the antithesis of *chibanda.*

Wynne wished she could buy into his superstitions so easily. "How do you know?"

"*Nkalamo ya musidi* can no longer hunt. His men see his weakness. His *chibanda* no longer strong and *nkalamo ya musidi* only a lion now." Aja frowned, stretching the leathery wrinkles on his face. "He'll not give up his power easily."

"Is that a warning?" Wynne popped the top on her can of beans and ate them with her fingers as the other guards and bearers had done.

Aja nodded, opening his beans, the heavy chains hanging from his wrists clanking against the can. She watched the fire's reflection shifting in his eyes and saw concern building in them.

At that moment, Tungana slipped out of the tent. He walked toward Wynne, his face etched with firm resolve.

Uh-oh. Here we go. Wynne eyed the little man with all the contempt she could muster.

"*BaK para* want you." He pointed at her.

Wynne felt every eye in camp on her. The tension in the air was thick. "Tell Hellstrom that if he wants me, he'll have to come out here and get me."

"Don't you listen? Come now." Tungana motioned wildly at her. "He not in good mood."

"Well, you know what, neither am I."

"Come." He reached down to grab the chain connecting her wrists.

Wynne shifted so he'd have to reach across her to grab them.

He froze, unwilling to cross the imaginary line she'd just drawn.

"That's right. I wouldn't do that if I were you." Wynne warned him with a look. "Didn't I make myself clear?"

Tungana's eyes widened to egg size. He nodded, bit his lip and stepped back from her. "Yes, yes."

"Now go and tell him what I said."

Tungana almost ran back into the tent.

Aja finished his beans and said, "If the lion senses weakness he will attack, remember that lesson?"

Wynne nodded. She remembered it very well. Aja made her track lions as part of her training. She'd accidentally come face-to-face with one in the bush. It had been a heart-stopping moment for her, staring for the first time into the face of a wild lion. She'd seen the ones at her dad's zoo, but it was different facing one in the wild, unfettered by a cage or iron bars. The lion had roared in her face. She had felt his angry bellow rumble inside her chest, looked at his massive fangs, and smelled the feral bloody scent of a fresh kill on his breath. She had wanted to run like hell. But she remembered the lesson, "If the lion senses weakness, he will attack." So she'd forced herself to freeze, to stare into the lion's eyes. She didn't blink until he'd backed away and went to the zebra he'd killed. It was a test of wills. She'd passed by the skin of her teeth, and it had taught her a valuable lesson about bravery, and all the appearances of it.

She saw that the men in camp were watching her with worry and something close to respect. She glanced toward the tent. Hellstrom was moving inside, his silhouette unmistakable behind the canvas. He picked up his pistol, strapped the belt around his hips, then walked out of the tent.

Tension slid along her neck and shoulders as she watched him approach her. He'd shaved and put on a new change of pants and shirt. His belongings must not have gone down river with Kanopi. In the firelight his eyes glinted with a challenging, pitiless light. He reminded Wynne of the lion she had faced. This would be another test of wills.

He pulled his pistol and paused far enough away from

her that he could shoot her before she attacked him. He noticed she and Aja were eating and turned to glower at the men in camp.

They looked everywhere but at him.

"Who fed the prisoners?"

Everyone studied the ground, especially Akid.

Wynne knew Hellstrom would press the issue until he found and shot the guilty man, so she said, "I stole the food. They didn't know I had it until after we'd eaten it."

He spoke without taking his eyes off the men. "I bloody well know you're lying."

"Believe what you like." Wynne shrugged, indifferent. She didn't feel indifferent. Her heart pounded and the smoke from the fire settled in the back of her throat like bile.

His cheeks inflated with anger, moving in and out like the gills of a fish. "I'll find out which one of you did this." He shook the barrel of the gun at them. "I'll brook no insubordination in my ranks. Am I clear?"

They nodded, their gazes disapproving, seeing their leader as the desperate man he'd become. He'd lost their respect and he had only intimidation to get it back.

"Aren't you out here to threaten me?" Wynne asked.

He wheeled to face her. "Bloody right. Tungana said you refused my request."

"That's right." Wynne's gaze shifted between his eyes and the Glock. "I'm not up for your games tonight."

"I've been too patient with you." He pointed the pistol at her. "Now get up."

"I can't." Wynne pointed to the chains binding her ankles. She was sitting with her knees bent in front of her. "They make it impossible to rise from this angle."

He aimed at her heart.

Was this it? So much for Aja's *Mipashi* theory. She'd rather take a bullet now than fulfill Hellstrom's fantasies in that disgusting red dress. She'd never give him that. She wanted to flinch, to cower, but she concentrated on staring into his leonine eyes.

At the last moment he lowered the gun and fired.

Wynne felt bits of grass and wet soil hitting her bare ankles and realized he hadn't hit her. He'd aimed for the chain holding her ankles together.

He fired again, cutting the chain completely in half. "Now, get up."

Could she push him a little more? Rather than lose face in front of his men, he'd probably shoot her. He hadn't realized yet that he already had lost their respect. So she rose and caught Aja's encouraging nod as she walked in front of Hellstrom. The chains dragged between her ankles and sounded like the metallic rattle of nails.

Once inside the tent, Wynne spotted the dress. A stick had been shoved between the spaghetti straps and a piece of twisted reed made up the handle of the makeshift coat hanger. It hung from the center pole, in front of the light, right where Hellstrom had ordered Tungana to place it so she could see the shadow.

She looked around. Only a grass mat on the ground, no mosquito netting, no lawn chairs or radio. Wynne said, "What, no wine?"

"So sorry about that." His voice was as frigid as an iceberg. "Put it on." He motioned toward the dress with the pistol.

"What is it with this dress?"

"And you're going to bloody well put it on, or die now."

"What do you plan to do? Dress up a corpse and get off?"

His eyes narrowed. "Put the dress on."

"Nothing has changed, I'm not putting on this dress." Wynne grabbed the dress and ripped it all the way to the hem.

Hellstrom looked astounded as if he couldn't believe she'd defied him.

"Do you think for one minute I'd enjoy your little fantasy? You must really be insane. I know you now, Hellstrom. You're nothing but a coward—"

His surprise turned to rage and he lunged at her.

Wynne kicked at him, but he was ready for it and grabbed her leg. She fell backward, and he fell on top of her.

"Bitch...you dirty bitch." He slapped her again and again.

Wynne schooled her features into granite. She gritted her teeth, tightened her neck, feeling his powerful hand connecting with her face. She glared at him as she had the lion she had faced...test of wills. Who'd win?

Finally he spent his anger. He glowered down at her. She felt his weight pressing her irons wrist chains into her stomach, her shoulders straining. She couldn't move. Her face stung, and she felt her lip bleeding.

"See, you've gone and made me angry." His rapid breaths burned her face.

"Does that make you feel more like a man?" Wynne asked, her voice ragged. "Like your father. Is this how your father treated your mother while you ran into your closet to hide?"

"Shut up." He grabbed her chin and tried to kiss her.

Wynne spit in his face.

He wiped the bloody spittle from his mouth and nose. "That wasn't very civil."

And using her for a punching bag was? He was trying to change the topic of his parents. It was the heart of his cowardice, shame and anger. The narcissist in him had fought all his life to hide it. She wouldn't let him hide now. "Did you hear your mother getting beaten? Did you want to help her?"

"I wanted to help her, but I couldn't. Like you, she wouldn't cry, and it made him beat her more. She defied him at every turn. That's why he kept beating the hell out of her."

"So he just kept hitting her and hitting her."

"That's right. Hitting her." He gave her face a long measuring once-over. His brows met as if he realized the extent of what he'd just done. He touched her swollen lip, an almost tender emotion in his eyes, the expression of a frightened boy looking at his mother in the aftermath. The face of a man coming to the realization that he'd somehow become his father, a man he hated.

Wynne wanted to wince from the sting of his finger on her lip but wouldn't give in to it. "I won't stop fighting you, either. I'll fight you with my last breath."

His gaze scoured her eyes for a tense moment, then he rolled off her, grabbed the gun where it had fallen in the struggle, and said, "Get out and leave me alone."

Wynne struggled to her feet. She could only walk bent over and staggered out of the tent.

"Tungana," Hellstrom's bellow sounded behind her.

Tungana had been sitting near the fire, eating. He dropped his bean can and ran toward the tent.

Wynne flopped down by the fire, the guards watching her. A ghost of a smile played across Aja's lips. He looked pleased about something.

Tungana ran out of the tent, carrying the torn dress. He tossed it on the fire.

Wynne watched it go up in flames. She might have cheered, but she'd been lucky tonight. She had appealed to the little boy and won a reprieve. When the man took over again and regretted the boy's actions, he'd want to dominate her again. She had to find the right moment to take Hellstrom and his men down. And get back to Hellstrom's central bush meat camp and stop MacKay from picking up that shipment. She remembered her promise to Eieb. Somehow she had to keep that promise.

Chapter 17

Swack, swack, swack. Wynne listened to Bucktooth's machete cutting through the dense foliage. Hellstrom strode behind him, swinging a machete, too, catching the foliage Bucktooth had missed. The force and anger behind Hellstrom's blows made Wynne wonder if he wasn't imagining swinging his knife at her neck. Thankfully, he had ignored her all day.

They'd been walking for several hours in some of the densest woodland Wynne had ever encountered. They were in the deepest heart of Hidden Valley. The Bemba tribe she had visited with Aja lived in the scarp mountains to the west, where it wasn't as dense. This forest was near the foot of the hills at a lower altitude.

The woodland here teemed with life. Exotic parrots squawked from the trees overhead. And a troop of Angola black and white colobus monkeys leaped from limb to limb. They were considered rare in Zambia. A vine snake had curled on a branch, waiting for the rains, and it watched her carefully as she passed by. This forest was an oasis for animals, a pristine vision of how nature could survive when left untouched by man.

Through the leaves overhead, Wynne saw heat lightning flashing on the edges of ragged dark clouds. It would rain again soon. She wiped away the sweat from her forehead and wondered how far they'd walk before Hellstrom tired and made camp?

She glanced behind her at the guards. The bearers brought up the rear, their arms laden with gear and trunks. They'd fallen behind from fatigue. She felt the watch rubbing against her rib and it reminded her MacKay would be picking up that shipment soon. She had to find the moment to make her move.

Ceetik-ceetik. She heard the call of a greater honey bird, a small black-throated gray bird. It had followed them all day. Aja walked in front of her and Wynne bent forward and whispered, "Have you been listening to that honey guide?"

"Yes, but he keeps his distance."

Honey guides led humans to beehives so they could extract the honey, and while the nest was open, the honey bird ate the bees. It was a pretty good setup for the smart little birds, but they could become annoying if someone didn't follow them, calling and flapping in the trees, sometimes swooping near the person.

"It's strange that the guide never came close to us. He's stayed two hundred feet away. That's not like them."

Aja nodded in agreement. "They not timid birds."

"Do you think someone is following us and the bird is following them?"

"Unless honey guide lost his mind, he calls to someone."

Her hope of the Anti-Crime Commission's help had died with Eieb, so she said, "Maybe the Bemba chief is following Bucktooth to exact a little of his own retribution for breaking faith with the tribe." She could only hope for such a diversion.

Aja shook his head. "Chiti-Mukulu believe scimitar will do punishing. It not chief, or his warriors."

Who was the honey guide following then? She glanced once again at the jungle around them, saw nothing strange then asked, "Do the scimitar exist?" Would Aja answer her now? She held her breath waiting.

"You will soon know." He wore that same cryptic look that irritated her.

A roar rebounded through the forest. Birds fluttered up from the trees. The monkeys disappeared behind leaf cover. Wynne froze in the deathly silence, her heart still feeling the rumble. She had heard plenty of lions before, but this roar sounded like cannon fire. It couldn't be a scimitar, could it? She glanced at Aja for confirmation. He wore a gloating expression. She had her answer. Her gaze combed the dense forest for signs of movement.

Nothing but tree trunks and vegetation.

Bucktooth held up his hand for silence. The machete wobbled in his trembling hand. His gaze shifted in all directions, and his eyes were huge with terror.

A wide smile split Hellstrom's lips. His gaze trolled the forest for his prey.

After the heart-stopping moment, Bucktooth seemed unable to rein in his fear any longer. He dropped the machete, wheeled around and bolted down the path.

Hellstrom tackled him near Wynne's feet, wrenched him in a headlock, and put his gun to his head. "Where do you think you're going?"

Though Bucktooth had the Remington draped across his chest, he seemed to have forgotten it was there. "That warning. No go near *mweo mfumu*." Perspiration broke out on his forehead.

"I paid you to guide me to the bloody cats and that's what you're going to do." He shoved Bucktooth forward, then motioned to one of the bearers to bring him his rifle case.

He extracted a .300 Weatherby. The rifle was a powerful hunting weapon, but could it bring down the magnificent creature Wynne had heard? She prayed not. She couldn't allow Hellstrom to kill one of them and profit from its death.

Bucktooth slipped the machete back into the sheath hanging from his waist, then began walking again, a strangle hold on his Remington rifle.

Hellstrom grabbed Wynne and shoved her ahead of him. "Ladies first."

It was rare when Wynne didn't feel at home in a forest, but having never encountered these animals, she didn't know what to expect. Their musky scent where they'd marked their territory permeated the air. It smelled like a regular lion's scent only more potent. The odor stimulated a primitive flight or fight response in her, and she felt the hairs on the back of her neck tingling. As she walked behind the guide, she could almost believe these animals had avoided man and survived because they had some other-worldly power granted to them by the jungle. Her chains and Aja's rattled like leaky pipes in the silence. She thought Aja was rattling his on purpose.

Bucktooth stopped and pointed at them. "Chains have to go."

Hellstrom motioned for Tungana. "Take them off."

Tungana unlocked Wynne's manacles first. Then Aja's. Wynne rubbed the abrasions on her wrists.

"One wrong move and you're both dead. Get moving."
Hellstrom motioned them forward with the rifle.

"Silence now." Bucktooth warned everyone with a
glower, then he moved deeper into the forest. He paused to
sniff what looked like lion spoor and to examine several broken branches, then he gulped and moved toward a stream.

He followed the stream, up a steep embankment. The
land became rocky, the thick vegetation butting right up to
the rocks.

Wynne thought she heard the soft pad of footsteps, but
when she glanced around…

Nothing.

She didn't hear the honey guide, either. She had never
heard the forest this quiet. There was an eeriness about it
that made a shiver go down her spine. She could almost
feel the scimitar's eyes on her.

Bucktooth came to the crest of a twenty-foot waterfall.
Rocks protruded on either side and sloped down a ravine
to a crystal-clear blue pool. He squatted behind a rock and
motioned for everyone to stop. He pointed to the waterfall
and mouthed. *"Mweo mfumu."*

Wynne glanced beyond his shoulder to a rocky ledge behind the falls, and got her first glimpse of a scimitar.

Wynne stared, openmouthed at a female and cub as they
sauntered along the ledge. The cub shook off the spray
from the falls. The water cascaded down to the pool below,
but only the spray touched the ledge where mother and cub
walked. The ledge seemed to extend the length of the falls.
Was their den hidden behind the wall of water in a cavern?

Bulkier than a lion and several hundred pounds worth
of muscle heavier, the female scimitar was a magnificent
predator. It shared the same markings and color of a lion,

golden with a white blaze on her chest. A tuft of fur formed a point on the tips of her ears like a mountain lion. But it was those large fangs, the weaponry of a killing machine, from which Wynne could not look away.

A recent kill, a civet cat, swayed in the female's jaws. The scimitar's massive mouth encompassed almost all on the long-haired, thick body of the civet. Wynne could only see the civet's striped black legs and head.

The cub smelled the kill and tugged at its leg. The mother plopped the civet in front of the cub and the hungry youngster ripped into the meat.

It was amazing to watch the cub eat with its elongated fangs. It chewed food more with its center teeth.

The mother raised her nose and scented the air. She caught a whiff of human, glanced toward Wynne, then grabbed the cub by its neck. Amazingly she caught the cub between those long fangs and the youngster dangled by its neck as she retreated back behind the waterfall, most likely to a cavern hidden by the water. The cub was not happy at losing a meal and growled and snarled at its mother.

Wynne realized she had witnessed a wonder of nature, a living fossil thought extinct since the Ice Age. It was believed scimitars only existed on the North American continent and Europe. But here they were, contrary to the pretentious, dogmatic, scientific understanding of man, beautiful living specimens in Africa, the Cradle of All Life. Nature had a way of astounding and humbling man and she was witnessing it.

Wynne saw that Hellstrom stood speechless beside her, caught by the wonder of the animals. After a moment his golden eyes seemed to blaze with greed, calculating the amount of money to be made off the cats. It was eerie, but his eyes resembled those of the scimitar. He clutched the rifle and started toward the cavern.

"Don't go down," Bucktooth grabbed Hellstrom's arm.

"I can't shoot the bloody thing up here, you fool," Hellstrom whispered. "And you're going with me."

Wynne wasn't about to let him shoot the scimitar. She caught movement to her left and was startled to see MacKay creeping toward the guards. He had his pistol drawn and a knife between his teeth. He wore camouflaged pants, but no shirt. His face and upper body were painted jungle green and brown. His hair was muddy. He looked like a stunt double off the set of *Predator*. The down-home persona was gone. It was scary seeing the cold hard battle expression on his face. MacKay? Was he helping her?

She looked at Aja in a silent communication. Aja saw MacKay. The bearers saw him too and dropped baskets and trunks and ran for cover.

Aja attacked the guard behind him.

MacKay charged into the other guards. Akid turned and punched the guard next to him in the mouth. He was helping MacKay.

Bent on killing the scimitar, Hellstrom hadn't noticed what was happening until it was too late. He was already climbing down the side of the waterfall. Bucktooth was in front of him.

Wynne dived on Hellstrom from behind.

She and Hellstrom tumbled down the rocks. They plowed into Bucktooth and he plummeted with them. Jagged edges pounded her body, but she held on to Hellstrom's neck. They landed at the base of a large boulder near the pool.

Hellstrom had a death grip on the rifle and thrust the stock at her head.

She dodged the thrust, but he came across with his fist and hit her jaw. She lost her grip on his neck.

He scrambled to his feet. "Bitch," he yelled over the roar of the falls. "You're dead."

He raised the rifle to shoot her.

Wynne glimpsed a massive blur of gold, fangs and claws before the male scimitar attacked Hellstrom. The rifle fell from his hands as the huge cat knocked him over and went for his jugular.

Hellstrom's scream died in his throat.

Wynne heard bone and flesh tearing from the savage power as the animal protected its den. Hellstrom was way beyond her help. She backed slowly away, feeling her legs and arms trembling, her heart pounding against her chest. If the scimitar noticed her, he'd charge. She stepped past Bucktooth, who didn't stir. His neck was at an unhealthy angle. The chief's words came back to her, "If you go to the *mweo mfumu* with evil in your heart, you die." It almost made her a believer. Almost.

She reached the boulders bordering the falls and MacKay stood there waiting for her. He reached down from the boulder above and grabbed her hand.

He pulled her up and whispered, "Can you climb?"

"Try and stop me."

He nodded and waited for her to go first, then they wasted no time in getting to the top of the falls. Wynne couldn't look down. She felt only relief that Hellstrom was dead; the boy he once was she could almost mourn.

The bearers and the guards were already bound. Some of the guards had battered faces and cuts on their cheeks and hands. Aja and Akid were hurrying them into the forest, away from the scimitar den. Tungana held the guards' rifles and scurried behind them, looking back at the falls, his face a mask of terror.

Wynne and MacKay trailed them.

She watched MacKay's muscles rippling beneath the leather shoulder holster strung across his back as he moved through the woods. The green and brown paint he'd used on his body gleamed over the contoured ridges of his muscular back. His back looked like a taut mountain range, and she tried not to recall rubbing his back and how it felt beneath her palms.

"You owe me a big time explanation, Lone Star," Wynne whispered at his broad back.

"You got one coming, darlin'." He glanced over his shoulder and winked at her, his eyes full of devilment. A lazy sensual grin turned up the corners of his mouth, then he turned back around.

Was that look just another come on? She couldn't forget his scathing words when talking about her, "She ain't bad to look at, but she's not my type. Too bossy, and a damned cold fish. Gotta be Rambo's sister to live like she does out in the bush. I like my women warm, soft and giving." Suddenly her body ached all over and the bullet wound in her side was throbbing.

When they were several miles away, Wynne grabbed MacKay's bicep. It was like grabbing a supersized softball. She could only get her hand halfway around it. "Okay, spill the truth," she said, pausing.

He wheeled and faced her. "What do you want to know?"

She realized she was still holding his arm and dropped it. "You can start with who you are." Even behind the green and brown paint and the mud he'd slathered on his hair for camouflage, he looked wickedly handsome. The front of his chest was better than the back, and she couldn't take her eyes off his pecs or the six pack along his stomach. Abruptly the distance between them seemed to close in, and she forced her eyes to his face.

"All righty then. I'm a bounty hunter who works undercover to stop poaching. Right now I'm under contract with President Mwiinga."

"You're working for the president?" Wynne wanted to punch him for good measure. "Why didn't you tell me?"

"I didn't know if I could trust you."

"So that's why you were hitting on me?" Nothing like point-blank bluntness. Well, she had to know didn't she? And she was tired of being a pawn.

He shrugged as if it was an everyday occurrence to seduce women. "I knew Hellstrom and Kaweki were dirty. I didn't know if you were, too."

"So you tried to get close to me to find out what I knew and rule me out as a suspect." She jammed her fists on her hips.

"Pretty much. When I first met you, I gotta say, you were coming on strong to Hellstrom."

"I was only trying to find out if my suspicions about him were correct." Wynne stepped closer to him.

"I realized that after you stormed Hellstrom's camp."

"But you still didn't tell me."

"I couldn't risk breaking my cover. I was too close to infiltrating his operation. He has poachers working for him all over Africa. I know of at least eight camps operating right here in Zambia."

Wynne felt sick at hearing the number. "How did Mwiinga hire you?"

"He learned of Hellstrom's bush meat poaching through one of the LZCG board members."

"Which one?"

"Mwiinga wouldn't say. It seemed it was a person who regularly reports to him. I hear he has informants in a lot of places throughout the country."

Wynne wondered which of the board had ratted on Hellstrom. They deserved a medal. "How did the board member find out about his poaching?"

"Evidently he was skimming money from the trust."

Wynne wasn't surprised at Hellstrom's greed. "So that night I found you at Sausage Tree Camp, you were looking for poachers."

"That's right. I knew about the shipment and wanted to learn how Hellstrom moved the meat and who was involved. And I found you there. Another reason I couldn't trust you."

She could understand his caution. "What's your real name?"

"Jackson Garrison."

"Jackson. Oh, I get it. Jack came from Jackson."

"Right. You don't sound as if you like my first name." He looked as if he almost cared what she thought.

"You look more like a MacKay."

"Call me anything you like, darlin'. It really doesn't matter."

Why should it? He was going his way and she would be going hers. "And I guess that stuff about the orphanage was all lies."

"No, that's pretty much the truth about my childhood. I found it hard to lie to you." His eyes twinkled with a playful light.

Why didn't he control those flirting looks? He probably couldn't. He was like a wind-up toy around women. Flirt. Look handsome. Call her darlin'. She saw that the others were about two hundred yards ahead and she began walking, feeling uncomfortable now at the way he eyed her.

She heard his light footsteps fall in behind her, and asked, "I guess that freaking out episode in the clinic was fake, too?"

"It was real. What about that kiss of yours, was that real?"

God, he had to bring that up. "I was just playing you to find out what you were doing with Hellstrom?"

"Got it." Was there disappointment in his voice?

She quickly changed the subject. "So how did you get into the bounty hunting business." She knew he hadn't been lying about being an ex-SEAL. She kept walking back along the path Bucktooth and Hellstrom had cut earlier, not looking at him.

"I came over here about five years ago on a hunting safari. I saw the corruption in the game-managed areas. The scouts could be bought for hardly nothing. They weren't doing their jobs, allowing poachers to kill unchecked." His voice turned thoughtful. "We had to drive for days to find animals to hunt. I knew I had to do something to stop it. So I formed the African Wildlife Trust, an antipoaching organization. I'm based in Dallas."

"And you make your living doing this?" Wynne found it hard to believe as poor as Zambia and a lot of African countries were that he made enough money to live on and cover his travel expenses.

"Not really. I got a hankering to look up my parents, to find out why they gave me away. I came across my real great-aunt. Lived right outside of Lubbock." He cleared his throat as though the memory bothered him. "Anyway, she didn't have any family and she told me I was her niece's baby. My mother was sixteen when she had me, so she gave me away." His words trailed off, caught on a tide of emotion.

Wynne kept walking, listening to his heavy footfalls behind her. She didn't want to see the sorrow on his face, because she would want to comfort him.

After a moment he continued. "My aunt died a while back and left me her oil rights and her mansion. I do okay."

Okay? He must be a millionaire. "What about your mother?"

"Died of breast cancer when she was forty. Her aunt was the last of my family. I always wanted a family, though. Hope to settle down and have one some day."

Did he have a fiancée back in Texas? She wanted to ask, but what difference did it make. That was his personal life, and she wouldn't delve any deeper in it. She already knew too much about him as it was. Wynne frowned and said, "There are some papers in Hellstrom's office that you might want to give Mwiinga. Hellstrom was shipping the meat all over the world."

"You found those, too?"

"I guess you got there before me."

"Found them the first night in Hellstrom's compound." A teasing grin pulled at his mouth. "The police already have them."

"Oh." Wynne hesitated a moment, then she asked about what was really bothering her. "Why did you leave me and not help me escape Hellstrom?"

"Didn't want to blow my cover. I had to get backup and contact Mwiinga—by the way, I came across some officers with the Anti-Crime Commission. They helped me secure both poaching camps and the bush meat cave operation. We've got a lot of men to interrogate."

"But you could have left me with a weapon, at least."

"I did. Akid can be a pretty handy weapon. He was an Army ranger, until he came to work for me. I knew he'd make sure nothing happened to you. And if Hellstrom was correct about the scimitar, I knew you, Akid and Aja could protect them."

"And why'd you leave me the watch?"

"An added precaution. I wanted to track you."

"The watch has a tracking device in it?"

He nodded. "State of the art."

"How did you know I'd keep it?" Wynne turned to glower at him.

"Ain't seen a woman yet that didn't like to hang on to jewelry."

"It's a man's watch." Her words flew out like darts.

"Still practical. You don't seem like the pink frilly type to me." A sultry grin curved his lips.

"I can be frilly."

"Now that is rich." He looked amused.

Not frilly? A man's watch? If she were being honest, she might have bought a watch like that for working out in the bush. Still, not frilly? She could be feminine. She could be frilly. He had the insight of a trash can lid. She jerked up her shirt and snatched out the watch. She slapped it in his hand. "Thanks, I don't need it now."

"You're bleeding." He reached to touch her wound. "We should get that looked at."

She was bleeding but it wasn't from the bullet wound. She knocked his hand away. "I'll take care of it when I get back to camp."

She almost jogged down the trail to get away from him. She was good at keeping her distance. Hadn't she kept her distance from her mother? From men? Now she knew just what he thought of her. Why did it make her feel like she'd failed some kind of MacKay femininity test. God, if any test should be easy to win it would be MacKay's—or whatever his name was. He didn't discriminate when it came to women. He'd jump anything that wasn't cold yet. She didn't care, she told herself, she'd never see him again. Let him take his test and stick

it right back in Texas. She'd survive, like she had survived her life in Africa, despite her mother's lack of faith
in her.

Wynne and Garrison—she couldn't get used to his real
name—hadn't spoken since the frilly conversation. They
came to the area where Kanopi had lost his life and Hellstrom had left his Land Cruiser. The river was five feet
lower and calmer now. She noticed a Hummer parked behind the Cruiser. It must be Garrison's.

Garrison strode up to Akid and Aja and said, "The prisoners will ride with me."

Hellstrom's men obediently slipped into the back of the
Hummer.

Wynne walked up to Garrison. He didn't have that lover
boy persona in place. It was as if the disclosure of his real
name had turned him into an entirely different man. A sto-
ical look hardened the handsome edges of his face. "What
are you going to do with these men?" she asked. "They
know about the scimitar."

"I'm arresting them."

"I can't have them blabbing about what they saw."

"You want me to get rid of them?" He frowned at her.

"No, I've got a better idea." Wynne stuck her head in and
looked at the eleven men, twelve counting Tungana. "We'll
be needing help back in my base camp. I'll see you're not
arrested and that you'll all have jobs, but you must keep
silent about the big cats. Can I trust you?" She wasn't
naive enough to believe they would stay silent forever, but
she could keep an eye on them in camp.

They looked at each other, then back at her, then they
nodded in unison.

"Good." She turned back to Garrison. "If you don't mind, drop them at base camp."

"You sure about that?"

"Yes."

"I guess this is where we part company," Wynne said.

"Yeah." He slapped a piece of paper in her hand. "There's a surprise waiting for you there."

She opened up the paper and read an address in Lusaka. It didn't seem familiar to her. "What is it?"

"Wouldn't be a surprise if I told you." He motioned to Hellstrom's Cruiser. "I hotwired it. All you need to do is touch the wires together to get it going."

"Okay." She paused. "Can I trust you not to say anything about the scimitar?"

"The what?" A sly grin twisted a corner of his mouth.

Wynne looked into those liquid blue eyes. They gave away nothing. "I didn't say thank you. Thank you."

His smile faded. "You didn't have to." He turned and hopped into the Hummer.

No "darlin'." She missed hearing it roll off his tongue. She felt a tightening in her chest and throat. She walked over to Aja and her voice cracked with emotion, "We need to see the Bemba chief again. I need to speak to him about moving the scimitar to protect them." They had kept the scimitar safe from man for thousands of years, and she hoped they would help her protect them in the future.

Aja looked at her. "That what troubles you?"

"Yes." Wynne heard the Hummer start up and she watched Garrison turn it around. He didn't look her way. "Do you think I can convince the chief to help me?"

"I do not know."

Wynne strode toward the Cruiser, forcing herself to forget Garrison. She had the scimitar to think about, not some Texas playboy who had two-stepped into her life, made her care about him, then just left. No goodbye. Not a glance. He was an expert at leaving, too.

She saw something white flash near the Cruiser, and Snow appeared. Wynne's joy at seeing Snow brought a wide smile to her face, though she didn't feel at all like smiling. The big cat bounded toward Wynne and leaped up on her shoulders. Wynne hugged the cat around her neck and buried her face in the soft fur of Snow's neck. Tears stung her eyes. She didn't know if they were from her happiness at finding Snow unharmed, or from Garrison's departure.

Chapter 18

A week later Wynne walked down the Men's ward in the University Teaching Hospital in Lusaka and discovered her surprise. Rows of beds lined the walls and her eyes scanned the patients until...

Eieb glanced up at her. His eyes looked heavy with sedation, a bandage covered his head and chest, and IV poles and tubes draped his bed, but he was smiling at her. And he was alive.

At the sight of him, joy filled Wynne's heart. She sorely regretted the choice names she'd called Garrison in the past week. She hadn't heard squat from him. Not a call. A letter. Nada. She had wondered many times during the week whether he'd meant what he said about her to Hellstrom, or if he had been hamming it up for Hellstrom. Now she was growing more convinced that he had meant every word. Did he even think of her as much as she thought of him?

Eieb took in her black skirt and her white peasant shirt and a broad grin broke out on his face. "Ohhh, woman, you are getting jiggy with it."

He'd gotten it right. Wynne smiled and felt a blush sting her cheeks. If he was teasing her, everyone in camp would. "It's a different look for me," she said flatly.

"I have never seen you in a skirt. Did you think I'd died and you were coming to my funeral? Is that it?"

"Very funny. I see you're not too sick to joke around." Wynne grinned and pecked him on the cheek.

"Did something happen I need to know about, young lady?"

Not frilly. A man's watch. She didn't pass the test. That's what happened. "Nothing," she said.

"Something happened. You're not the same Wynne I knew."

She beamed a smile at him, emotion in her voice. "When I heard Hellstrom's thugs say they'd killed you, I thought you were gone."

"It's amazing, isn't it? I did, too. If Garrison hadn't found me—"

"He found you?"

"He didn't tell you?"

"No. He just said there was a surprise here for me. I didn't know you were here until the hospital called trying to locate your family."

"I would have died if he hadn't found me. Those three goons who broke out of jail shot me in the chest. Garrison found me and piloted me here in his helicopter."

"Helicopter?" Wynne frowned. She wasn't that surprised. Every time she turned around she found out something new about him.

"He owns an airplane, too."

"Oh." Wynne felt a little annoyed that Eieb knew more about him than she did, then chided herself for it. She was just glad Eieb was alive.

"So did you tie up all the loose ends with Hellstrom's ring?"

"Everyone's facing charges here in Lusaka. I wish you could have been there when they slapped the handcuffs on Zhieka and Kaweki. President Mwiinga was there, too."

"Was he?" Eieb's eyes brightened.

"Oh, yeah. And the press." Wynne handed him the *Times of Zambia.* Mwiinga stood next to a handcuffed Kaweki. The headline read, "President Thwarts International Bush Meat Ring."

"Ah, he did it all alone." Eieb read the headline. "Odd, I did not see him with us."

"Can't deny the man his free press. I didn't mind. Technically, Garrison worked for Mwiinga. Without his help, we wouldn't have arrested all the poachers involved here in Zambia."

"There are more?" Eieb frowned, the wrinkles on his brow disappearing beneath his bandage.

"Hellstrom had poachers all over Africa." Wynne said. "Mwiinga had all of Hellstrom's assets here in Zambia confiscated and they found evidence that he was not only into bush meat and ivory poaching, but he was also exporting exotic animals."

"I know."

"You do?" She looked puzzled.

"Yes, Garrison told me."

"You've seen him?"

"He called to see how I was doing. He's a stand-down guy. He told me he was in Zimbabwe following leads he'd gleaned from interrogating the poachers the government arrested."

She was going to correct Eieb's misuse of stand-up, but she suddenly felt deflated. Nice of Garrison to call someone.

"He also told me you were running things in base camp now." Eieb dropped the newspaper on his chest.

"Yeah, I got Kaweki's job and cleaned house. Every ranger there knows what will happen if they take bribes." Wynne had hired the guards who had worked for Hellstrom and hoped they kept their word. "Things will be different now. We'll have more patrols. The LZCG has already promised to help me find funding for a DNA lab—"

"You are not going to be one of those nagging female bosses."

"I'll only require of my employees what I require from myself."

"You'll work us all to death."

Wynne grinned at him. "I can't wait to have you back."

"What about the scimitar? Do they exist?"

Wynne hoped Eieb didn't hate her one day for the answer she was about to give him, but the fewer people who knew about the scimitar the better. She had talked the Bemba chief into helping her relocate the cats and they had found almost an identical cavern upstream. Only she, Aja, and the Bemba knew the location, and Wynne trusted the chief would help her keep them safe.

"No, they don't exist," she said, hoping she'd covered the lie in her voice. "Oh, I forgot." She pulled his Garfield cap out of her pocket book. "Here. I was going to give this to Kidaya, when I thought you'd died, but you can give it to her yourself."

Wynne glanced up and saw Kidaya standing in the ward doorway. She wore a bright pink sundress with white stripes. She looked shyly toward Eieb and nervously rubbed her hands. Wynne motioned her to come in.

Tears glistened in Eieb's eyes as he turned the cap over in his hands, then he blinked up at her. "I thought this was lost."

"Funny how things turn up." Wynne grinned at him, and as she looked into the glowing face she thought she'd never see again, she knew Garrison had given her a gift she could never repay. She moved aside as Kidaya came to stand near Eieb's bed.

"Eya mukwai," Kidaya said, then bent and kissed Eieb. Her lips lingered on Eieb's mouth in a tender kiss.

Their relationship might have begun out of Eieb's sense of guilt at killing Mehan, but no two people seemed more suited to each other. Kidaya would make him a good wife. And she needed a husband to provide for her children. There wasn't a better man than Eieb. He'd have the family he wanted. Sometimes fate got it right.

Wynne left them alone and headed down the corridor, aware of the patients who were awake and watching her, yet she felt utterly alone. She glanced back and saw Eieb take Kidaya's hands. They were smiling, their eyes full of each other. Wynne's loneliness turned into emptiness.

Three weeks later, Wynne stood before the House of Representatives of the United States. A sea of faces stared at her. Along the gallery were spectators, world dignitaries, and board members from almost every ecological society in the world. It seemed everyone who cared about animals and the environment had put in an appearance. The lobbyists had certainly done their job.

She had approached the World Fund for Animals in hopes of getting funding for her DNA lab and struck up a friendship with the President of WFA. He'd asked her to speak before the House because she was so dedicated and had practical experience out in the field. So here she was, standing on the speaker's dais, staring at hundreds of people, almost at the end of her speech. At first she had been terrified out of her wits, but once she had begun speaking, she had forgotten about her own discomfort and thought only of the wild animals she was here to save. And no one had fallen asleep yet. Always a good sign. If she pulled this off maybe she could get more funding.

She finished her last comment on the statistical data of bush meat poaching, then glanced at the massive screen next to her. A slide she had taken at Hellstrom's cave was splayed across it. The picture showed a herd of zebra carcasses, vultures picking at the leftover skin and bones. She clicked on her PowerPoint presentation and another slide popped up, one of people on a photography safari in Zambia.

She concluded with, "So you see, developing countries could realize a far more lucrative profit by keeping wildlife alive rather than allowing them to be slaughtered for bush meat. Kenya is a prime example. They have done an excellent job in policing poachers and have made millions of dollars on their tourism trade.

"I'm asking you, ladies and gentleman, to put the pressure on our American delegates at the United Nations Convention for International Trade in Endangered Species. As you know, they will meet in Bangkok in October of this year. We need an amendment that will create a worldwide policing organization that can end bush meat poaching and sales and educate the people of these developing countries about alternative protein sources and the benefits of tourism. Save our wildlife. Save our future.

"I'll leave you with the words of American Indian Chief Seattle:

'All things are connected. Whatever befalls the earth befalls the sons of the earth. Man did not weave the web of life. He is merely a strand in it. Whatever he does to the web, he does to himself.'"

Wynne glanced out at the sea of faces.

Silence.

Not a paper rustle. Not a cough. Complete and utter silence. The kind of silence that could break a comedian. Then someone in the balcony began clapping. Wynne glanced up and saw Maria Van Warren-Sperling. Her mother was wearing a beige suit, tailored to her body, not a wrinkle anywhere. Diamonds sparkled around her neck, ears, and wrist. She gazed at Wynne with large hazel eyes, so much like her own. Her mother stood up and was actually smiling now and clapping. For her. The rogue daughter.

Cody was with her mother and stood up, too, applauding. She was a miniature version of Wynne, her blond hair falling straight to her shoulders. She was wearing gold-rim glasses now, a new distinguished-college-student look for her. The kids at the Habitat had made Cody a set of African beads for her fudge and clothes donations, and the bright beads draped her neck. She gave Wynne a thumbs-up.

Wynne returned it.

A wave of applause sifted over the rotunda, then grew to a roar.

Cody put her fingers in her mouth and gave out a whistle. Wynne saw her mother lean over and admonish Cody.

Wynne grinned. Her mother had come to hear her. Her mother. She felt a wave of warmth spreading through her, and a realization that she'd missed Maria Van Warren-Sperling. Terribly. Even though they were like oil and water, Wynne had missed her.

* * *

Wynne waited for her mother and Cody on the Capitol steps, getting cautious glances from the guards posted at the doors.

Suddenly Cody walked through the doors. A smile bright enough to light up the whole city flashed on her face as she bounded toward Wynne. She flung her arms around Wynne's neck. "I'm so glad you're home—oh, man, you looked great up there."

"Thanks, kiddo." Wynne hugged Cody back, breathing in the herbal scent of her hair. It felt so good to hug her sister again.

"You were fantastic, Wynnie. I couldn't believe that was you down there. You gave them hell. Way to go." Some of the exuberance on Cody's face waned. "Dad wanted to come, but he called me and said he had emergency surgery at the zoo."

Wynne wished he had come, but she knew he was there in spirit. "I'll see him tonight at dinner," she said.

Cody stepped back from Wynne, far enough to survey Wynne's black business suit. "You've gone establishment on me."

Wynne pulled at Cody's baggy World Wildlife Fund T-shirt. "I'd prefer to be wearing this, but it isn't everyday I address Congress. And I thought I'd at least try for presentable."

"You look great." Cody grimaced at her T-shirt and jeans. "I, on the other hand, didn't pass muster this morning."

At that moment, Wynne saw her mother standing in front of the doors, watching her and Cody. There was the usual severity in her demeanor, but she also appeared self-conscious. Her hazel eyes warily surveying Wynne before she walked over and joined them.

"Hello, Wynne," she said, a current brewing under her voice.

"Mom."

"You'll be staying at home for a few days before you leave?" Her voice had a courtroom interrogating authority in it.

"Okay, sure." Wynne couldn't say no to the demand.

Her mother's lips thinned. She fought with some kind of inner turmoil for a few seconds, then her self-command took on several more coats of armor. She stared hard at Wynne and blurted, "You scared the life out of me. Do you know that? My God, I thought you'd died."

"You did?"

"Don't act so innocent. When I got that letter from the embassy, I almost went crazy."

"They weren't supposed to mail it unless something happened." Wynne grimaced. "I'm sorry."

"You damn well should be." She grabbed Wynne and hugged her, her voice never losing its direct quality. "I thought I wouldn't get to say goodbye, or tell you I love you, or how proud I am of you."

Wynne couldn't remember the last time they'd hugged. Her mother loved her. She was proud of her. And as she held this petite woman who'd been like a stranger to her all her life, Wynne felt the strength within her. It defined Maria Van Warren-Sperling. It's what Wynne admired most about her—no, loved about her.

"Look's like I'm late for something."

Wynne jumped at the deep sensual voice. It was the last voice she ever expected to hear.

She glanced over her mother's shoulder and saw Garrison grinning at her. He was wearing tight jeans, a chambray blue shirt, his gold-toed cowboy boots, and a cowboy hat. The afternoon sun reflected in his blue eyes like cut glass. He couldn't have been more handsome had he been the poster model for a Texas tourism ad.

Wynne and her mother separated.

Cody saw Garrison and grinned. "Do we know you, Mr. Cowboy?"

"I'm a friend of Wynne's. The name's Jackson Garrison, ma'am." He extended his hand. "And you are?"

"Cody, the little sister."

"You don't look too little to me, darlin'." He graced her with one of his lady-killer grins, dimples and white teeth flashing.

Cody took his hand and seemed to melt. "Where's Wynne been keeping you?" She turned to Wynne and mouthed, "You didn't tell me about him."

Wynne ignored her. "Mom, this is someone I know from Africa."

Her mother took in his clothes and didn't seem to approve. "You look like you have a lot of catching up to do. We'll see you at home, Wynne."

Wynne's mother grabbed Cody's arm and pulled her down the steps. Cody kept eyeing Garrison as if she couldn't take her eyes off him.

"What are you doing here?" Wynne asked, feeling embarrassed now and awkward around him.

"I had to hear you speak to Congress." He checked her out in the suit.

Wynne felt suddenly self-conscious and a blush stung her cheeks. "How did you know I'd be here?" she asked, trying not to look at his eyes.

"I spoke to Eieb."

He hadn't said a word. Some friend. These days he was preoccupied with Kidaya. Wynne could forgive him.

"You look very nice today."

"Thanks." She saw his eyes undressing her, and a hot ache began building inside her. She could almost feel his hands on her body.

They lapsed into an uncomfortable silence.

"I should get going," Wynne said, ready to escape.

"Wait a minute." Garrison grabbed her and pulled her into his arms. "I'm not letting you go as easily as I did in Africa, darlin'," he said, the blue in his eyes deepening.

It felt nice to be in his arms. Nice to be called darlin' again. "I could make you let me go," she taunted.

"You could try," he said, a velvety roughness in his words.

"You sound pretty confident there, Lone Star."

"Damn straight, when it comes to something I want. Nobody keeps me from it. We've got unfinished business, darlin'."

"We do?"

"Oh, yeah." He bent and kissed her, languorous at first as if he were savoring the taste of her mouth. Then he deepened the kiss.

Wynne felt the heat of it all the way to her knees. The power of it sucked her breath away and made her heart pound against her ribs. His tongue dove into her mouth and Wynne was kissing him back, not only with her mouth, but with her whole body. Her fingers tangled in the hair on his collar, while she pressed her breasts against his hard chest. She grew aware of his arms encircling her waist and pulling her so close she could barely breathe.

He groaned and pulled back to gaze at her. An intense light flared in his eyes as he looked at her. "I've missed you.

I tried to forget you, but I couldn't. You're all I can think about."

Was she hearing him correctly? He'd missed her? She was all he could think about? Her. No frills, Sperling. She cocked her head to one side and said, "You told Hellstrom I wasn't your type. I believe you said I was bossy, a cold fish, and you mentioned Rambo's sister."

"You heard that?" His brows met in a frown. "It was an act." He paused and seemed to realize something. "So that's why you were so cold to me."

"I wasn't cold."

"Naw, you weren't cold." He chuckled.

She felt the vibrations of his upper body against her breasts. She put her hands on his muscular chest and felt the laughter leave him. His heartbeat thumped beneath her palms, and she couldn't believe he was really here. "Okay, a little," she said. "Why do you care for me, anyway?" She had to hear him say it.

He captured both her cheeks in his wide palms. His warm breath brushed her lips as he spoke, "Because you're the bravest woman I've ever known. And you use your strength to fight for what you believe in." His voice lowered to a reverent murmur. "You're a rare breed, darlin', the rarest of them all."

She found herself staring into his bottomless blue eyes. The tender fierceness she saw there made her want to get lost in them.

At her silence, he said, "You're the reason I'm thinking of moving my operation from Texas to Zambia." His fingers traced the outline of her cheek as he spoke. "You think it's big enough for the both of us?"

"I don't know about bounty hunters. I don't think I trust any of them." Wynne taunted him with a smile.

"I promise to keep you updated on my jobs."

"Then I guess we shouldn't get in each others way. And I could always use your help fighting poachers."

"You got it—oh, I got you something. And it's not a man's watch." He winked at her, looking amused. "I know how you feel about them now." He pulled a velvet box out of his jeans pocket.

Wynne opened it and blinked at a gold necklace with a diamond leopard slide attached to it. Her tears blurred the diamonds into shiny blobs.

"You don't like it?" he asked, worried. "It reminded me of Snow. Did you find her? Was she all right?"

"Yes." Wynne thought of Snow. Before she had left for America, the cat had been staying away and hunting for days at a time. Soon, Snow wouldn't come back at all. Wynne fingered the necklace, blinking back tears. "It's beautiful, I love it, but I can't keep this. ZWA needs money too badly. I'd feel terrible when I wore it."

He kissed her lips and whispered against them in a husky voice, "Do what you like with it, darlin'. Won't hurt my feelings. All I care about is being with you—"

She slipped her arms around his neck and pulled his mouth hard against hers, cutting off his words with a kiss that let him know how much she needed him. With him by her side, she'd be starting an entirely new chapter of her life in Africa. It would really feel like home to her now.

Epilogue

A month later Wynne left Garrison to move into his new office near base camp, while she went in search of Snow. The leopard hadn't come home for two weeks now, and Wynne needed to know that she was adjusting to her new life.

Wynne drove along the Lubonga River Plain. A white leopard had been spotted in the area, and it had brought her there today. She hoped this trip wasn't just another wild-leopard chase.

She passed an enormous buffalo herd grazing near the river. A ranger had said he'd seen the white leopard following the herd. Wynne spotted something white moving through the elephant grass and stopped. The grass thinned near the river and Snow slunk out toward the bank to drink.

Wynne's heart leaped at the sight of her. She looked thinner than when Wynne had last seen her, but she was alive and okay. Wynne leaped out of the new Rover she had purchased while in Washington. She started toward Snow, but a male leopard stepped out of the grass.

Snow scented Wynne immediately and lifted her head. Wynne motioned for her to come.

Snow bounded toward her, then leaped up on Wynne's shoulders. She rubbed her furry face against Wynne's cheek.

The familiar feral scent of the cat broke Wynne's heart. Tears stung her eyes as she said, "You remember, don't you?"

Snow licked Wynne's face and she felt the cat's rough tongue on her skin.

The male gave a warning growl at Wynne and prowled forward.

"Looks like Mr. Paws wants to keep you safe. Better go." She gave Snow the hand signal to leave.

Snow leaped down and faced her new beau, protecting Wynne if the need arose.

Wynne slipped her slingshot free from her waist and eased back into the Rover, keeping her eyes on the male. This would be the last time she could get this close to Snow. But at least she'd been able to say goodbye. They were both ready to say goodbye.

* * * * *

A brand new Bombshell miniseries is coming your way!
The ladies of the exclusive Gotham Roses society club for
women have a secret—they are spies who use their access
to the elite circles of society to take down the richest,
most elusive criminals in the world....

Turn the page for an exclusive
excerpt from the first book
in THE IT GIRLS *miniseries*
starting next month:

THE GOLDEN GIRL
by Erica Orloff

On sale September 2005
at your favorite retail outlet.

Olivia, Renee's personal secretary, greeted her warmly, kissing her on each cheek. "So glad you could make the trip in these circumstances, Madison. Renee's waiting for you in the sunroom. Tea will be served in just a few minutes now that you're here."

Madison nodded and made her way down the hallway to the sunroom in the back of the brownstone. The French doors were open and there sat Renee Dalton-Sinclair, head of the exclusive Gotham Roses society club for women, her auburn hair in an elegant bun and dressed to perfection in an Oscar de la Renta suit. She rose and extended her hand. Though Madison knew she was in her forties, her beauty was timeless in a Grace Kelly sort of way.

"Hello, Madison. Thank you so much for coming." Renee leaned forward and kissed Madison's cheek as the two women clasped hands.

"Sit down. How are you feeling?"

Madison was unused to making more than small talk with Renee, but she was also weary. She opened up a bit.

"To be honest…awful. I haven't slept." Madison ran her fingers through her long golden blond hair. "And…Claire and I had a falling out over her relationship with my father. They had hidden it for months, and…well, it was hard to accept. So I feel terribly that she's gone and things hadn't been right between us."

Renee nodded, her royal blue eyes conveying empathy.

"Anyway," Madison said, waving a hand, "the Pruitts are nothing if not tough."

Renee pursed her lips and clasped her hands together. She gave a nearly imperceptible nod and one of her staff wheeled in a tea cart with a beautiful bone china tea set on it. Madison was always amazed at how Renee's crew forgot nothing. There were two hundred members of the Gotham Roses, but Maddie assumed the staff kept a catalogue of each member's likes and dislikes, because without asking, she got a cup of tea with lemon, no sugar, no cream—exactly as she liked it.

After the staff help had served Renee, she retreated from the sunroom, shutting the French Doors behind her.

"Madison, perhaps you're wondering why I've brought you here in the midst of your crisis. I want to know what really makes Madison Taylor-Pruitt tick. Madison, do you believe your father had nothing to do with Claire's death?"

"Absolutely."

"Then why was she shot at a property your father was negotiating for?"

"I don't know. What I do know is I want the killer or killers brought to justice soon because this kind of publicity Pruitt & Pruitt can do without."

"What if I was to say I can offer you the chance to do just that?"

"Just what?"

"Find the killer. Would the Madison Taylor-Pruitt I think I know—nerves of steel and a resolve unlike anyone else's—would she take me up on the offer?"

"Yes. Though I don't know how you can offer that, so it's a hypothetical, Renee." Madison lifted her tea cup and sipped.

"Madison, the Gotham Roses was an idea close to my heart. In my wilder youth, I was in the Peace Corps, and I saw firsthand what good people with high ideals can do. But after I married Preston, I also saw what ruthless people with low ideals can do. The Sinclair family, his own flesh and blood, took advantage of his honesty and decency, and they framed him, made him a scapegoat. It nearly destroyed me. Until I received my own unusual offer—similar to the one I am making you today."

Renee paused, then continued. "I was contacted by a woman named The Governess. Never directly—though we've spoken on the phone. Through representatives. And this person—and even I'm unsure who she is—wields unprecedented power. You, your father, Preston, myself— we deal with money and boardrooms and power. But this is power with the strength of the government and FBI behind it—resources I still find amazing."

Madison tried to follow what Renee was driving at. "Are you saying you work for the government?"

"In a manner of speaking, yes. The offer—early release for Preston—came with strings attached. The strings involved running a secret organization that reports only to the Governess. With backing and support from the FBI, the CIA and other law enforcement entities—including Scotland Yard and Interpol, this organization is now embedded in the Gotham Roses. Among you are about fifteen or six-teen hand-picked women with talents and ambitions needed to bring down various criminal activities."

"But why the Roses? Why not the FBI or the CIA or…the regular police? Why involve a bunch of—no offense—wealthy young women? What do we—or you—bring to the table?"

"Do you know how to use a lobster fork, Madison?"

Maddie laughed a little. "Sure."

"Can you waltz, fox trot, discuss the Bauhaus move-ment in art, and converse with a diplomat—in his or her native language usually?"

"Sure."

"Well, shocking as this may be to you, Madison, this world we live in, this bubble, if you will, isn't easily penetrated."

"So?"

Renee leaned forward. "It would be impossible for the FBI or law enforcement, to penetrate the society pages, to blend in with us, to fall into step with our world, if they had to solve a crime in our midst."

"So you're saying these women have been working as…spies? Cops?"

"Agents. They're able to blend in and solve major finan-cial and banking cases, even drug dealing among the elite. They can do what the FBI can't—namely infiltrate the path of crime among mind-boggling wealth without being perceived as interlopers."

"And if I say yes to this?"

"Your life will never be the same. But you will have both the chance to discover who killed Claire, to discover the truth behind her love affair with your father, and to make peace with it all."

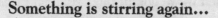

Coming this September

In the first of Charlotte Douglas's Maggie Skerritt mysteries, an experienced police detective has to predict a serial killer's next move while charting her course for the future. But will Maggie's longtime friend and confidant add another life-altering event to the mix?

PELICAN BAY
Charlotte Douglas

COMING NEXT MONTH

#57 TOUCH OF THE WHITE TIGER by Julie Beard
An Angel Baker Novel

Times were tough in Chicago in the year 2104. As a Certified Retribution Specialist, Angel Baker had the responsibility of making criminals pay for their crimes. But now she and her fellow specialists were the targets—of smear campaigns, lies, even assassination. Not even her cop boyfriend trusted her. Only Angel could bring the mastermind of this twisted plot to justice before she became the next victim.

#58 THE GOLDEN GIRL by Erica Orloff
The It Girls

Real-estate heiress Madison Taylor-Pruitt had it all—money in the bank, the looks and labels to die for and her pick of eligible bachelors. But when her own father was named prime suspect in her coworker's murder, Madison's reversal of fortune seemed like a done deal—until the elite Gotham Rose spy ring asked her to find the real killer. Could the savvy socialite stay on the A-list *and* keep her father off the Most-Wanted list?

#59 BEYOND THE RULES by Doranna Durgin

For once in Kimmer Reed's life, all the pieces were falling into place. She had a dream job with the Hunter Agency, and a man she actually trusted at her back. Then her deadbeat brother showed up on her doorstep with a sob story and gunmen in hot pursuit. Now a major crime organization had Kimmer in its sights and her love life was on the rocks. It was enough to make this undercover gal bend the rules one more time....

#60 MEDUSA RISING by Cindy Dees
The Medusa Project

When terrorists hijacked the *Grand Adventure* cruise ship and took all the women and children on board hostage, the all-female Medusa Special Forces team quickly infiltrated and made plans to take back the ship. But Medusa medic Aleesha Gautier soon found out that one of the hijackers wasn't who he seemed to be. Could she trust his offer of help, or was she bringing a viper into their midst before the final showdown?